Marietta Holley

Sweet Cicely

Or, Josiah Allen as a politician

Marietta Holley

Sweet Cicely
Or, Josiah Allen as a politician

ISBN/EAN: 9783337068592

Printed in Europe, USA, Canada, Australia, Japan

Cover: Foto ©Andreas Hilbeck / pixelio.de

More available books at **www.hansebooks.com**

SWEET CICELY

OR

JOSIAH ALLEN

AS A

POLITICIAN

BY

"JOSIAH ALLEN'S WIFE"

(MARIETTA HOLLEY)

WITH ILLUSTRATIONS

FUNK & WAGNALLS

NEW YORK
10 & 12 DEY STREET

1885

LONDON
44 FLEET STREET

TO

THE SAD-EYED MOTHERS,

WHO, LIKE CICELY,

ARE LOOKING ACROSS THE CRADLE OF THEIR
BOYS INTO THE GREAT WORLD OF
TEMPTATION AND DANGER,

This Book is Dedicated.

PREFACE.

JOSIAH and me got to talkin' it over. He said it wuzn't right to think more of one child than you did of another.

And I says, "That is so, Josiah."

And he says, "Then, why did you say yesterday, that you loved sweet Cicely better than any of the rest of your thought-children? You said you loved 'em all, and was kinder sorry for the hull on 'em, but you loved her the best: what made you say it?"

Says I, "I said it, to tell the truth."

"Wall, what did you do it *for?*" he kep' on, determined to get a reason.

"I did it," says I, a comin' out still plainer, — "I did it to keep from lyin'."

"Wall, when you say it hain't right to feel so, what makes you?"

"I don't know, Josiah," says I, lookin' at him, and be-yend him, way into the depths of emotions and feelin's we can't understand nor help, —

"I don't know why, but I know I do."

And he drawed on his boots, and went out to the barn.

CONTENTS.

SWEET CICELY.

CHAPTER I.

IT was somewhere about the middle of winter, along in the forenoon, that Josiah Allen was telegrafted to, unexpected. His niece Cicely and her little boy was goin' to pass through Jonesville the next day on her way to visit her aunt Mary (aunt on her mother's side), and she would stop off, and make us a short visit if convenient.

We wuz both tickled, highly tickled; and Josiah, before he had read the telegraf ten minutes, was out killin' a hen. The plumpest one in the flock was the order I give; and I wus a beginnin' to make a fuss, and cook up for her.

We loved her jest about as well as we did Tirzah Ann. Sweet Cicely was what we used to call her when she was a girl. Sweet Cicely is a plant that has a pretty white posy. And our niece Cicely was prettier and purer and sweeter than any posy that ever grew: so we thought then, and so we think still.

Her mother was my companion's sister, — one of a pair of twins, Mary and Maria, that thought the world of each other, as twins will. Their mother died when they wus

"

JOSIAH TELLING THE NEWS TO SAMANTHA.

both of 'em babies; and they wus adopted by a rich aunt, who brought 'em up elegant, and likely too: that I will say for her, if she wus a 'Piscopal, and I a Methodist. I am both liberal and truthful — very.

Maria wus Cicely's ma, and she wus left a widow when she wus a young woman; and Cicely wus her only child. And the two wus bound up in each other as I never see a mother and daughter in my life before or sense.

The third year after Josiah and me wus married, Maria wusn't well, and the doctor ordered her out into the country for her health; and she and little Cicely spent the hull of that summer with us. Cicely wus about ten; and how we did love that girl! Her mother couldn't bear to have her out of her sight; and I declare, we all of us wus jest about as bad. And from that time they used to spend most all of their summers in Jonesville. The air agreed with 'em, and so did I: we never had a word of trouble. And we used to visit them quite a good deal in the winter season: they lived in the city.

Wall, as Cicely got to be a young girl, I used often to set and look at her, and wonder if the Lord could have made a prettier, sweeter girl if he had tried to. She looked to me jest perfect, and so she did to Josiah.

And she knew so much, too, and wus so womanly and quiet and deep. I s'pose it wus bein' always with her mother that made her seem older and more thoughtful than girls usially are. It seemed as if her great dark eyes wus full of wisdom beyend — fur beyend — her years, and sweetness too. Never wus there any sweeter eyes under the heavens than those of our niece Cicely.

She wus very fair and pale, you would think at first;

but, when you would come to look closer, you would see there was nothing sickly in her complexion, only it was very white and smooth, — a good deal like the pure white leaves of the posy Sweet Cicely. She had a gentle, tender mouth, rose-pink; and her cheeks wuz, when she would get rousted up and excited about any thing; and then it would all sort o' die out again into that pure white. And over all her face, as sweet and womanly as it was, there was a look of power, somehow, a look of strength, as if she would venture much, dare much, for them she loved. She had the gift, not always a happy one, of loving, — a strength of devotion that always has for its companion-trait a gift of endurance, of martyrdom if necessary.

She would give all, dare all, endure all, for them she loved. You could see that in her face before you had been with her long enough to see it in her life.

Her hair wus a soft, pretty brown, about the color of her eyes. And she wus a little body, slender, and sort o' plump too; and her arms and hands and neck wus soft and white as snow almost.

Yes, we loved Cicely: and no one could blame us, or wonder at us for callin' her after the posy Sweet Cicely; for she wus prettier than any posy that ever blew, enough sight.

Wall, she had always said she couldn't live if her mother died.

But she did, poor little creeter! she did.

Maria died when Cicely wus about eighteen. She had always been delicate, and couldn't live no longer: so she died. And Josiah and me went right after the poor child, and brought her home with us.

She lived, Cicely did, because she wus young, and couldn't die. And Josiah and me wus dretful good to

CICELY.

her; and many's the nights that I have gone into her room when I'd hear her cryin' way along in the night; many's the times I have gone in, and took her in my arms, and held her there, and cried with her, and soothed her, and got her to sleep, and held her in my arms like a baby till mornin'.

Wall, she lived with us most a year that time; and it wus about two years after, while she wus to some of her father's folks'es (they wus very rich), that she met the young man she married, — Paul Slide.

He wus a handsome young man, well-behaved, only he would drink a little once in a while: he'd got into the habit at college, where his mate wus wild, and had his turns. But he wus very pretty in his manners, Paul was, — polite, good-natured, generous-dispositioned, — and very rich.

And as to his looks, there wuzn't no earthly fault to find with him, only jest his chin. And I told Josiah, that how Cicely could marry a man with such a chin wus a mystery to me.

And Josiah said, "What is the matter with his chin?"

And I says, "Why, it jest sets right back from his mouth: he hain't got no chin at all hardly," says I. "The place where his chin ort to be is nothin' but a holler place all filled up with irresolution and weakness. And I believe Cicely will see trouble with that chin."

And then — I well remember it, for it was the very first time after marriage, and so, of course, the very first time in our two lives — Josiah called me a fool, a "dumb fool," or jest the same as called me so. He says, "I wouldn't be a dumb fool if I was in your place."

I felt worked up. But, like warriors on a battle-field, I grew stronger for the fray; and the fray didn't scare me none.

PAUL SLIDE.

But I says, "You'll see if you live, Josiah Allen;" and he did.

But, as I said, I didn't see how Cicely ever fell in love with a man with such a chin. But, as I learned afterwards, she fell in love with him under a fur collar. It wus on a slay-ride. And he wuz very handsome from his mouth up, very: his mouth wuz ruther weak. It wus a case of love at first sight, which I believe in considerable; and she couldn't help lovin' him, women are so queer.

I had always said that when Cicely did love, it would go hard with her. Many's the offers she'd had, but didn't care for 'em. But I knew, with her temperament and nater, that love, if it did come to her, would come to stay, and it would come hard and voyalent. And so it did.

She worshipped him, as I said at first, under a fur collar. And then, when a woman once gets to lovin' a man as she did, why, she can't help herself, chin or no chin. When a woman has once throwed herself in front of her idol, it hain't so much matter whether it is stuffed full of gold, or holler: it hain't so much matter *what* they be, I think. Curius, hain't it?

It hain't the easiest thing in the world for such a woman as Cicely to love, but it is a good deal easier for her than to unlove, as she found out afterwards. For twice before her marriage she saw him out of his head with liquor; and it wus my advice to her, to give him up.

And she tried to unlove him, tried to give him up.

But, good land! she might jest as well have took a piece of her own heart out, as to take out of it her love for him: it had become a part of her. And he told her she could save him, her influence could redeem him, and it wus the only thing that could save him.

And Cicely couldn't stand such talk, of course ; and she believed him — believed that she could love him so well, throw her influence so around him, as to hold him back from any evil course.

It is a beautiful hope, the very beautifulest and divinest piece of folly a woman can commit. Beautiful enough in the sublime martyrdom of the idee, to make angels smile ; and vain enough, and foolish enough in its utter uselessness, to make sinners weep. It can't be done — not in 98 cases out of a 100 at least.

Why, if a man hain't got love enough for a woman when he is tryin' to win her affection, — when he is on probation, as you may say, — to stop and turn round in his downward course, how can she expect he will after he has got her, and has let down his watch, so to speak ?

But she loved him. And when I warned her with tears in my eyes, warned her that mebby it wus more than her own safety and happiness that wus imperilled, I could see by the look in her eyes, though she didn't say much, that it wusn't no use for me to talk ; for she wus one of the constant natures that can't wobble round. And though I don't like wobblin', still I do honestly believe that the wobblers are happier than them that can't wobble.

'I could see jest how it wuz, and I couldn't bear to have her blamed. And I would tell folks, — some of the relations on her mother's side, — when they would say, " What a fool she wus to have him ! " — I'd say to 'em, " Wall, when a woman sees the man she loves goin' down to ruination, and tries to unlove him, she'll find out jest how

much harder it is to unlove him than to love him in the
first place : they'll find out it is a tough job to tackle."

I said this to blamers of Cicely (relatives, the best
blamers you can find anywhere). But, at the same time,

SAMANTHA AND THE "BLAMERS."

it would have been my way, when he had come a courtin'
me so far gone with liquor that he could hardly stand up —
why, I should have told him plain, that I wouldn't try
to set myself up as a rival to alcohol, and he might pay to
that his attentions exclusively hereafter.

But she didn't. And he promised sacred to abstain,

and could, and did, for most a year; and she married
him.

But, jest before the marriage, I got so rousted up
a thinkin' about what I had heard of him at college, —
and I studied on his picture, which she had sent me, took
sideways too, and I could see plain (why, he hadn't no
chin at all, as you may say; and his lips was weak and
waverin' as ever lips was, though sort o' amiable and fascinating), — and I got to forebodin' so about that chin,
and my love for her wus a hunchin' me up so all the time,
that I went to see her on a short tower, to beset her on
the subject. But, good land! I might have saved my
breath, I might have saved my tower.

I cried, and she cried too. And I says to her before I
thought, —

"He'll be the ruin of you, Cicely."

And she says, "I would rather be beaten by his hand,
than to be crowned by another. Why, I love him, aunt
Samantha."

You see, that meant a awful sight to her. And as she
looked at me so earnest and solemn, with tears in them
pretty brown eyes, there wus in her look all that that
word could possibly mean to any soul.

But I cried into my white linen handkerchief, and
couldn't help it, and couldn't help sayin', as I see that
look, —

"Cicely, I am afraid he will break your heart — kill
you " —

"Why, I am not afraid to die when I am with him. I
am afraid of nothing — of life, or death, or eternity."

Well, I see my talk was no use. I see she'd have him,

chin or no chin. If I could have taken her up in my arms, and run away with her then and there, how much misery I could have saved her from! But I couldn't: I had the rheumatiz. And I had to give up, and go home disapp'inted, but carryin' this thought home with me on my tower, — that I had done my duty by our sweet Cicely, and could do no more.

As I said, he promised firm to give up drinking. But, good land! what could you expect from that chin? That chin couldn't stand temptation if it came in his way. At the same time, his love for Cicely was such, and his good heart and his natural gentlemanly intuitions was such, that, if he could have been kep' out of the way of temptation, he would have been all right.

If there hadn't been drinking-saloons right in front of that chin, if it could have walked along the road without runnin' right into 'em, it would have got along. That chin, and them waverin'-lookin', amiable lips, wouldn't have stirred a step out of their ways to get ruined and disgraced: they wouldn't have took the trouble to.

And for a year or so he and the chin kep' out of the way of temptation, or ruther temptation kep' out of their way; and Cicely was happy, — radiently happy, as only such a nature as hern can be. Her face looked like a mornin' in June, it wus so bright, and glowing with joy and happy love.

I visited her, stayed 3 days and 2 nights with her; and I almost forgot to forebode about the lower part of his face, I found 'em so happy and prosperous and likely.

Paul wus very rich. He wus the only child: and his pa left 2 thirds of his property to him, and the other third to his ma, which wus more than she could ever use while she wus alive; and at her death it wus to go to Paul and his heirs.

They owned most all of the village they lived in. His pa had owned the township the village was built on, and had built most all the village himself, and rented the buildings. He owned a big manufactory there, and the buildings rented high.

Wall, it wus in the second year of their marriage that that old college chumb — (and I wish he had been chumbed by a pole, before he had ever gone there). He had lost his property, and come down in the world, and had to work for a livin'; moved into that village, and opened a drinking-saloon and billiard-room.

He had been Paul's most intimate friend at college, and his evil genius, so his mother said. But he was bright, witty, generous in a way, unprincipled, dissipated. And he wanted Paul's company, and he wanted Paul's money; and he had a chin himself, and knew how to manage them that hadn't any.

Wall, Cicely and his mother tried to keep Paul from that bad influence. But he said it would look shabby to not take any notice of a man because he wus down in the world. He wouldn't have much to do with him, but it wouldn't do to not notice him at all. How curius, that out of good comes bad, and out of bad, good. That was a good-natured idee of Paul's if he had had a chin that could have held up his principle; but he didn't.

So he gradually fell under the old influence again. He didn't mean to. He hadn't no idee of doin' so when he begun. It was the chin.

He begun to drink hard, spent his nights in the saloon, gambled, — slipped right down the old, smooth track worn by millions of jest such weak feet, towards ruin. And Cicely couldn't hold him back after he had got to slippin': her arms wuzn't strong enough.

She went to the saloon-keeper, and cried, and begged of him not to sell her husband any more liquor. He was very polite to her, very courteous: everybody was to Cicely. But in a polite way he told her that Paul wus his best customer, and he shouldn't offend him by refusing to sell him liquor. She knelt at his feet, I hearn, — her little, tender limbs on that rough floor before that evil man, — and wept, and said, —

"For the sake of her boy, wouldn't he have mercy on the boy's father."

But in a gentle way he gave her to understand that he shouldn't make no change.

And he told her, speakin' in a dretful courteous way, "that he had the law on his side: he had a license, and he should keep right on as he was doing."

And so what could Cicely do? And time went on, carryin' Paul further and further down the road that has but one ending. Lower and lower he sunk, carryin' her heart, her happiness, her life, down with him.

And they said one cold night Paul didn't come home at all, and Cicely and his mother wus half crazy; and they wus too proud, to the last, to tell the servants more than they could help: so, when it got to be most mornin', them two delicate women started out through the deep snow, to try to find him, tremblin' at every little heap of snow that wus tumbled up in the path in front of 'em; tremblin'

CICELY IN THE SALOON.

and sick at heart with the agony and dread that wus rackin' their souls, as they would look over the cold fields of snow stretching on each side of the road, and thinkin' how that face would look if it wus lying there staring with lifeless eyes up towards the cold moonlight, — the face they had kissed, the face they had loved, — and thinkin', too, that the change that had come to it — was comin' to it all the time — was more cruel and hopeless than the change of death.

So they went on, clear to the saloon; and there they found him, — there he lay, perfectly stupid, and dead with liquor.

And they both, the broken-hearted mother and the broken-hearted wife, with the tears running down their white cheeks, besought the saloon-keeper to let him alone from that night.

The mother says, "Paul is so good, that if you did not tempt him, entice him here, he would, out of pity to us, stop his evil ways."

And the saloon-keeper was jest as polite as any man wus ever seen to be, — took his hat off while he told 'em, so I hearn, "that he couldn't go against his own interests: if Paul chose to spend his money there, he should take it."

"Will you break our hearts?" cried the mother.

"Will you ruin my husband, the father of my boy?" sobbed out Cicely, her big, sorrowful eyes lookin' right through his soul — if he *had* a soul.

And then the man, in a pleasant tone, reminded 'em, —

"That it wuzn't him that wus a doin' this. It wus the law: if they wanted things changed, they must look further than him. He had a license. The great Government of the United States had sold him, for a few dollars, the right to do just what he was doing. The law, and all the respectability that the laws of our great and glorious Republic can give, bore him out in all his acts. The law was responsible for all the consequenses of his acts: the men were responsible who voted for license — it was not him."

"But you *can* do what we ask if you will, out of pity to Paul, pity to us who love him so, and who are forced to stand by powerless, and see him going to ruin — we who would die for him willingly if it would do any good. You *can* do this."

He was a little bit intoxicated, or he wouldn't have gin 'em the cruel sneer he did at the last, — though he sneered polite, — a holdin' his hat in his hand.

"As I said, my dear madam, it is not I, it is the law; and I see no other way for you ladies who feel so about it, only to vote, and change the laws."

`"Would to God I *could!*" said the old white-haired mother, with her solemn eyes lifted to the heavens, in which was her only hope.

"Would to God I could!" repeated my sweet Cicely, with her eyes fastened on the face of him who had promised to cherish her, and comfort her, and protect her, layin' there at her feet, a mark for jeers and sneers, unable to speak a word, or lift his hand, if his wife and mother had been killed before him.

But they couldn't do any thing. They would have lain their lives down for him at any time, but that wouldn't do any good. The lowest, most ignorant laborer in their employ had power in this matter, but they had none. They had intellectual power enough, which, added to their utter helplessness, only made their burden more unendurable; for they comprehended to the full the knowledge of what was past, and what must come in the future unless help came quickly. They had the strength of devotion, the strength of unselfish love.

They had the will, but they hadn't nothin' to tackle it onto him with, to draw him back. For their prayers, their midnight watches, their tears, did not avail, as I said: they went jest so far; they touched him, but they lacked the tacklin'-power that was wanted to grip holt of him, and draw him back. What they needed was the justice of the law to tackle the injustice; and they hadn't got it, and couldn't get holt of it: so they had to set with hands folded, or lifted to the heavens in wild appeal, — either way didn't help Paul any, — and see him a sinkin' and a sinkin', slippin' further and further down; and they had to let him go.

He drunk harder and harder, neglected his business, got quarrelsome. And one night, when the heavens was curtained with blackness, like a pall let down to cover the accursed scene, he left Cicely with her pretty baby asleep on her bosom, went down to the saloon, got into a quarrel with that very friend of hisen, the saloon-keeper, over a game of billiards, — they was both intoxicated, — and then and there Paul committed *murder*, and would have been hung for it if he hadn't died in State's prison the night before he got his sentence.

Awful deed! Dreadful fate! But no worse, as I told Josiah when he wus a groanin' over it; no worse, I told the

PAUL SHOOTING HIS FRIEND.

children when they was a cryin' over it; no worse, I told
my own heart when the tears wus a runnin' down my
face like rain-water, — no worse because Cicely happened
to be our relation, and we loved her as we did our own
eyes.

And our broad land is *full* of jest such sufferin's, jest
such crimes, jest such disgrace, caused by the same cause;
— as I told Josiah, suffering, disgrace, and crime made
legal and protected by the law.

And Josiah squirmed as I said it; and I see him squirm,
for he believed in it: he believed in licensing this shame
and disgrace and woe; he believed in makin' it respectable, and wrappin' round it the mantilly of the law, to keep
it in a warm, healthy, flourishin' condition. Why, he had
helped do it himself; he had helped the United States lift
up the mantilly; he had voted for it.

He squirmed, but turned it off by usin' his bandana hard,
and sayin', in a voice all choked down with grief, —

" Oh, poor Cicely ! poor girl ! "

" Yes," says I, " ' poor girl ! ' and the law you uphold
has made her ' poor girl ' — has killed her; for she won't
live through it, and you and the United States will see
that she won't."

He squirmed hard; and my feelin's for him are such that
I can't bear to see him squirm voyalently, as much as I
blamed him and the United States, and as mad as I was at
both on 'em.

So I went to cryin' agin silently under my linen handkerchief, and he cried into his bandana. It wus a awful
blow to both on us.

Wall, she lived, Cicely did, which was more than we any

one of us thought she could do. I went right there, and
stayed six weeks with her, hangin' right over her bed,
night and day; and so did his mother, — she a broken-
hearted woman too. Her heart broke, too, by the United
States; and so I told Josiah, that little villain that got
killed was only one of his agents. Yes, her heart was
broke; but she bore up for Cicely's sake and the boy's.
For it seemed as if she felt remorsful, and as if it was for
them that belonged to him who had ruined her life, to help
her all they could.

Wall, after about three weeks Cicely begun to live.
And so I wrote to Josiah that I guessed she would keep
on a livin' now, for the sake of the boy.

And so she did. And she got up from that bed a
shadow, — a faint, pale shadow of the girl that used to
brighten up our home for us. She was our sweet Cicely
still. But she looked like that posy after the frost has
withered it, and with the cold moonlight layin' on it.

Good and patient she wuz, and easy to get along with;
for she seemed to hold earthly things with a dretful loose
grip, easy to leggo of 'em. And it didn't seem as if she
had any interest at all in life, or care for any thing that
was a goin' on in the world, till the boy wus about four
years old; and then she begun to get all rousted up about
him and his future. "She *must* live," she said: "she had
got to live, to do something to help him in the future.

"She couldn't die," she told me, "and leave him in a
world that was so hard for boys, where temptations and
danger stood all round her boy's pathway. Not only hidden perils, concealed from sight, so he might possibly escape them, but open temptations, open dangers, made as

alluring as private avarice could make them, and made as respectable as dignified legal enactments could make them, —all to draw her boy down the pathway his poor father

CICELY AND THE BOY.

descended." For one of the curius things about Cicely wuz, she didn't seem to blame Paul hardly a mite, nor not so very much the one that enticed him to drink. She went back further than them: she laid the blame onto our laws; she laid the responsibility onto the ones that made 'em, directly and indirectly, the legislators and the voters.

Curius that Cicely should feel so, when most everybody said that he could have stopped drinking if he had wanted to. But then, I don't know as I could blame her for feelin' so when I thought of Paul's chin and lips. Why, anybody that had them on 'em, and was made up inside and outside accordin', as folks be that have them looks; why, unless they was specially guarded by good influences, and fenced off from bad ones, — why, they *could not* exert any self-denial and control and firmness.

Why, I jest followed that chin and that mouth right back through seven generations of the Slide family. Paul's father wus a good man, had a good face; took it from his mother: but his father, Paul's grandfather, died a drunkard. They have got a oil-portrait of him at Paul's old home: I stopped there on my way home from Cicely's one time. And for all the world he looked most exactly like Paul, — the same sort of a irresolute, handsome, weak, fascinating look to him. And all through them portraits I could trace that chin and them lips. They would disappear in some of 'em, but crop out agin further back. And I asked the housekeeper, who had always lived in the family, and wus proud of it, but honest; and she knew the story of the hull Slide race.

And she said that every one of 'em that had that face had traits accordin'; and 'most every one of 'em got into trouble of some kind.

One or two of 'em, specially guarded, I s'pose, by good influences, got along with no further trouble than the loss of the chin, and the feelin' they must have had inside of 'em, that they wuz liable to crumple right down any minute.

And as they wus made with jest them looks, and jest them traits, born so, entirely unbeknown to them, I don't know as I can blame Cicely for feelin' as she did. If temptation hadn't stood right in the road in front of him, why, he'd have got along, and lived happy. That's Cicely's idee. And I don't know but she's in the right ont.

But as I said, when her child wus about four years old, Cicely took a turn, and begun to get all worked up and excited by turns a worryin' about the boy. She'd talk about it a sight to me, and I hearn it from others.

She rousted up out of her deathly weakness and heartbroken, stunted calm, — for such it seemed to be for the first two or three years after her husband's death. She seemed to make an effort almost like that of a dead man throwin' off the icy stupor of death, and risin' up with numbed limbs, and shakin' off the death-robes, and livin' agin. She rousted up with jest such a effort, so it seemed, for the boy's sake.

She must live for the boy; she must work for the boy; she must try to throw some safeguards around his future. What *could* she do to help him? That wus the question that was a hantin' her soul.

It wus jest like death for her to face the curius gaze of the world again; for, like a wounded animal, she had wanted to crawl away, and hide her cruel woe and disgrace in some sheltered spot, away from the sharp-sot eyes of the babblin' world.

But she endured it. She came out of her quiet home, where her heart had bled in secret; she came out into society again; and she did every thing she could, in her gentle, quiet way. She joined temperance societies, — helped push 'em forward with her money and her influence. With other white-souled wimmen, gentle and refined as she was, she went into rough bar-rooms, and knelt on their floors, and prayed what her sad heart wus full of, — for pity and mercy for her boy, and other mothers' boys, — prayed with that fellowship of suffering that made her sweet voice as pathetic as tears, and patheticker, so I have been told.

But one thing hurt her influence dretfully, and almost broke her own heart. Paul had left a very large property, but it wus all in the hands of an executor until the boy wus of age. He wus to give Cicely a liberal, a very liberal, sum every year, but wus to manage the property jest as he thought best.

He wus a good business man, and one that meant to do middlin' near right, but wus close for a bargain, and sot, awful sot. And though he wus dretful polite, and made a stiddy practice right along of callin' wimmen "angels," still he would not brook a woman's interference.

Wall, he could get such big rents for drinkin'-saloons, that four of Cicely's buildings wus rented for that purpose; and there wus one billiard-room. And what made it worse for Cicely seemin'ly, it wus her own property, that she brought to Paul when she wus married, that wus invested in these buildings. At that time they wus rented for dry-goods stores, and groceries. But the business of the manufactories had increased greatly; and there wus

three times the population now there wus when she went
there to live, and more saloons wus needed ; and these
buildings wus handy ; and the executer had big prices
offered to him, and he would rent 'em as he wanted to.
And then, he wus something of a statesman ; and he felt,
as many business men did, that they wus fairly sufferin'
for more saloons to enrich the government.

Why, out of every hundred dollars that them poor
laboring-men had earned so hardly, and paid into the
saloons for that which, of course, wus ruinous to themselves and families, and, of course, rendered them inca-
pable of all labor for a great deal of the time, — why, out
of that hundred dollars, as many as 2 cents would go to
the government to enrich it.

Of course, the government had to use them 2 cents right
off towards buyin' tight-jackets to confine the madmen
the whiskey had made, and poorhouse-doors for the idiots
it had breeded, to lean up aginst, and buryin' the paupers,
and buyin' ropes to hang the murderers it had created..

But still, in some strange way, too deep, fur too deep,
for a woman's mind to comprehend, it wus dretful profit-
able to the government.

Now, if them poor laborin'-men had paid that 2 cents
of thiern to the government themselves, in the first place,
in direct taxation, why, that wouldn't have been states-
manship. That is a deep study, and has a great many
curius performances, and it has to perform.

Cicely tried her very best to get the executor to change
in this one matter; but she couldn't move him the width
of a horse-hair, and he a smilin' all the time at her, and
polite. He liked Cicely : nobody could help likin' the

UNCLE SAM ENRICHING THE GOVERNMENT.

gentle, saintly-souled little woman. But he wus sot: he wus makin' money fast by it, and she had to give up.

And rough men and women would sometimes twit her of it, — of her property bein' used to advance the liquor-traffic, and ruin men and wimmen; and she a feelin' like death about it, and her hands tied up, and powerless. No wonder that her face got whiter and whiter, and her eyes bigger and mournfuller-lookin'.

Wall, she kep' on, tryin' to do all she could: she joined the Woman's Temperance Union; she spent her money free as water, where she thought it would do any good, and brought up the boy jest as near right as she could possibly bring him up; and she prayed, and wept right when she wus a bringin' of him, a thinkin' that *her* property wus a bein' used every day and every hour in ruinin' other mothers' boys. And the boy's face almost breakin' her heart every time she looked at it; for, though he wus jest as pretty as a child could be, the pretty rosy lips had the same good-tempered, irresolute curve to 'em that the boy inherited honestly. And he had the same weak, waverin' chin. It was white and rosy now, with a dimple right in the centre, sweet enough to kiss. But the chin wus there, right under the rosy snow and the dimple; and I foreboded, too, and couldn't blame Cicely a mite for her forebodin', and her agony of sole.

I noticed them lips and that chin the very minute Josiah brought him into the settin'-room, and set him down; and my eyes looked dubersome at him through my specks. Cicely see it, see that dubersome look, though I tried to turn it off by kissin' him jest as hearty as I could after I had took the little black-robed figure of his mother, and hugged her close to my heart, and kissed her time and time agin.

She always dressed in the deepest of mournin', and always would. I knew that.

Wall, we wus awful glad to see Cicely. I had had the old fireplace fixed in the front spare room, and a crib put in there for the boy; and I went right up to her room with her. And when we had got there, I took her right in my arms agin, as I used to, and told her how glad I wus, and how thankful I wus, to have her and the boy with us.

The fire sparkled up on the old brass handirons as warm as my welcome. Her bed and the boy's bed looked white and cozy aginst the dark red of the carpet and the cream-colored paper. And after I had lowered the pretty ruffled muslin curtains (with red ones under 'em), and pulled a stand forward, and lit a lamp, — it wus sundown, — the room looked cheerful enough for anybody, and it seemed as if Cicely looked a little less white and broken-hearted. She wus glad to be with me, and said she wuz. But right there — before supper; and we could smell the roast chicken and coffee, havin' left the stair-door open — right there, before we had visited hardly any, or talked a mite about other wimmen, she begun on what she wanted to do, and what she *must* do, for the boy.

I had told her how the boy had grown, and that sot her off. And from that night, every minute of her time almost, when she could without bein' impolite and trouble-some (Cicely wus a perfect lady, inside and out), she would talk to me about what she wanted to do for the boy, what she must do. She must work for him; she must try

THE SPARE ROOM.

to have the laws changed before he grew up; she didn't
dare to let him go out into the world with the laws as
they was now, with temptation on every side of him.

"You know, aunt Samantha," she says to me, "that I wanted to die when my husband died; but I want to live now. Why, I *must* live; I cannot die; I dare not die until my boy is safer. I will work, I will die if necessary, for him."

It wus the same old Cicely, I see, not carin' for herself, but carin' only for them she loved. Lovin' little creeter, good little creeter, she always wuz, and always would be. And so I told Josiah.

Wall, we had the boy set between us to the supper-table, Josiah and me did, in Thomas Jefferson's little high-chair. I had new covered it on purpose for him with bright copperplate calico.

And that night at supper, and after supper, I judged, and judged calmly, — we made the estimate after we went to bed, Josiah and me did, — that the boy asked 3 thousand and 85 questions about every thing under the sun and moon, and things over 'em, and outside of 'em, and inside.

Why, I panted for breath, but wouldn't give in. I was determined to use Cicely first-rate, and we loved the boy too. But, oh! it was a weary love, and a short-winded love, and a hoarse one.

We went to bed tuckered completely out, but good-natured: our love for 'em held us up. And when we made the estimate, it wuzn't in a cross tone, but amiable, and almost winnin'. Josiah thought they went up into the trillions. But I am one that never likes to set such things too high; and I said calmly, 3,000 and 85. And finally he gin in that mebby it wuzn't no more than that.

Cicely told me she couldn't stay with us very long now; for her aunt Mary wuz expectin' to go away to the Mich-

igan pretty soon, to see a daughter who wus out of
health, — had been out of it for some time, — and she
wanted a visit from her neice Cicely before she went. But
she promised to come back, and make a good visit on her
way home.

And so it was planned. The next day was Sunday, and
Cicely wus too tired with her journey to go to meetin'.
But the boy went. He sot up, lookin' beautiful, by the
side of me on the back seat of the Democrat; his uncle
Josiah sot in front; and Ury drove. Ury Henzy, he's our
hired man, and a tolerable good one, as hired men go.
His name is Urias; but we always call him Ury, — spelt
U-r-y, Ury, — with the emphasis on the U.

Wall, that day Elder Minkly preached. It wus a powerful sermon, about the creation of the world, and how
man was made, and the fall of Adam, and about Noah and
the ark, and how the wicked wus destroyed. It wus a
middlin' powerful sermon; and the boy sot up between
Josiah and me, and we wus proud enough of him. He
had on a little green velvet suit and a deep linen collar;
and he sot considerable still for him, with his eyes on
Elder Minkly's face, a thinkin', I guess, how he would put
us through our catechism on the way home. And, oh!
didn't he, didn't he do it? I s'pose things seem strange
to children, and they can't help askin' about 'em.

But 4,000 wus the estimate Josiah and me calculated on
our pillows that night wus the number of questions the
boy asked on our way home, about the creation, how the
world wus made, and the ark — oh, how he harressed my
poor companion about the animals! "Did they drive 2 of
all the animals in the world in that house, uncle Josiah?"

GOING TO MEETING.

" Yes," says Josiah.

" 2 elfants, and rinosterhorses, and snakes, and snakes, and bears, and tigers, and cows, and camels, and hens ? "

" Yes, yes."

" And flies, uncle Josiah ? — did they drive in two flies ? and mud-turkles ? and bumble-bees ? and muskeeters ? Say, uncle Josiah, did they drive in muskeeters ? "

" I s'pose so."

" *How* could they drive in two muskeeters ? "

" Oh ! less stop talkin' for a spell — shet up your little mouth," says Josiah in a winnin' tone, pattin' him on his head.

" I can shut up my mouth, uncle Josiah, but I can't shut up my thinker."

Josiah sithed ; and, right while he wus a sithin', the boy commenced agin on a new tack.

" What for a lookin' place was paradise ? " And then follered 800 questions about paradise. Josiah sweat, and offered to let the boy come back, and set with me. He had insisted, when we started from the meetin'-house, on havin' the boy set on the front seat between him and Ury.

But I demurred about any change, and leaned back, and eat a sweet apple. I don't think it is wrong Sundays to eat a sweet apple. And the boy kep' on.

" What did Adam fall off of ? Did he fall out of the apple-tree ? "

" No, no ! he fell because he sinned."

But the boy went right on, in a tone of calm conviction, —

" No big man would be apt to fall a walking right along. He fell out of the apple-tree."

And then he says, after a minute's still thought, —

"I believe, if I had been there, and had a string round Adam's leg, I could kep' him from fallin' off; — and say, where was the Lord? Couldn't He have kept him? say, couldn't He?"

"Yes: He can do any thing."

"Wall, then, why didn't He?"

Josiah groaned, low.

"If Adam hadn't fell, I wouldn't have fell, would I? — nor you — nor Ury — nor anybody?"

"No: I s'pose not."

"Wall, wouldn't it have paid to kept Adam up? Say, uncle Josiah, say!"

"Oh! less talk about sunthin' else," says my poor Josiah. "Don't you want a sweet apple?"

"Yes; and say! what kind of a apple was it that Adam eat? Was it a sweet apple, or a greening, or a sick-no-further? And say, was it *right* for all of us to fall down because Adam did? And how did *I* sin just because a man eat an apple, and fell out of an apple-tree, when I never saw the apple, or poked him offen the tree, or jog-gled him, or any thing — when I wasn't there? Say, how was it wrong, uncle Josiah? When I wasn't *there!*"

My poor companion, I guess to sort o' pacify him, broke out kinder a singin' in a tone full of fag, "'In Adam's fall, we sinnèd all.'" Josiah is sound.

"And be I a sinning now, uncle Josiah? and a falling? And is everybody a sinning and a falling jest because that one · man eat one apple, and fell out of an apple-tree? Say, is it *right*, uncle Josiah, for you and me, and every-body that is on the earth, to keep a falling, and keep

a falling, and bein' blamed, and every thing, when we
hadn't done any thing, and wasn't *there?*   And *say*, will
folks always keep a falling?"

"Yes, if they hain't good."

"*How* can they keep a falling?   If Adam fell out of the
apple-tree, wouldn't he have struck on the ground, and got

JOSIAH CLOSING THE CONVERSATION.

up agin?   And if anybody falls, why, why, mustn't they
come to the bottom sometime?   If there is something to
fall off of, mustn't there be something to hit against?
And *say*" —

Here the boy's eyes looked dreamier than they had
looked, and further off.

"Was I made out of dirt, uncle Josiah?"

" Yes: we are all made out of dust."

" And did God breathe our souls into us? Was it His own self, His own life, that was breathed into us?"

" Yes," says Josiah, in a more fagged voice than he had used durin' the intervue, and more hopelesser.

" Wall, if God is in us, how can He lose us again? Wouldn't it be a losing His own self? And how could God lose Himself? And what did He find us for, in the first place, if He wus going to lose us again?"

Here Josiah got right up in the Democrat, and lifted the boy, and sot him over on the seat with me, and took the lines out of Ury's hands, and drove the old mair at a rate that I told him wus shameful on Sunday, for a perfessor.

" IT WUS ON A SLAY-RIDE " (p. 8).

CHAPTER II.

Wall, Cicely and the boy staid till Tuesday night. Tuesday afternoon the children wus all to home on a invitation. (I had a chicken-pie, and done well by 'em.)

And nothin' to do but what Cicely and the boy must go home with 'em: they jest think their eyes of Cicely. And I couldn't blame 'em for wantin' her, though I hated to give her up.

She laid out to stay a few days, and then come back to our house for a day or two, and then go on to her aunt Mary's. But, as it turned out, the children urged her so, she stayed most two weeks.

And the very next day but one after Cicely went to the children's — And don't it beat all how, if visitors get to comin', they'll keep a comin'? jest as it is if you begin to have trials, you'll have lots of 'em, or broken dishes, or any thing.

Wall, it wus the very next mornin' but one after Cicely had gone, and my voice had actually begun to sound natural agin (the boy had kep' me hoarse as a frog answerin' questions). I wus whitewashin' the kitchen, havin' put it off while Cicely wus there; and there wus a man to work a patchin' up the wall in one of the chambers,

— and right there and then, Elburtus Smith Gansey come. And truly, we found him as clever a critter as ever walked the earth.

It wus jest before korkuss; and he wus kinder visatin' round amongst his relations, and makin' himself agreable. He is my 5th cousin, — 5th or 6th. I can't reely tell which, and I don't know as I care much; for I think, that, after you get by the 5th, it hain't much matter anyway. I sort o' pile 'em all in promiscous. Jest as it is after anybody gets to be 70 years old, it hain't much matter how much older they be: they are what you may call old, anyway.

But I think, as I said prior and beforehand, that he wus a 5th. His mother wus a Butrick, and her mother wus a Smith. So he come to make us a visit, and sort o' ellectioneer round. He wanted to get put in county judge; and so, the korkuss bein' held in Jonesville, I s'pose he thought he'd come down, and endear himself to us, as they all do.

I am one that likes company first-rate, and I always try to do well by 'em; but I tell Josiah, that somehow city folks (Elburtus wus brought up in a city) are a sort of a bother. They require so much, and give you the feelin', that, when you are a doin' your very best for 'em, they hain't satisfied. You see, some folks'es best hain't nigh so good as other folks'es 3d or 4th.

But this feller — why! I liked him from the first minute I sot my eyes on him. I hadn't seen him before sence I wus a child, and so didn't feel so awful well acquainted with him; or, that is, I didn't, as it were, feel intimate. You know, when you don't see anybody from the time you are babies till you are married, and have lost a good many teeth, and considerable hair, you can't feel over and above intimate with 'em at first sight.

But I liked him, he wus so unassuming and friendly, and took every thing so peaceable and pleasant. And he deserved better things than what happened to him.

You see, I wus a cleanin' house when he come, cleanin' the kitchen at that out-of-the-way time of year on account of Cicely's visit, and on account of repairin' that had promised to be done by Josiah Allen, and delayed from week to week, and month to month, as is the way with men. But finally he had got it done, and I wus ready to the minute with my brush and scourin'-cloth.

I wus a whitewashin' when he come, and my pail of whitewash wus hung up over the kitchen-door; and I stood up on a table, a whitewashin' the ceilin, when I heard a buggy drive up to the door, and stop. And I stood still, and listened; and then I heard a awful katouse and rumpus, and then I heard hollerin'; and then I heard Josiah's voice, and somebody else's voice, a talkin' back and forth, sort o' quick and excited.

. Now, some wimmen would have been skairt, and acted skairt; but I didn't. I jest stood up on that table, cool and calm as a statue of Repose sculped out of marble, and most as white (I wus all covered with whitewash), with my brush held easy and firm in my right hand, and my left ear a listenin'.

Pretty soon the door opened right by the side of the table, and in come Josiah Allen and a strange man. He introduced him to me as Elburtus Gansey, my 4th cousin; and I made a handsome curchy. I s'pose, bein' up on the

EXCELLENT LIME.

table, the curchy showed off to better advantage than it would if I had been on the floor: it looked well. But I felt that I ort to shake hands with him; and, as I went to step down into a chair to get down (entirely unbeknown to me), my brush hit against that pail, and down come that pail of whitewash right onto his back. (If it had been his head, it would have broke it.)

I felt as if I should sink.

But he took it the best that ever wus. He said, when Josiah and me wus a sweepin' him off, and a rubbin' him off with wet towels, that "it wusn't no matter at all." And he spoke up so polite and courteous, that "it seemed to be first-rate whitewash: he never see better, whiter lime in his life, than that seemed to be." And then he sort o' felt of it between his thumb and finger, and asked Josiah "where did he get that lime, and if they had any more of it. He didn't believe they could get such lime outside of Jonesville." He acted like a perfect gentleman.

And he told me, in that same polite, pleasant tone, how Josiah's old sheep had knocked him over 3 times while he wus a comin' into the house. He said, with that calm, gentle smile, "that no sooner would he get up, than he would stand off a little, and then rush at him with his head down, and push him right over."

Says I, "It is a perfect shame and a disgrace," says I. "And I have told you, Josiah Allen, that some stranger would get killed by that old creeter; and I should think you would get rid of it."

"Wall, I lay out to, the first chance I get," says he.

Elburtus said "it would almost seem to be a pity, it

was so strong and healthy a sheep." He said he never met a sheep under any circumstances that seemed to have a sounder, stronger constitution. He said of course the sheep and he hadn't met under the pleasantest of circumstances, and it wusn't over and above pleasant to be knocked down by it three or four times; but he had found that he couldn't have every thing as he wanted it in this world, and the only way to enjoy ourselves wus to take things as they come.

Says I, " I s'pose that wus the way you took the sheep ; " and he said, " It was."

And then he went on to say in that amiable way of hisen, "that it probably made it a little harder for him jest at that time, as he wus struck by lightnin' that mornin'." (There had been a awful thunder-storm.)

Says Josiah, all excitement, "Did it strike you sensible?"

Says I, " You mean senseless, Josiah Allen."

" Wall, I said so, didn't I ? Did it strike you senseless, Mr. Gansey?"

"No," he said: it only stunted him. And then he went on a praisin' up our Jonesville lightnin'. He said it wus about the cleanest, quickest lightnin' he ever see. He said he believed we had the smartest lightnin' in our county that you could find in the nation.

So good he acted about every thing. It beat all. Why, he hadn't been in the house half an hour when he offered to help me whitewash. I told him I wouldn't let him, for it would spile his clothes, and he hadn't ever been there a visitin' before, and I didn't want to put him to work. But he hung on, and nothin' to do but what he had got to take hold and whitewash. And I had to give up and let him; for I thought it wus better manners to put a visiter to work, than it wus to dispute and quarrel with 'em: and, of course, he wusn't used to it, and he filled one eye most full of lime. It wus dretful painful, dretful.

But I swabbed it out with viniger, and it got easier about the middle of the afternoon. It bein' work that he never done before, the whitewashin' looked like fury; but I done it all over after him, and so I got along with it, though it belated me. But his offerin' to do it showed his good will, anyway.

I shouldn't have done any more at all after Elburtus had come, only I had got into the job, and had to finish it; for I always think it is better manners, when visitors come unexpected, and ketch you in some mean job, to go on and finish it as quick as you can, ruther than to set down in the dirt, and let them, ditto, and the same.

And Josiah was ketched jest as I wus, for he had a piece of winter wheat that wus spilin' to be cut; and he had got the most of it down, and had to finish it: it wus lodged so he had to cut it by hand, — the machine wouldn't work on it. And jest as quick as Elburtus had got so he could see out of that eye, nothin' to do but what he had got to go out and help Josiah cut that wheat. He hadn't touched a scythe for years and years, and it wusn't ten minutes before his hands wus blistered on the inside. But he would keep at it till the blisters broke, and then he had to stop anyway.

He got along quite well after that: only the lot where Josiah wus to work run along by old Bobbet'ses, and he had carried a jug of sweetened water and viniger and ginger out into the lot, and Elburtus had talked so polite

ELBURTUS ENDEARIN' HIMSELF TO MR. BOBBET.

and cordial to him, a conversin' on politics, that he got attached to him, and treated him to the sweetened water.

And Elburtus, not wantin' to hurt his feelin's, drinked about 3 quarts. It made him deathly sick, for it went aginst his stomach from the first: he never loved it. And Miss Bobbet duz fix it dretful sickish, — sweetens it with sale mollasses for one thing.

Oh, how sick that feller wus when he come in to supper! had to lay right down on the lounge.

Says I, "Elburtus, what made you drink it, when it went aginst your stomach?" says I.

"Why," says he in a faint voice, and pale round his lips as any thing, "I didn't want to hurt his feelin's by refusin'."

Says I, out to one side, "Did you ever, Josiah Allen, see such goodness in your life?"

"I never see such dumb foolishness," says he. "I'd love to have anybody ketch me a drinkin' three or four quarts of such stuff out of politeness."

"No," says I coldly: "you hain't good enough."

Wall, that night his bed got a fire. It seemed as if every thing under the sun wus a goin' to happen to that man while he wus here. You see, the house wus all tore up a repairin', and I had to put him up-stairs: and the bed had been moved out by carpenters, to plaster a spot behind the bed; and, unbeknown to me, they had set it too near the stove-pipe. And the hot pipe run right up by the side of it, right by the bed-clothes. It took fire from the piller-case.

We smelt a dretful smudge, and Josiah run right up-stairs: it had only jest ketched a fire, and Elburtus was sound asleep; and Josiah, the minute he see what wus the matter, he jest ketched up the water-pitcher, and throwed the water over him ; and bein' skairt and tremblin', the pitcher flew out of his hand, and went too, and hit Elburtus on the end of his nose, and took a piece of skin right off.

He waked up sudden ; and there he wus, all drownded out, and a piece gone off of his nose.

Now, most any other man would have acted mad. Josiah would have acted mad as a mad dog, and madder. But you ort to see how good Elburtus took it, jest as quick as he got his senses back. Josiah said he could almost take his oath that he swore out as cross a oath as he ever heard swore the first minute before he got his eyes opened, but I believe he wus mistaken. But anyway, the minute his senses come back, and he see where he wuz, you ort to see how he behaved. Never, never did I hear of such manners in all my born days ! Josiah told me all about it.

There Elburtus stood, with his nose a bleedin', and his whiskers singed, and a drippin' like a mushrat. But, instead of jawin' or complainin', the first thing he said wuz, " What a splendid draft our stove must have, or else the stove-pipe wouldn't be so hot ! " (I had done some cookin' late in the evenin', and left a fire in the stove.)

And he said our stove-wood must be of the very best quality; and he asked Josiah where he got it, and if he had to pay any thing extra for that kind. He said he'd give any thing if he could get holt of a cord of such wood as that !

Josiah said he felt fairly stunted to see such manners ; and he went to apologisin' about how awful bad it was for him to get his whiskers singed so, and how it wus a pure axident his lettin' the pitcher slip out of his hand, and he wouldn't have done it for nothin' if he could have helped it, and he wus afraid it had hurt him more than he thought for.

And such manners as that clever critter showed then! He said he was a calculatin' to get his whiskers cut that very day, and it was all for the best; he persumed they wus singed off in jest the shape he wanted 'em: and as for his nose, he wus always ashamed of it; it wus always too long, and he should be glad if there wus a piece gone off of it: Josiah had done him a favor to help him get rid of a piece of it.

Why, when Josiah told it all over to me after he come down, I told him "I believed sunthin' would happen to that man before long. I believed he wus too good for earth."

Josiah can't bear to hear me praise up any mortal man only himself, and he muttered sunthin' about "he bet he wouldn't be so tarnel good after 'lection."

But I wouldn't hear no such talk; and says I, —

"If there wus ever a saint on earth, it is Elburtus Smith Gansey;" and says I, "If you try to vote for anybody else, I'll know the reason why."

"Wall, wall! who said J wus a goin' to? I shall probable vote in the family; but he hain't no more saint than I be."

I gin him a witherin' look; but, as it wus dark as pitch in the room, he didn't act withered any. And I spoke out agin, and says I, in a low, deep voice, —

"If it wus one of the relations on your side, Josiah Allen, you would say he acted dretful good."

And he says, "There is such a thing, Samantha, as bein' *too* good — too *dumb* good."

I didn't multiply any more words with him, and we went to sleep.

Wall, that is jest the way that feller acted for the next five days. Why, the neighbors all got to lovin' him so, why, they jest about worshipped him. And Josiah said that there wuzn't no use a talkin', Elburtus would get the nomination unanimous; for everybody that had seen him appear (and he had been all over the town appearin' to 'em, and endearin' himself to 'em, cleer out beyond Jonesville as far as Spoon Settlement and Loontown), why, they jest thought their eyes of him, he wus so thoughtful and urbane and helpful. Why, there hain't no tellin' how much helpfuler he wuz than common folks, and urbaner.

Why, Josiah and me drove into Jonesville one day towards night; and Elburtus had been there all day. Josiah had some cross-gut saws that he wanted to get filed, and had happened to mention it before Elburtus; and nothin' to do but he must go and carry 'em to the man in Jonesville that wus goin' to do it, and help him file 'em. Josiah told him we wus goin' over towards night with the team, and could carry 'em as well as not; and he hadn't better try to help, filin' saws wus such a sort of a raspin' undertakin'. But Elburtus said "he should probably go through more raspin' jobs before he died, or got the nomination; and Josiah could have 'em to bring home that night." So he sot out with 'em walkin' a foot.

Wall, when we drove in, I see Elburtus a liftin' and a luggin', a loadin' a big barrell into a double wagon for a farmer; and I says, —

"What under the sun is Elburtus Gansey a doin'?"

And Josiah says, in a gay tone, —

ELBURTUS APPEARIN'.

"He is a electionerin', Samantha : 'see him sweat," says he. "Salt is heavy, and political life is, wearin', when anybody goes into it deep, and tackles it in the way Elburtus tackles it."

He seemed to think it wus a joke ; but I says, —

" He is jest a killin' himself, Josiah Allen ; and you would set here, and see him."

" I hain't a runnin'," says he in a calm tone.

"No," says I : "you wouldn't run a step to help anybody. And see there," says I. " How good, how good that man is ! "

Elburtus had finished loadin' the salt, and now he wus a holdin' the horses for the man to load some spring-beds. And the horses wus skairt by 'em, and wuz jest a liftin' Elburtus right up offen his feet. Why, they pranced, and tore, and lifted him up, and switched him round, and then they'd set him down with a crash, and whinner.

But that man smiled all the time, and took off his hat, and bowed to me : we went by when he wus a swingin' right up in the air. I never see the beat of his goodness. Why, we found out afterwards, that, besides filin' them saws, he had loaded seven barrells of salt that day, besides other heavy truck. That night he wus perfectly beat out — but good.

Josiah said that Philander Dagget'ses wive's brother wouldn't have no chance at all. He wanted the nomination awful, and Philander had been a workin' for him all he could ; and if Elburtus hadn't come down to Jonesville, and showed off such a beautiful demeanor and actions, why, we all thought that Philander's wive's brother would have got it. And I couldn't help feelin' kind o' sorry for him, though highly tickled for Elburtus. We both of us, Josiah and me, felt very pleased and extremely tickled to think that Elburtus wus so sure of it; for there wus a good deal of money in the office, besides honor, sights of honor.

Wall, when the mornin' of town-meetin' came, that critter wus so awful clever that nothin' to do but what he must help Josiah do the chores.

And amongst other chores Josiah had to do that mornin', wus to carry home a plow that belonged to old Dagget. And old Dagget wanted Josiah, when he had got through with it, to carry it to his son Philander's: and Philander had left word that he wanted it that mornin'; and he wanted it carried down to his lower barn, that stood in a meadow a mile away from any house. Philander'ses land run in such a way that he had to build it there to store his fodder.

Wall, time run along, and it got time to start for town-meetin', and Elburtus couldn't be found. I hollered to him from the back stoop, and Josiah went out to the barn and hollered; but nothin' could be seen of him. And Josiah got all ready, and waited, and waited; and I told him that Elburtus had probable got in such a hurry to get there, that he had started on a foot, and he had better drive on, and he would overtake him. So finally he did; and he drove along clear to Jonesville, expectin' to overtake him every minute, and didn't. And the hull day passed off, and no Elburtus. And nobody had seen him. And everybody thought it looked so curius in him, a disapearin' as he did, when they all knew that he had come down to our part of the county a purpose to get the nom-

ELBURTUS HOLDING THE HORSES.

ination. Why, his disapearin' as he did looked so awful strange, that they didn't know what to make of it.

And the opposition side, Philander Daggets'es wive's brother's friends, started the story that he wus arrested for stealin' a sheep, and wus dragged off to jail that mornin'.

Of course Josiah tried to dispute it; but, as he wus as much in the dark as any of 'em as to where he wuz, his disputin' of it didn't amount to any thing. And then, Josiah's feelin' so strange about Elburtus made his eyes look kinder glassy and strange when they wus talkin' to him about it; and they got up the story, so I hearn, that Josiah helped him off with the sheep, and wus feelin' like death to have him found out.

And the friends of Philander Daggets'es wive's brother had it all thier own way, and he wus elected almost unanimous.

Wall, Josiah come home early, he wus so worried about Elburtus. He thought mebby he had come back home after he had got away, and wus took sick sudden. And his first words to me wuz, —

" Where is Elburtus? Have you seen Elburtus? "

And then wus my time to be smit and horrow-struck. And the more we got to thinkin' about it, the more wonderful did it seem to us, that that man had dissapeared right in broad daylight, jest as sudden and mysterious as if the ground had opened, and swallowed him down, or as if he had spread a pair of wings, and flown up into the sky.

Not that I really thought he had. I couldn't hardly associate the idee of heaven and endless repose with a short frock-coat and boots, and a blue necktie and a stiff shirt-collar.

But, oh! how strange and mysterious it did seem to be! We talked it over and over, and we could not think of any thing that could happen to him. He knew enough to keep out of the creek; and there wusn't no woods nigh where he could get lost, and he wus too old to be stole. And so we thought and thought, and racked our 2 brains.

And finally I says, "Wall! it hain't happened for several thousand years, but I don't know what to think. We read of folks bein' translated up to heaven when they get too good for earth, and you know I have told you several times that he wus too clever for earth. I have thought he wus not of the earth, earthy."

"And I have thought," says he, sort o' snappish, "that he wus of politics, politicky."

Says I, "Josiah Allen, I should be afraid, if I wus in your place, to talk in that way in such a time as this," says I. "I have felt, when I see his actions when he wus knocked over by that sheep, and covered with lime, and sot fire to, I have felt as if we wus entertainin' a angel unawares."

"Yes," says he, "it *wuz unawares*, entirely *unawares* to me."

His axent wus dry, dry as chaff, and as full of ironry as a oven-door or flat-iron.

"Wall," says I, "mebby you will see the time, before the sun rises on your bald head again, that you will be sorry for such talk." Says I, "If it wus one of the relation on your side, mebby you would talk different about him." That touched him; and he snapped out, —

"What do you s'pose I care which side he wus on? And I should think it wus time to have a little sunthin' to eat: it must be three o'clock if it is a minute."

Says I, "Can you eat, Josiah Allen, in such a time as this?"

"I could if I could *get* any thing to eat," says he; "but there don't seem to be much prospect of it."

Says I, "The best thing you can do, Josiah Allen, is to foller his tracks. The ground is kinder soft and spongy, and you can do it," says I. "Where did he go to last from here?"

"Down to Philander Daggets'es, to carry home his plow."

"That angel man!" says I.

"That angel fool!" says Josiah. "Who asked him to go?"

Says I, "When a man gets too good for earth, there is other ways to translate him besides chariots of fire. Who knows but what he has fell down in a fit! And do you go this minute, Josiah Allen, and foller his tracks!"

"I sha'n't foller nobody's tracks, Samantha Allen, till I have sunthin' to eat."

I knew there wuzn't no use of reasonin' no further with him then; for when he said Samantha Allen in that axent, I knew he wus as sot as a hemlock post, and as hard to move as one. And so my common sense bein' so firm and solid, even in such a time as this, I reasoned it right out, he wouldn't stir till he had sunthin' to eat, and so the sooner I got his supper, the sooner he would go and foller Elburtus'es tracks. So I didn't spend no more strength a arguin', but kep' it to hurry up; and my reason is such, strong and vigorous and fur-seein', that I knew the better supper he had, the more animated would be his search. So I got a splendid supper, but quick.

HUNTING FOR ELBURTUS.

But, oh! all the time I wus a gettin' it, this solemn and awful question wus a hantin' me, — What had become of Elburtus Smith Gansey? What had become of the relation on my side? Oh, the feelin's I felt! Oh, the emotions I carried round with me, from buttery to teakettle, and from teapot to table!

But finally, after eatin' longer than it seemed to me he ever eat before (such wus my feelin's), Josiah started off acrost the lot, towards Daggets'es barn. And I stood in the west door, with my hand over my eyes, a watchin' him most every minute he wus gone. And when that man come back, he come a laughin'. And I wus that madded, to have him look in that sort of a scorfin' way, that I wouldn't say a word to him; and he come into the house a laughin', and sot down and crossed his legs a laughin', and says he, —

"What do you s'pose has become of the relation on your side?" And says he, snickerin' agin, —

"You wus in the right on it, Samantha, — he did asscend: he went up!" And agin he snickered loud. And says I coldly, cold as ice almost, —

"If I wuzn't a perfect luny, or idiot, I'd talk as if I knew sunthin'. You know I said that, as one who allegores. If you have found Elburtus Gansey, I'd say so, and done with it."

"Wall," says he, "you *wuz* in the right of it, and that is what tickles me. He got locked up in Dagget's barn. He asscended, jest as I told you. He went up the ladder over the hay, to throw down fodder, and got locked up *axidental.*" And, as he said "axidental," he snickered worse than ever.

And I says, "It is a mean, miserable, good for nothin', low-lived caper! And Philander Dagget done it a purpose to keep Elburtus from the town-meetin', so his wive's brother would get the election. And, if I wus Elburtus Gansey, I'd sue him, and serve a summons on him, and prosicute him."

"Why," says Josiah, in the same hilarious axent, and the same scorfin' look onto him, "Philander says he never felt so worked up about any thing in his life, as he did when he unlocked the barn-door to-night, and found Elburtus there. He said he felt as if he should sink, for he wus so afraid that some evil-minded person might say he done it a purpose. And he said what made him feel the worst about it wuz to think that he should have shut him up axidental when he wus a helpin' so good."

Says I, "The mean, impudent creeter! As good as Elburtus wuz!"

"Wall," says Josiah, "you know what I told you, — there is such a thing as bein' *too* good."

I wouldn't. multiply no more words on the subject, I wus that wrought up and excited and mad; and I wouldn't give in a mite to Josiah Allen, and wouldn't want it repeated now so he could hear it, but I do s'pose that wus the great trouble with Elburtus, — he wus a leetle *too* good.

And, come to think it over, I don't s'pose Philander had laid any plot to keep him away from 'lection; but he is a great case for fun, and he had laughed and tickled about Elburtus bein' so polite and helpful, and had made a good deel of fun of him. And then, he thinks a awful sight of his wive's brother, and wanted him to get the election.

And I s'pose the idee come to him after Elburtus had got down to the barn where he wus a fodderin' his sheep.

You see, if Elburtus had let well enough alone, and not been *too* good, every thing would have gone off right then; but he wouldn't. Nothin' to do but he must help Philander get down his fodder. And I s'pose then the idee come to him that he would shet him up, and keep him there till after 'lection wus over. For I don't believe a word about its bein' a axident. And I don't believe Josiah duz, though he pretends he duz. But every time he says that word "axident," he will laugh out so sort o' aggravatin'. That is what mads me to this day.

But, as Josiah says, who would have thought that Elburtus would have offered to carry that plow home, and throw down the fodder?

But, at any rate, Philander turned the key on him while he wus up over-head, and locked him in there for the day. A meaner, low-liveder, miserabler caper, I never see nor heard of.

But the way Philander gets out of it (he is a natural liar, and has had constant practice), he don't deny lockin' the door, but he says he wus to work on the outside of the barn, and he s'posed Elburtus had gone out, and gone home; and he locked the door, and went away.

He says (the mean, sneakin', hippocritical creeter!) that he feels like death about it, to think it happened so, and on that day too. And he says what makes him feel the meanest is, to think it was his wive's brother that wus up on the other side, and got the nomination. He says it leaves room for talk.

And there it is. You can't sue a man for lockin' his

own barn-door. And Elburtus wouldn't want it brought into court, anyway; for folks would be a wonderin' so what under the sun he wus a prowlin' round for up overhead in Philander Daggets'es barn.

So he wus obliged to let the subject drop, and Philander has it all his own way. And they say his wive's brother give him ten silver dollars for his help. And that is pretty good pay for turnin' one lock, about 2 seconts' work.

Wall, anyway, that wus the last thing that happened to Elburtus in Jonesville; and whether he took it polite and easy, or not, I don't know. For that night, when Philander went down to the barn to fodder, jest before Josiah went there, and let him out (and acted perfectly suprised and horrified at findin' him there, Philander did, so I have been told), Elburtus started a bee-line for the depo, and never come back here at all; and he left a good new handkerchief, and a shirt, and 3 paper collars.

And whether he has kep' on a sufferin', or not, I don't know. Mebby he had his trials in one batch, as you may say, and is now havin' a spell of enjoyments. I am sure, I hope so; for a cleverer, good-natureder, polite-appearin'er creeter, *I* never see, nor don't expect to see agin in my life; and so I tell Josiah.

CHAPTER III.

T_{HE} next evenin' follerin' after the exodus of Elburtus Gansey, Josiah and I, thinkin' that we needed a relaxation to relax our two minds, rode into Jonesville. We went in the Democrat, at my request; for I wus in hopes Cicely would come home with us.

And she did. We had a good ride. I sot in front with Josiah at his request; and what made it pleasanter wuz, the boy stood up in the Democrat behind me a good deal of the way, with his arms round my neck, a kissin' me.

And when I waked up in the mornin', I wus glad to think they wus there. Though Cicely wuzn't well: I could see she wuzn't. I felt sad at the breakfast-table to see how her fresh young beauty wus bein' blowed away by the sharp breath of sorrow's gale.

But she wus sweet and gentle as ever the posy wus we had named her after. No Sweet Cicely blow wus ever sweeter and purer than she wuz. After I got my work all done up below, — she offerin' to help me, and a not lettin' her lift her finger, — I went up into her room, where there wus a bright fire on the hearth, and every thing looked cozy and snug.

The boy, havin' wore himself out a harrowin' his uncle

Josiah and Ury with questions, had laid down on the crimson rug in front of the fire, and wus fast asleep, gettin' strength for new labors.

And Cicely sot in a little low rockin'-chair by the side of him. She had on a white flannel mornin'-dress, and a thin white zephyr worsted shawl round her; and her silky brown hair hung down her back, for she had been a brushin' it out; and she looked sweet and pretty enough to kiss; and I kissed her right there, before I sot down, or any thing.

And then, thinks'es I as I sot down, we will have a good, quiet visit, and talk some about other wimmen. (No runnin' 'em: I'd scorn it, and so would she.)

But I thought I'd love to talk it over with her, about what good housekeepers Tirzah Ann and Maggie wuz. And I wanted to hear what she thought about the babe, and if she could say in cander that she ever see a little girl equal her in graces of mind and body.

And I wanted to hear all about her aunt Mary and her aunt Melissa (on her father's side). I knew she had had letters from 'em. And I wanted to hear how she that was Jane Smith wuz, that lived neighbor to her aunt Mary's oldest daughter, and how that oldest daughter wuz, who wus s'posed to be a runnin' down. And I wanted to hear about Susan Ann Grimshaw, who had married her aunt Melissy's youngest son. There wus lots of news that I felt fairly sufferin' for, and lots of news that I felt like disseminatin' to her.

But, if you'll believe it, jest as I had begun to inquire, and take comfort, she branched right off, a lady-like branch, and a courteous one, but still a branch, and begun to talk about "what should she do — what could she do — for the boy."

And she looked down on him as he lay there, with such a boundless love, and a awful dread in her eyes, that it was pitiful in the extreme to see her; and says she, —

"What will become of him in the future, aunt Samantha, with the laws as they are now?"

And with such a chin and mouth as he has got, says I

THE BABY.

to myself, lookin' down on him; but I didn't say it out loud. I am too well bread.

"It must be we can get the laws changed before he grows up. I dare not trust him in a world that has such temptations, such snares set ready for him. Why," says she — And she fairly trembled as she said it. She would always throw her whole soul into any thing she undertook;

and in this she had throwed her hull heart, too, and her hull life — or so it seemed to me, to look at her pale face, and her big, glowin' eyes, full of sadness, full of resolve too.

' "Why, just think of it! How he will be coaxed into those drinking-saloons! how, with his easy, generous, good-natured ways, — and I know he will have such ways, and be popular, — a bright, handsome young man, and with plenty of money. Just think of it! how, with those open saloons on every side of him, when he can't walk down the street without those gilded bars shining on every hand; and the friends he will make, gay, rich, thoughtless young men like himself — they will laugh at him if he refuses to do as they do; and with my boy's inherited tastes and temperament, his easiness to be led by those he loves, what will hinder him from going to ruin as his poor father did? What will keep him, aunt Samantha?"

And she busted out a cryin'.

I says, "Hush, Cicely," layin' my hand on hern. It wus little and soft, and trembled like a leaf. Some folks would have called her nervous and excitable; but I didn't, thinkin' what she had went through with the boy's father.

Says I, "There is One who is able to save him. And, instead of gettin' yourself all worked up over what may never be, I think it would be better to ask Him to save the boy."

"I do ask Him, every day, every hour," says she, sobbin' quieter like.

"Wall, then, hush up, Cicely."

And sometimes she would hush up, and sometimes she wouldn't.

But how she would talk about what she wanted to do for him! I heard her talkin' to her uncle Josiah one day.

You see, she worried about the boy to that extent, and loved him so, that she would have been willin' to have had her head took right off, if that would have helped him, if it would have insured him a safe and happy future; but it wouldn't: and so she was willin' to do any other hard job if there wus any prospect of its helpin' the boy.

She wus willin' to vote on the temperance question.

But Josiah wus more sot than usial that mornin' aginst wimmen's votin'; and he had begun himself on the subject to Cicely; had talked powerful aginst it, but gentle: he loved Cicely as he did his eyes.

He had been to a lecture the night before, to Toad Holler, a little place between Jonesville and Loontown. He and uncle Nate Burpy went up to hear a speech aginst wimmen's suffrage, in a Democrat.

Josiah said it wus a powerful speech. He said uncle Nate said, "The feller that delivered it ort to be President of the United States:" he said, "That mind ort to be in the chair."

And I said I persumed, from what I had heard of it, that his mind wuz tired, and ort to set down and rest.

I spoke light, because Josiah Allen acted so high-headed about it. But I do s'pose it wus a powerful effort, from what I hearn.

He talked dretful smart, they say, and used big words.

The young feller that gin the lecture, and his sister, wus left orphans and poor; and she wus a good deal the

A GREAT EFFORT.

oldest, and she set her eyes by him. She had took care
of the old folks, supported 'em and lifted 'em round herself; took all the care of 'em in every way till they died:
and then this boy didn't seem to have much faculty for
gettin' along; so she educated him, sewed for tailors'
shops, and got money, and sent him to school and college,
so he could talk big.

And it was such a comfort to that sister, to sort o' rest
off for an evenin' from makin' vests and pantaloons, cheap,
to furnish him money!—it was so sort o' restful to her to
set and hear him talk large aginst wimmen's suffrage and
the weakness and ineficiency of .wimmen!

He said, the young chap did, and proved it right out, so
they said, "that the franchise was too tuckerin' a job for
wimmen to tackle, and that wimmen hadn't the earnest-
ness and persistency and deep forethought to make her
valuable as a franchiser—or safe."

You see, he had his hull strength, the young chap did;
for his sister had clothed him, as well as boarded him, and
educated him: so he could talk powerful. He could use up
quantities of wind, and not miss it, havin' all his strength.

His speech made a deep impression on men and wimmen. His sister bein' so wore out, workin' so hard, wept
for joy, it was so beautiful, and affected her so powerful.
And she said "she never realized till that minute how
weak and useless wimmen really was, and how strong and
powerful men was."

It wus a great effort. And she got a extra good supper
for him that night, I heard, wantin' to repair the waste in
his system, caused by eloquence. She wus supportin' him
till he got a client: he wus a studyin' law.

Wall, Josiah wus jest full of his arguments; and he talked 'em over to Cicely that mornin'.

But she said, after hearin' 'em all, "that she wus willin' to vote on the temperance question. She had thought it all over," she said. "Thought how the nation lay under the curse of African slavery until that race of slaves were freed. And she believed, that when women who were now in legal bondage, were free to act as their heart and reason dictated, that they, who suffered most from intemperance, would be the ones to strike the blow that would free the land from the curse."

Curius that she should feel so, but you couldn't get the idee out of her head. She had pondered over it day and night, she said, — pondered over it, and prayed over it.

And, come to think it over, I don't know as it wus so curius after all, when I thought how Paul had ruined himself, and broke her heart, and how her money wus bein' used now to keep grog-shops open, four of her buildin's rented to liquor-dealers, and she couldn't help herself.

Cicely owned lots of other landed property in the village where she lived; and so, of course, her property wus all taxed accordin' to its worth. And its bein' the biggest property there, of course it helped more than any thing else did to keep the streets smooth and even before the saloon-doors, so drunkards could get there easy; and to get new street-lamps in front of the saloons and billiard-rooms, so as to make a real bright light to draw 'em in and ruin 'em.

There wus a few — the doctor, who knew how rum ruined men's bodies; and the minister, he knew how it ruined men's souls — they two, and a few others, worked awful hard to get the saloons shut up.

But the executor, who wanted the town to go license, so's he could make money, and thinkin' it would be for her interest in the end, hired votes with her money. Her money used to hire liquor-votes! So she heard, and believed. The idee!

So her money, and his influence, and the influence of low appetites, carried the day; and the liquor-traffic won. The men who rented her houses, voted for license to a man. Her property used agin to spread the evil! She labored with these men with tears in her eyes. And they liked her. She was dretful good to 'em. (As I say, she held the things of this world with a loose grip.)

They listened to her respectful, stood with their hats in their hands, answerin' her soft, and went soft out of her presence — and voted license to a man. You see, they wus all willin' to give her love and courtesy and kindness, but not the right to do as her heaven-learnt sense of right and wrong wanted her to. She had a fine mind, a pure heart: she had been through the highest schools of the land, and that higher, heavenly school of sufferin', where God is the teacher, and had graduated from 'em with her lofty purposes refined and made luminous with somethin' like the light of Heaven.

But those men — many of 'em who did not know a letter of the alphabet, whose naturally dull minds had become more stupified by habitual vice — those men, who wus her inferiors, and her servants in every thing else, wus each one of 'em her king here, and she his slave; and they compelled her to obey thier lower wills.

Wall, Cicely didn't think it wus right. Curius she should think so, some folks thought, but she did.

But all this that wore on her wus as nothin' to what she felt about the boy, — her fears for his future. "What could she do — what *could* she do for the boy, to make it safer for him in the future?"

And I had jest this one answer, that I'd say over and over agin to her, —

"Cicely, you can pray! That is all that wimmen can do. And try to influence him right now. God can take care of the boy."

"But I can't keep him with me always; and other influences will come, and beat mine down. And I have prayed, but God don't hear my prayer."

And I'd say, calm and soothin', "How do you know, Cicely?"

And she says, "Why, how I prayed for help when my poor Paul went down to ruin, through the open door of a grog-shop! If the women of the land had it in their power to do what their hearts dictate, — what the poorest, lowest *man* has the right to do, — every saloon, every low grog-shop, would be closed."

She said this to Josiah the mornin' after the lecture I speak of. He sot there, seemin'ly perusin' the almanac; but he spoke up then, and says, —

"You can't shet up human nater, Cicely: that will jump out any way. As the poet says, 'Nater will caper.'"

But Cicely went right on, with her eyes a shinin', and a red spot in her white cheeks that I didn't like to see.

"A thousand temptations that surround my boy now, could be removed, a thousand low influences changed into better, helpful ones.　There are drunkards who long, who pray, to have temptations removed out of their way, — those who are trying to reform, and who dare not pass the door of a saloon, the very smell of the liquor crazing them with the desire for drink.　They want help, they pray to be saved; and we who are praying to help them are powerless.　What if, in the future, my boy should be like one of them, — weak, tempted, longing for help, and getting nothing but help towards vice and ruin?　Haven't mothers a right to help those they love in *every* way, — by prayer, by influence, by legal right and might?"

"It would be a dangerous experiment, Cicely," says Josiah, crossin' his right leg over his left, and turnin' the almanac to another month.　"It seems to me sunthin' unwomanly, sunthin' aginst nater.　It is turnin' the laws of nater right round.　It is perilous to the domestic nature of wimmen."

"I don't think so," says I.　"Don't you remember, Josiah Allen, how you worried about them hens that we carried to the fair?　They wus so handsome, and such good layers, that I really wanted the influence of them hens to spread abroad.　I wanted other folks to know about 'em, so's to have some like 'em.　But you worried awfully. You wus so afraid that carryin' the hens into the turmoil of public life would have a tendency to keep 'em from wantin' to make nests and hatch chickens!　But it didn't. Good land! one of 'em made a nest right there, in the coop to the fair, with the crowd a shoutin' round 'em, and laid two eggs.　You can't break up nature's laws; *they* are laid too deep and strong for any hammer we can get holt of to touch 'em ; all the nations and empires of the world can't move "em round a notch.

"A true woman's deepest love and desire are for her home and her loved ones, and planted right in by the side

SAMANTHA'S HENS.

of these two loves of hern is a deathless instinct and desire to protect and save them from danger.

"Good land ! I never heard a old hen called out of her spear, and unhenly, because she would fly out at a hawk, and cackle loud, and cluck, and try to lead her chickens off into safety.　And while the rooster is a steppin' high, and struttin' round, and lookin' surprised and injured, it is the old hen that saves the chickens, nine times out of ten.

"It is against the evil hawks, — men-hawks, — that are ready to settle down, and tear the young and innocent out of the home nest, that wimmen are tryin' to defend thier children from.　And men may talk about wimmen's gettin' too excited and zealous ; but they don't cluck and cackle half so loud as the old hen does, or flutter round half so earnest and fierce.

"And the chicken-hawk hain't to be compared for danger to the men-hawks Cicely is tryin' to save her boy from.　And I say it is domestic love in her to want to protect him, and tenderness, and nature, and grace, and — and — every thing."

I wus wrought up, and felt deeply, and couldn't express half what I felt, and didn't much care if I couldn't. I wus so rousted up, I felt fairly reckless about carin' whether Josiah or anybody understood me or not.　I knew the Lord understood me, and I knew what I felt in my own mind, and I didn't much care for any thing else. Wimmen do have such spells.　They get fairly wore out a tryin' to express what they feel in thier souls to a gainsayin' world, and have that world yell out at 'em, "Unwomanly ! unwomanly !"　I say, Cicely wuzn't unwomanly. I say, that, from the very depths of her lovin' little soul, she wus pure womanly, affectionate, earnest, tender-hearted, good ; and, if anybody tells me she wuzn't, I'll know the reason why.

But, while I wus a reveryin' this, my Josiah spoke out agin', and says, —

"Influence the world through your child, Cicely! influence him, and let him influence the world. Let him make the world better and purer by your influencein' it through him."

"Why not use that influence *now, myself?* I have it here right in my heart, all that I could hope to teach to my boy, at the best. And why wait, and set my hopes of influencing the world through him, when a thousand things may happen to weaken that influence, and death and change may destroy it? Why, my one great fear and dread is, that my boy will be led away by other, stronger influences than mine, — the temptations that have overthrown so many other children of prayer — how dare I hope that my boy will withstand them? And death may claim him before he could bear my influence to the world. Why not use it now, myself, to help him, and other mothers' boys? If it is, as you say, an experiment, why not let mothers try it? It could not do any harm; and it would ease our poor, anxious hearts some, to make the effort, even if it proved useless. No one can have a deeper interest in the children's welfare than their mothers. Would they be apt to do any thing to harm them?"

And then I spoke up, entirely unbeknown to myself, and says, —

"Selfishness has had its way for years and years in politics, and now why not let unselfishness have it for a change? For, Josiah Allen," says I firmly, "you know, and I know, that, if there is any unselfishness in this selfish world, it is in the heart of a mother."

"It would be apt to be dangerous," says Josiah, crossin' his left leg over his right one, and turnin' to a new month in the almanac. "It would most likely be apt to be."

" *Why?* " says Cicely. · " Why is it dangerous? Why is it wrong for a women to try to help them she would die for? Yes," says she solemnly, " I would die for Paul any time if I knew it would smooth his pathway, make it easier for him to be a good man."

" Wall, you see, Cicely," says Josiah in a soft tone, — his love for her softenin' and smoothin' out his axent till it sounded almost foolish and meachin', — " you see, it would be dangerous for wimmen to vote, because votin' would be apt to lower wimmen in the opinion of us men and the public generally. In fact, it would be apt to lower wimmen down to mingle in a lower class. And it would gaul me dretfully," says Josiah, turnin' to me, " to have our sweet Cicely lower herself into a lower grade of society : it would cut me like a knife."

And then I spoke right up, for I can't stand too much foolishness at one time from man or woman ; and I says, —

" I'd love to have you speak up, Josiah Allen, and tell me how wimmen would go to work to get any lower in the opinion of men ; how they could get into any lower grade of society than they are minglin' with now. They are ranked now by the laws of the United States, and the will of men, with idiots, lunatics, and criminals. And how pretty it looks for you men to try to scare us, and make us think there is a lower class we could get into ! *There hain't any lower class that we can get into* than the ones we are in now ; and you know it, Josiah Allen. And you sha'n't scare Cicely by tryin' to make her think there is."

He quailed. He knew there wuzn't. He knew he had said it to scare us, Cicely and me, and he felt considerable

meachin' to think he had got found out in it. But he
went on in ruther of a meek tone, —

"It would be apt to make talk, Cicely."

"What do I care for talk?" says she. "What do I
care for honor, or
praise, or blame? I
only want to try to
save my boy."

And she kep' right
on with her tender,
earnest voice, and
her eyes a shinin'
like stars, —

"Have I not a
right to help him?
Is he not *my* child?
Did not God give me
a *right* to him, when
I went down into the
darkness with God
alone, and a soul was
given into my hands?
Did I not suffer for
him? Have I not
been blessed in him?
Why, his little hands
held me back from
the gates of death.

CICELY AND HER PEERS.

By all the rights of heavenliest joy and deepest agony —
is he not *mine?* Have I not a *right* to help him in his
future?

"Now I hold him in my arms, my flesh, my blood, my life. I hold him on my heart now: he is *mine.* I can shield him from danger: if he should fall into the flames, I could reach in after him, and die with him, or save him. God and man give me that right now: I do not have to ask for it.

"But in a few years he will go out from me, carrying my own life with him, my heart will go with him, to joy or to death. IIe will go out into dangers a thousand-fold worse than death, — dangers made respectable and legal, — and I can't help him.

"*I,* his mother, who would die for him any hour — I must stand with my eyes open, but my hands bound, and see him rushing headlong into flames tenfold hotter than fire ; see him on the brink of earthly and eternal ruin, and can't reach out my hand to hold him back. My *boy!* My *own!* Is it right? Is it just?"

And she got up, and walked the room back and forth, and says, —

"IIow can I bear the thought of it? IIow can I live and endure it? And how can I die, and leave the boy?"

And her eyes looked so big and bright, and that spot of red would look so bright on her white cheeks, that I would get skairt. And I'd try to sooth her down, and talk gentle to her. And I says, —

"All things are possible with God, and you must wait and hope."

But she says, "What will hope do for me when my boy is lost? I want to save him now."

It did beat all, as I told Josiah, out to one side, to see

such hefty principles and emotions in such a little body. Why, she didn't weigh much over 90, if she did any.

And Josiah whispered back, "All women hain't like Cicely."

And I says in the same low, deep tones, "All men hain't like George Washington! Now get me a pail of water."

And he went out. But it did beat all, how that little thing, when she stood ready, seemin'ly, to tackle the nation — I've seen her jump up in a chair, afraid of a mice. The idee of anybody bein' afraid of a mice, and ready to tackle the Constitution!

And she'd blush up red as a rosy if a stranger would speak to her. But she would fight the hull nation for her boy.

And I'd try to sooth her (for that red spot on her cheeks skairt me, and I foreboded about her). I said to her after Josiah went out, a holdin' her little hot hands in mine, — for sometimes her hands would be hot and feverish, and then, agin, like two snowflakes, —

"Cicely, women's voting on intemperance would, as your uncle Josiah says, be a experiment. I candidly think and believe that it would be a good thing, — a blessin' to the youth of the land, a comfort to the females, and no harm·to the males. But, after all, we don't know what it would do " —

"*I know*," says she. And her eyes had such a far-off, prophetic look in 'em, that I declare for't, if I didn't almost think she *did* know. I says to myself, —

" She's so sweet and unselfish and good, that I believe she's more than half-ways into heaven now. The Holy Scriptures, that I believe in, says, ' Blessed are the pure

in heart, for they shall see God.' And it don't say where
they shall see Him, or when. And it don't say that the
light that fell from on high upon the blessed mother of our
Lord, shall never fall again on other heart-broken mothers,
on other pure souls beloved of Him."

And it is the honest truth, that it would not have surprised me much sometimes, as she wus settin' in the twilight with the boy in her arms, if I had seen a halo round
her head; and so I told Josiah one night, after she had
been a settin' there a holdin' the boy, and a singin' low to
him, —

> " ' A charge to keep I have, —
> A God to glorify;
> A never-dying soul to save,
> And fit it for the sky.' "

It wuzn't *her* soul she wus a thinkin' of, I knew. She
didn't think of herself: she never did.

And after she went to bed, I mentioned the halo. And
Josiah asked what that was. And I told him it was " the
inner glory that shines out from a pure soul, and crowns a
holy life."

And he said " he s'posed it was some sort of a head-
dress. Wimmen was so full of new names, he thought it
was some new kind of a crowfar."

I knew what he meant. He didn't mean crowfar, he
meant *crowfure*. That is French. But I wouldn't hurt
his feelin's by correctin' him; for I thought "fur" or
"fure," it didn't make much of any difference.

Wall, the very next day, when Josiah came from Jonesville, — he had been to mill, — he brought Cicely a letter

"A CHARGE TO KEEP I HAVE."

from her aunt Mary. She wanted her to come on at once; for her daughter, who wus a runnin' down, wus supposed to be a runnin' faster than she had run. And her aunt Mary was goin' to start for the Michigan very soon, — as soon as she got well enough : she wasn't feelin' well when she wrote. And she wanted Cicely to come at once.

So she went the next day, but promised that jest as quick as she got through visitin' her aunt and her other relations there, she would come back here.

So she went; and I missed her dretfully, and should have missed her more if it hadn't been for the state my companion returned in after he had carried Cicely to the train.

He come home rampant with a new idee. All wrought up about goin' into politics. He broached the subject to me before he onharnessed, hitchin' the old mair for the purpose. He wanted to be United-States senator. He said he thought the nation needed him.

"Needs you for what?" says I coldly, cold as a ice suckle.

"Why, it needs somebody it can lean on, and it needs somebody that can lean. I am a popular man," says he. "And if I can help the nation, I will be glad to do it; and if the nation can help me, I am willin'. The change from Jonesville to Washington will be agreeable and relaxin', and I lay out to try it."

Says I, in sarkastick tones, "It is a pity you hain't got your free pass to go on : — you remember that incident, don't you, Josiah Allen?"

"What of it?" he snapped out. "What if I do?"

"Wall, I thought then, that, when you got high-headed

and haughty on any subject agin, mebby you would remember that pass, and be more modest and unassuming."

He riz right up, and hollered at me, —

"Throw that pass in my face, will you, at this time of
year?"

And he started for the barn, almost on the run.

But I didn't care. I wus bound to break up this idee
of hisen at once. If I hadn't been, I shouldn't have mentioned the free pass to him. For it is a subject so gaulin'
to him, that I never allude to it only in cases of extreme
danger and peril, or uncommon high-headedness.

Now I have mentioned it, I don't know but it will be
expected of me to tell about this pass of hisen. But, if I
do, it mustn't go no further; for Josiah would be mad, mad
as a hen, if he knew I told about it.

I will relate the history in another epistol.

CHAPTER IV.

THIS free pass of Josiah Allen's wus indeed a strange incident, and it made sights and sights of talk.

But of course there wus considerable lyin' about it, as you know the way is. Why, it does beat all how stories will grow.

Why, when I hear a story nowadays, I always allow a full half for shrinkage, and sometimes three-quarters; and a good many times that hain't enough. Such awful lyin' times! It duz beat all.

But about this strange thing that took place and happened, I will proceed and relate the plain and unvarnished history of it. And what I set down in this epistol, you can depend upon. It is the plain truth, entirely unvarnished: not a mite of varnish will there be on it.

A little over two years ago Josiah Allen, my companion, had a opportunity to buy a wood-lot cheap. It wus about a mild and a half from here, and one side of the lot run along by the side of the railroad. A Irishman had owned it previous and prior to this time, and had built a little shanty on it, and a pig-pen. But times got hard, the pig died, and owing to that, and other financikal difficulties, the Irishman had to sell the place, "ten acres more or

JOSIAH'S WOOD-LOT.

less, runnin' up to a stake, and back again," as the law
directs.

Wall, he beset my companion Josiah to buy it; and as
he had plenty of money in the Jonesville bank to pay
for it, and the wood on our wood-lot wus gettin' pretty
well thinned out, I didn't make no objection to the enter-
prize, but, on the other hand, I encouraged him in it.
And so he made the bargain with him, the deed wus made
out, the Irishman paid. And Josiah put a lot of wood-
choppers in there to work; and they cut, and drawed the
wood to Jonesville, and made money. Made more than
enough the first six months to pay for the expenditure
and outlay of money for the lot.

He did well. And he calculated to do still better; for
he said the place bein' so near Jonesville, he laid out,
after he had got the wood off, and sold it, and kep' what
he wanted, he calculated and laid out to sell the place for
twice what he give for it. Josiah Allen hain't nobody's
fool in a bargain, a good deal of the time he hain't. He
knows how to make good calculations a good deal of the
time. He thought somebody would want the place to
build on.

Wall, I asked him one day what he laid out to do with
the shanty and the pig-pen that wus on it. The pig-pen
wus right by the side of the railroad-track.

And he said he laid out to tear 'em down, and draw the
lumber home: he said the boards would come handy to
use about the premises.

Wall, I told him I thought that would be a good plan,
or words to that effect. I can't remember the exact words
I used, not expectin' that I would ever have to remember

back, and lay 'em to heart. Which I should not had it not been for the strange and singular things that occurred and took place afterwards.

Then I asked my companion, if I remember rightly, "When he laid out to draw the boards home?" For I mistrusted there would be some planks amongst 'em, and I wanted a couple to lay down from the back-door to the pump. The old ones wus gettin' all cracked up and broke in spots.

And he said he should draw 'em up the first day he could spare the team. Wall, this wus along in the first week in April that we had this talk: warm and pleasant the weather wus, exceedingly so, for the time of year. And I proposed to him that we should have the children come home on the 8th of April, which wus Thomas J.'s birthday, and have as nice a dinner as we could get, and buy a handsome present for him. And Josiah was very agreeable to the idee (for when did a man ever look scornfully on the idee of a good dinner?).

And so the next day I went to work, and cooked up every thing I could think of that would be good. I made cakes of all kinds, and tarts, and jellys. And I wus goin' to have spring lamb and a chicken-pie (a layer of chicken, and a layer of oysters. I can make a chicken-pie that will melt in your mouth, though I am fur from bein' the one that ort to say it); and I wus goin' to have a baked fowl, and vegetables of all kinds, and every thing else I could think of that wus good. And I baked a large plum-cake a purpose for Whitfield, with "Our Son" on it in big red sugar letters, and the dates of his birth and the present date on each side of it.

I do well by the children, Josiah says I do; and they see it now, the children do; they see it plainer every day, they say they do. They say, that since they have gone out into the world more, and seen more of the coldness and selfishness of the world, they appreciate more and more the faithful affection of her whose name wus once Smith.

Yes, they like me better and better every year, they say they do. And they treat me pretty, dretful pretty. I don't want to be treated prettier by anybody than the children treat me.

And their affectionate devotion pays me, it pays me richly, for all the care and anxiety they caused me. There hain't no paymaster like Love: he pays the best wages, and the most satisfyin', of anybody I ever see. But I am a eppisodin', and to resoom and continue on.

Wall! the dinner passed off perfectly delightful and agreeable. The children and Josiah eat as if— Wall, suffice it to say, the way they eat wus a great compliment to the cook, and I took it so.

Thomas J. wus highly delighted with his presents. I got him a nice white willow rockin'-chair, with red ribbons run all round the back, and bows of the same on top, and a red cushion,— a soft feather cushion that I made myself for it, covered with crimson rep (wool goods, very nice). Why, the cushion cost me above 60 cents, besides my work and the feathers.

Josiah proposed to get him a acordeun, but I talked him out of that; and then he wanted to get him a bright blue necktie. But I perswaided him to give him a handsome china coffee cup and saucer, with " To My Son " painted on it; and I urged him to give him that, with ten new silver dollars in it. Says I, "He is all the son you have got, and a good son." And Josiah consented after a parlay. Why, the chair I give him cost about as much as that; and it wuzn't none too good, not at all.

Wall, he had a lovely day. And what made it pleasanter, we had a prospect of havin' another jest as good. For in about 2 months' time it would be Tirzah's Ann's birthday; and we both told her, Josiah and me, both did, that she must get ready for jest another such a time. For we laid out to treat 'em both alike (which is both Christian and common sense). And we told 'em they must all be ready to come home that day, Providence and the weather permittin'.

Wall, it wus so awful pleasant when the children got ready to go home, that Josiah proposed that he and me should go along to Jonesville with 'em, and carry little Samantha Joe. And I wus very agreeable to the idee, bein' a little tired, and thinkin' such a ride would be both restful and refreshin'.

And, oh! how beautiful every thing looked as we rode along! The sun wus goin' down in glory; and Jonesville layin' to the west of us, we seemed to be a ridin' along right into that glory — right towards them golden palaces, and towers of splendor, that riz up from the sea of gold. And behind them shinin' towers wus shadowy mountain ranges of softest color, that melted up into the tender blue of the April sky. And right in the east a full moon wuz sailin', lookin' down tenderly on Josiah and me and the babe — and Jonesville and the world. And the comet sot there up in the sky like a silent and shinin' mystery.

The babe's eyes looked big and dreamy and thoughtful.
She has got the beautifulest eyes, little Samantha Joe has.
You can look down deep into 'em, and see yourself in 'em;
but, beyond yourself, what is it you can see?   I can't tell,
nor nobody.   The ellusive, wonderful beauty that lays in

GOD'S COMMA.

the innocent baby eyes of little Samantha Joe. The
sweet, fur-off look, as if she wus a lookin' right through
this world into a fairer and more peaceful one.

And how smart they be, who can answer their question-
ing, — questionin' about every thing. Nobody can't —

Josiah can't, nor I, nor nobody. Pretty soon she looked up at the comet; and says she, "Nama," — she can't say grandma, — "Nama, is that God's comma?"

Now, jest see how deep that wuz, and beautiful, very. The heavens wuz full of the writin' of God, writin' we can't read yet, and translate into our coarser language; and she, with her deep, beautiful eyes, a readin' it jest as plain as print, and puttin' in all the marks of punctuation. Readin' the marvellous poem of glory, with its tremblin' pause of flame.

Josiah says, it is because she couldn't say comet; but I know better. Says I, "Josiah Allen, hain't it the same shape as a comma?"

And he had to gin it up that it was. And in a minute or two she says agin, —

"Nama, what is the comma up there for?"

Now hear that, how deep that wuz. Who could answer that question? I couldn't, nor Josiah couldn't. Nor the wisest philosopher that ever walked the earth, not one of 'em. From them that kept their night-watches on the newly built pyramids, to the astronimers of to-day who are spending their lives in the study of the heavens. If every one of them learned men of the world, livin' and dead, if they all stood in rows in our door-yard in front of little Samantha Joe, they would have to bow their haughty heads before her, and put their finger on their lips. Them lips could say very large words in every language under the sun; but they couldn't answer my baby's question, not one of 'em.

But I am eppisodin' fearfully, fearfully; and to re-soom.

We left the children and the babe safe in their respective housen', and happy; and we went on placidly to Jonesville, got our usual groceries, and stopped to the post-office. Josiah went into the office, and come out with his "World," and one letter, a big letter with a blue envelope. I thought it had a sort of a queer look, but I didn't say nothin'. And it bein' sort o' darkish, he didn't try to open it till we got home. Only I says, —

"Who do you s'pose your letter is from, Josiah Allen?"

And he says, "I don't know: the postmaster had a awful time a tryin' to make out who it was to. I should think, by his tell, it wus the dumbdest writin' that ever wus seen. I should think, by his tell, it went ahead of yourn."

"Wall," says I, "there is no need of your swearin'." Says I, "If I wus a grandfather, Josiah Allen, I would choose my words with a little more decency, not to say morality."

"Wall, wall! your writin' is enough to make a man sweat, and you know it."

"I hain't disputed it," says I with dignity. And havin' laid the blame of the bad writin' of the letter he had got, off onto his companion, as the way of male pardners is, he felt easy and comfortable in his mind, and talked agreeable all the way home, and affectionate, some.

Wall, we got home; and I lit a light, and fixed the fire so it burnt bright and clear. And I drawed up a stand in front of the fire, with a bright crimson spread on it, for the lamp; and I put Josiah's rockin'-chair and mine, one on each side of it; and put Josiah's slippers in front of the hearth to warm. And then I took my knittin'-work,

JOSIAH READING THE LETTER.

and went to knittin'; and by that time Josiah had got his barn-chores all done, and come in.

And the very first thing he did after he come in, and drawed off his boots, and wondered "why under the gracious heavens it was, that the bootjack never could be found where he had left it" (which was right in the middle of the settin'-room floor). But he found it hangin' up in its usual place in the closet, only a coat had got hung up over it so he couldn't see it for half a minute.

And after he had his warm slippers on, and got sot down in his easy-chair opposite to his beloved companion, he grew calmer again, and more placider, and drawed out that letter from his pocket.

And I sot there a knittin', and a watchin' my companion's face at the same time; and I see that as he read the letter, he looked smut, and sort o' wonder-struck: and says I, —

"Who is your letter from, Josiah Allen?"

And he says, lookin' up on top of it, —

"It is from the headquarters of the Railroad Company;" and says he, lookin' close at it agin, "As near as I can make out, it is a free pass for me to ride on the railroad."

Says I, "Why, that can't be, Josiah Allen. Why should they give you a free pass?"

"I don't know," says he. "But I know it is one. The more I look at it," says he, growin' excited over it, — "the more I look at it, the plainer I can see it. It is a free pass."

Says I, "I don't believe it, Josiah Allen."

"Wall, look at it for yourself, Samantha Allen " (when

he is dretful excited, he always calls me Samantha Allen),
"and see what it is, if it hain't that;" and he throwed it
into my lap.

I looked at it close and severe, but not one word could
I make out, only I thought I could partly make out the

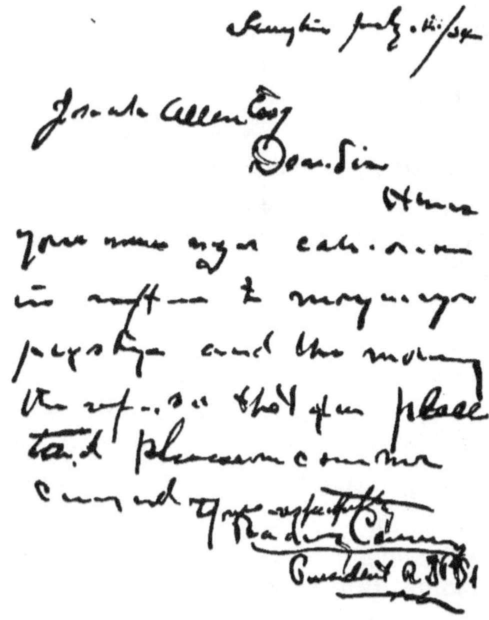

COPY OF THE LETTER: FREE PASS.

word "remove," and along down the sheet the word
"place," and there wus one word that did look like "free."
And Josiah jumped at them words; and says he, —

"It means, you know, the pass reads like this, for me to
remove myself from place to place, free. Don't you see
through it?" says he.

"No," says I, holdin' the paper up to the light. "No, I don't see through it, far from it."

"Wall," says he, highly excited and tickled, "I'll try it to-morrow, anyway. I'll see whether I am in the right, or not."

And he went on dreamily, "Lemme see — I have got to move that lumber in the mornin' up from my wood-lot. But it won't take me more'n a couple of hours, or so, and in the afternoon I'll take a start."

Says I, "What under the sun, Josiah Allen, should the Railroad Company give you a free pass for?"

"Wall," says he, "I have my thoughts."

He spoke in a dretful sort of a mysterious way, but proud; and I says, —

"What do you think is the reason, Josiah Allen?"

And he says, "It hain't always best to tell what you think. I hain't obleeged to," says he.

And I says, "No. As the poet saith, nobody hain't obleeged to use common sense unless they have got it;" and I says, in a meanin' tone, "No, I can't obleege you to tell me."

Wall, sure enough, the next day, jest as quick as he got that lumber drawed up to the house, Josiah Allen dressed up, and sot off for Jonesville, and come home at night as tickled a man as I ever see, if not tickleder.

And he says, "Now what do you think, Samantha Allen? Now what do you think about my ridin' on that pass?"

And I says, "Have you rode on it, Josiah Allen?"

And he says, "Yes, mom, I have. I have rode to Loontown and back; and I might have gone ten times as fur, and not a word been said."

And I says, "What did the conductor say?"

And he says, "He didn't say nothin'. When he asked me for my fare, I told him I had a free pass, and I showed it to him. And he took it, and looked at it close, and

LOOKING DUBERSOME.

took out his specks, and looked and looked at it for a number of minutes; and then he handed it back to me, and I put it into my pocket; and that wus all there was of it."

Says I, "How did the conductor look when he was a readin' it?"

And he owned up that he looked dubersome. But, says he, "I rode on it, and I told you that I could."

"Wall," says I, sithin', "there is a great mystery about it."

Says he, "There hain't no mystery to me."

And then I beset him agin to tell me what he thought the reason wus they give it to him.

And he said "he thought it was because he was so smart." Says he, "I am a dumb smart feller, Samantha, though I never could make you see it as plain as I wanted to." And then says he, a goin' on prouder and prouder every minute, —

"I am pretty-lookin'. I am what you might call a orniment to any car on the track. I kinder set a car off, and make 'em look respectable and dressy. And I'm what you might call a influential man, and I s'pose the rail-road-men want to keep the right side of me. And they have took the right way to do it. I shall speak well of 'em as long as I can ride free. And, oh! what solid comfort I shall take, Samantha, a ridin' on that pass! I calculate to see the world now. And there is nothin' under the sun to hender you from goin' with me. As long as you are the wife of such a influential and popular man as I be, it don't look well for you to go a mopein' along afoot, or with the old mare. We will ride in the future on my free pass."

"No," says I. "I sha'n't ride off on a mystery. I prefer a mare."

Says he, for he wus that proud and excited that you couldn't stop him nohow, —

"It will be a dretful savin' of money, but that hain't what I think of the most. It is the honor they are a heapin' onto me. To think that they think so much of me, set such a store by me, and look up to me so, that they send me a free pass without my makin' a move to ask for it. Why, it shows plain, Samantha, that I am one of the first men of the age."

And so he would go on from hour to hour, and from day to day; and I wus that dumbfoundered and wonderin' about it, that I couldn't for my life tell what to think of it. It worried me.

But from that day Josiah Allen rode on that pass, every chance he got. Why, he went to the Ohio on it, on a visit to his first wive's sister; and he went to Michigan on it, and to the South, and everywhere he could think of. Why, he fairly hunted up relations on it, and I told him so.

And after he got 'em hunted up, he'd take them onto that pass, and ride round with 'em on it.

And he told every one of 'em, he told everybody, that he thought as much agin of the honor as he did of the money. It showed that he wus thought so much of, not only in Jonesville, but the world at large.

Why, he took such solid comfort in it, that it did honestly seem as if he grew fat, he wus so puffed up by it, and proud. And some of the neighbors that he boasted so before, wus eat up with envy, and seemed mad to think he had come to such honor, and they hadn't. But the madder they acted, the tickleder he seemed, and more prouder, and high-headeder.

But I could not feel so. I felt that there wus sunthin'

strange and curius about it. And it wus very, very seldom that Josiah could get me to ride on it. Though I did take a few short journeys on it, to please him. But I felt sort o' uneasy while I was a ridin' on it, same as you feel when you are goin' up-hill with a heavy load and a little horse. You kinder stand on your feet, and lean forward, as if your bein' oncomfortable, and standin' up, helped the horse some.

I had a good deal of that restless feelin', and oneasy. And as I told Josiah time and time again, "that for stiddy ridin' I preferred a mare to a mystery."

Wall, it run along for a year; and Josiah said he s'posed he'd have to write on, and get the pass renewed. As near as he could make out, it run out about the 4th day of April. So he wrote down to the head one in New-York village; and the answer came back by return mail, and wrote in plain writin' so we could read it.

It seemed there wus a mistake. It wuzn't a free pass, it wus a order for Josiah Allen to remove a pig-pen from his place on the railroad-track within three days.

There it wuz, a order to remove a nuisence; and Josiah Allen had been a ridin' on it for a year, with pride in his mean, and haughtiness in his demeanor.

Wall, I never see a man more mortified and cut up than Josiah Allen wuz. If he hadn't boasted so over its bein' gin to him on account of his bein' so smart and popular and etcetery, he wouldn't have felt so cut up. But as it was, it bowed down his bald head into the dust (allegory).

But he didn't stay bowed down for any length of time: truly, men are constituted in such a way that mortification don't show on 'em for any length of time.

But it made sights and sights of talk in Jonesville. The Jonesvillians made sights and sights of fun of him, poked fun at him, and snickered. I myself didn't say much: it hain't my way. I merely says this: says I, —

"You thought you wus so awful popular, Josiah Allen, mebby you won't go round with so haughty a mean onto you right away."

"Throw my mean in my face if you want to," says he. "But I guess," says he, "it will learn 'em another time to take a little more pains with their duck's tracks, dumb 'em!"

Says I, "Stop instantly." And he knew what I meant, and stopped.

JOSIAH AND HIS RELATIONS ON THE PASS (p. 99).

CHAPTER V.

Josiah is as kind-hearted a man as was ever made. And he loves me with a devotion, that though hidden sometimes, like volcanic fires, and other married men's affections for their wives, yet it bursts out occasionally in spurts and jets of unexpected tenderness.

Now, the very next mornin' after Cicely left for her aunt Mary's, he gave me a flaming proof of that hidden fire that burns but don't consume him.

A agent come to our dwelling, and with the bland and amiable air of their sect, asked me, —

"If I would buy a encyclopedia?"

I was favorable to the idee, and showed it by my looks and words; but Josiah wus awful set against it. And the more favorable I talked about it, the more horrow-struck and skairt Josiah Allen looked. And finally he got behind the agent, and winked at me, and made motions for me to foller him into the buttery. He wunk several times before I paid much attention to 'em; but finally, the winks grew so violent, and the motions so imperious, yet clever, that I got up, and follered him into the buttery. He shet the door, and stood with his back against it; and says to me, with his voice fairly tremblin' with his emotions, —

"It will throw you, Samantha! you don't want to buy it."

"What will throw me? and when?" says I.

"Why," says he, "you can't never ride it! How should I feel to see you on one of 'em! It skairs me most to death to see a boy ride 'em; and at your age, and with your rheumatiz, you'd get throwed, and get your neck broke, the first day." Says he, "If you have got to have something more stylish, and new-fangled than the old mair, I'd ruther buy you a philosopher. They are easier-going than a encyclopedia, anyway."

"A philosopher?" says I dreamily.

"Yes, such a one as Tom Gowdey has got."

Says I, "You mean a velocipede!"

"Yes, and I'll get you one ruther than have you a ridin' round the country on a encyclopedia."

His tender thoughtfulness touched my heart, and I explained to him all about 'em. He thought it was some kind of a bycicle. And he brightened up, and didn't make no objections to my gettin' one.

Wall, that very afternoon he went to Jonesville, and come home, as I said, all rousted up about bein' a senator. I s'pose Elburtus'es bein' there, and talkin' so much on politics, had kinder sot him to thinkin' on it. Anyway, he come home from Jonesville perfectly rampant with the idee of bein' United-States senator. "He said he had been approached on the subject."

He said it in that sort of a haughty, high-headed way, such as men will sometimes assume when they think they have had some high honors heaped onto 'em.

Says I, "Who has approached you, Josiah Allen?"

JOSIAH BEING APPROACHED.

"Wall," he said, "it might be a foreign minister, and it might be uncle Nate Gowdey." He thought it wouldn't be best to tell who it was. "But," says he, "I am bound

to be senator.   Josiah Allen, M.C., will probable be wrote
on my letters before another fall.   I am bound to run."

Says I coldly, "You know you can't run.   You are as
lame as you can be.   You have got the rheumatiz the
worst kind."

Says he, "I mean runnin' with political legs — and I do
want to be a senator, Samantha.   I want to, like a dog.
I want the money there is in it, and I want the honor.
You know they have elected me path-master, but I hain't
a goin' to accept it.   I tell you, when anybody gets into
political life, ambition rousts up in 'em: path-master don't
satisfy me.   I want to be senator: I want to, like a dog.
And I don't lay out to tackle the job as Elburtus did, and
act too good."

"No!" says I sternly.   "There hain't no danger of
your bein' too good."

"No: I have laid my plans, and laid 'em careful.   The
relation on your side was *too* willin', and *too* clever.   And
witnessin' his campaign has learnt me some deep lessons.
I watched the rocks he hit aginst; and I have laid my
plans, and laid 'em careful.   I am going to act offish.   I
feel that offishness is my strong holt — and endearin' myself to the masses.   Educatin' public sentiment up to lovin'
me, and urgin' me not to be so offish, and to obleege 'em by
takin' a office — them is my 2 strong holts.   If I can only
hang back, and act onwillin', and get the masses fierce to
elect me — why, I'm made.   And then, I've got a plan in
my head."

I groaned, in spite of myself.

"I have got a plan in my head, that, if every other plan
fails, will elect me in spite of the old Harry."

Oh! how that oath grated against my nerve! And how I hung back from this idee! I am one that looks ahead. And I says in firm tones, —

"You never would get the nomination, Josiah Allen! And if you did, you never would be elected."

"Oh, yes, I should!" says he. But he continued dreamily, "There would have to be considerable wire-pullin'."

"Where would the wires be?" says I sternly. "And who would pull 'em?"

"Oh, most anywhere!" says he, lookin' dreamily up onto the kitchen ceilin', as if wires wus liable to be let down anywhere through the plasterin'.

Says I, "Should you have to go to pullin' wires?"

"Of course I should," says he.

"Wall," says I, "you may as well make up your mind in the first ont, that I hain't goin' to give my consent to have you go into any thing dangerous. I hain't goin' to have you break your neck, at your age."

Says he, "I don't know but my age is as good a age to break my neck in as any other. I never sot any particular age to break my neck in."

"Make fun all you are a mind to of a anxious Samantha," says I, "but I will never give my consent to have you plunge into such dangerous enterprizes. And talkin' about pullin' wires sounds dangerous: it sounds like a circus, somehow; and how would *you*, with your back, look and feel performin' like a circus?"

"Oh, you don't understand, Samantha! the wires hain't pulled in that way. You don't pull 'em with your hands, you pull 'em with your minds."

"Oh, wall!" says I, brightenin' up. "You are all right in that case: you won't pull hard enough to hurt you any."

I knew the size and strength of his mind, jest as well as if I had took it out of his head, and weighed it on the steel-yards. It was *not* over and above large. I knew it; and he knew that I knew it, because I have had to sometimes, in the cause of Right, remind him of it. But he knows that my love for him towers up like a dromedary, and moves off through life as stately as she duz — the drome-dary. Josiah was my choice out of a world full of men. I love Josiah Allen. But to resoom and continue on.

Josiah says, "Which side had I better go on, Saman-tha?" Says he, kinder puttin' his head on one side, and lookin' shrewdly up at the stove-pipe, "Would you run as a Stalwart, or a Half-breed?"

Says I, "I guess you would run more like a lame hen than a Stalwart or a Half-breed; or," says I, "it would depend on what breeds they wuz. If they wus half snails, and half Times in the primers, maybe you could get ahead of 'em."

"I should think, Samantha Allen, in such a time as this, you would act like a rational bein'. I'll be hanged if I know what side to go on to get elected!"

Says I, "Josiah Allen, hain't you got any principle? Don't you *know* what side you are on?"

"Why, yes, I s'pose I know as near as men in gineral. I'm a Democrat in times of peace. But it is human nater, to want to be on the side that beats."

I sithed, and murmured instinctively, "George Wash-ington!"

"George Granny!" says he.

I sithed agin, and kep' sithin'.

Says I, "It is bad enough, Josiah Allen, to have you talk about runnin' for senator, and pullin' wires, and etcetery. But, oh, oh! my agony to think my partner is destitute of principle."

"I have got as much as most political men, and you'll find it out so, Samantha."

My groans touched his heart — that man loves me.

"I am goin' to work as they all do. But wimmen hain't no heads for business, and I always said so. They don't look out for the profits of things, as men do."

I didn't say nothin' only my sithes, but they spoke volumes to any one who understood their language. But anon, or mebby before, — I hadn't kep' any particular account of time, but I think it wus about anon, — when another thought struck me so, right in my breast, that it most knocked me over. It hanted me all the rest of that day: and all that night I lay awake and worried, and I'd sithe, and sposen the case; and then I'd turn over, and sposen the case, and sithe.

Sposen he would be elected — I didn't really think he would, but I couldn't for my life help sposen. Sposen he would have to go to Washington. I knew strange things took place in politics. Strange men run, and run fur: some on 'em run clear to Washington. Mebby he would. Oh! how I groaned at the idee!

I thought of the awfulness of that place as I had heard it described upon to me; and then I thought of the weakness of men, and their liability to be led astray. I thought of the powerful blasts of temptation that blowed through them broad streets, and the small size of my pardner, and the light weight of his bones and principles.

And I felt, if things wuz as they had been depictered to me, he would (in a moral sense) be lifted right up, and blowed away — bones, principles, and all. And I trembled.

At last the idee knocked so firm aginst the door of my heart, that I had to let it in. That I *must,* I *must* go to Washington, as a forerunner of Josiah. I must go ahead of him, and look round, and see if my Josiah could pass through with no smell of fire on his overcoat — if there wuz any possibility of it. If there wuz, why, I should stand still, and let things take their course. But if my worst apprehensions wuz realized, if I see that it was a place where my pardner

JOSIAH BEING BLOWN AWAY.

would lose all the modest worth and winnin' qualities that first endeared him to me — why, I would come home, and throw all my powerful influence and weight into the scales, and turn 'em round.

Of course, I felt that I should have to make some pretext about goin': for though I wus as innocent as a babe of wantin' to do so, I felt that he would think he wus bein' domineered over by me. Men are so sort o' high-headed and haughty about some things! But I felt I could make a pretext of George Washington. That dear old martyr! I felt truly I would love to weep upon his tomb.

And so I told Josiah the next mornin', for I thought I would tackle the subject at once. And he says, —

"What do you want to weep on his tomb for, Samantha, at this late day?"

Says I, "The day of love and gratitude never fades into night, Josiah Allen: the sun of gratitude never goes down; it shines on that tomb to-day jest as bright as it did in 1800."

"Wall, wall! go and weep on it if you want to. But I'll bet half a cent that you'll cry onto the ice-house, as I've heard of other wimmen's doin'. Wimmen don't see into things as men do."

"You needn't worry, Josiah Allen. I shall cry at the right time, and in the right place. And I think I had better start soon on my tower."

I always was one to tackle hard jobs immejutly and to once, so's to get 'em offen' my mind.

"Wall, I'd like to know," says he, in an injured tone, "what you calculate to do with me while you are gone?"

"Why," says I, "I'll have the girl Ury is engaged to, come here and do the chores, and work for herself; they are goin' to be married before long: and I'll give her some rolls, and let her spin some yarn for herself. She'll be glad to come."

"How long do you s'pose you'll be gone? She hain't no cook. I'd as lives eat rolls, as to eat her fried cakes."

"Your pardner will fry up 2 pans full before she goes, Josiah; and I don't s'pose I'll be gone over four days."

"Oh, well! then I guess I can stand it. But you had better make some mince-pies ahead, and other kinds of pies, and some fruit-cake, and cookies, and tarts, and things: it is always best to be on the safe side, in vittles."

So it wus agreed on, — that I should fill two cubbard shelves full of provisions, to help him endure my absence.

I wus some in hopes that he might give up the idee of bein' United-States senator, and I might have rest from my tower; for I dreaded, oh, how I dreaded, the job! But as day by day passed, he grew more and more rampant with the idee. He talked about it all the time daytimes; and in the night I could hear him murmur to himself, —

"Hon. Josiah Allen!"

And once I see it in his account-book, "Old Peedick debtor to two sap-buckets to Hon. Josiah Allen."

And he talked sights, and sights, about what he wus goin' to do when he got to Washington, D.C. — what great things he wus goin' to do. And I would get wore out, and say to him, —

"Wall! you will have to get there first."

"Oh! you needn't worry. I can get there easy enough. I s'pose I shall have to work hard jest as they all do. But as I told you before, if every thing else fails, I have got a grand plan to fall back on — sunthin' new and uneek. Josiah Allen is nobody's fool, and the nation will find it out so."

Then, oh, how I urged him to tell his plan to his lovin' pardner! but he *wouldn't tell.*

But hours and hours would he spend, a tellin' me what

great things he wus goin' to do when he got to Washington.

Says he, "There is one thing about it. When I get
to be United-States senator, uncle Nate Gowdey shall be
promoted to some high and responsible place."

"Without thinkin' whether he is fit for it or not?"
says I.

"Yes, mom, without thinkin' a thing about it. I am
bound to help the ones that help me."

"You wouldn't have him examined," says I,—"wouldn't
have him asked no questions?"

"Oh, yes! I'd have him pass a examination jest as
the New-York aldermen do, or the civil-service men. I'd
say to him, 'Be you uncle Nate Gowdey?'

"'Yes.'

"'How long have you been uncle Nate Gowdey?'

"And he'd answer; and I'd say,—

"'How long do you calculate to be uncle Nate?'

"And he'll tell; and then I'll say,—

"'Enough: I see you have all the qualifications for
office. You are admitted.' That is what I would do."

I groaned. But he kep' on complacently, "I am goin'
to help the ones that elect me, sink or swim; and I calculate to make money out of the project,—money and
honor. And I shall do a big work there,—there hain't
no doubt of it.

"Now, there is political economy. I shall go in strong
for that. I shall say right to Congress, the first speech I
make to it, I shall say, that there is too much money spent
now to hire votes with; and I shall prove it right out,
that we can get votes cheaper if we senators all join in

together, and put our feet right down that we won't pay only jest so much for a vote. But as long as one man is willin' to pay high, why, everybody else has got to foller suit. And there hain't no economy in it, not a mite.

"Then, there is the canal question. I'll make a thorough end of that. There is one reform that will be pushed right through."

"How will you do it?" says I.

"I will have the hull canal cleaned out from one end to the other."

"I was readin' only yesterday," says I, "about the corruption of the canal question. But I didn't s'pose it meant that."

"That is because you hain't a man. You hain't got the mind to grasp these big questions. The corruption of the canal means that the bottom of the canal is all covered with dead cats and things; and it ort to be seen to, by men that is capable of seein' to such things. It ort to be cleaned out. And I am the man that has got the mind for it," says he proudly.

"Then, there is the Star Route. Nothin' but foolishness from beginnin' to end. They might have known they couldn't make any road through the stars. Why, the very Bible is agin it. The ground is good enough for me, and for any other solid man. It is some visionary chap that begun it in the first place. Nothin' but dumb foolishness; and so uncle Nate Gowdey said it was. We got to talkin' about it yesterday, and he said it was a pity wimmin couldn't vote on it. He said that would be jest about what they would be likely to vote for.

"He is a smart old feller, uncle Nate is, for a man of his

age.   He talked awful smart about wimmin's votin'.   He said any man was a fool to think that a woman would ever

JOSIAH'S STAR ROUTE.

have the requisit grasp of intellect, and the knowledge of public affairs, that would render her a competent voter.

" I tell you, you have got to *understand* things in order to tackle politicks. Politicks takes deep study.

" Now, there is the tariff question, and the revenue. I shall most probable favor 'em, and push 'em right through."

" How ? " says I.

" Oh, wall ! a woman most probable couldn't understand it. But I shall push 'em forward all I can, and lift 'em up."

" Where to ? " says I.

" Oh, keep a askin', and a naggin' ! That is what wears out us public men, — wimmin's questionin'. It hain't so much the public duties we have to perform that ages us, and wears us out before our time, — it is woman's weak curiosity on public topics, that her mind is too feeble to grasp holt of. It is wearin'," says he haughtily.

Says I, " Specially when they don't know what to answer." Says I, " Josiah Allen, you don't know this minute what tariff means, or revenue."

" Wall, I know what starvation means, and I know what vittles means, and I know I am as hungry as a bear."

Instinctively I hung on the teakettle. And as Josiah see me pare the potatoes, and grind the coffee, and pound the steak, he grew very pleasant again in his demeanor; and says he, —

" There will be some abuses reformed when I get to Washington, D.C.; and you and the nation will see that there will. Now, there is the civil-service law: Uncle Nate and I wus a talkin' about it yesterday. It is jest what we need. Why, as uncle Nate said, hired men hain't civil at all, nor hired girls either. You hire 'em to serve you, and to serve you civil; and they are jest as dumb uppish and impudent as they can be. And hotel-clerks — now, they don't know what civil-service means."

" Why, uncle Nate said when he went to the Ohio, last fall, he stayed over night to Cleveland, and the hotel-clerk sassed him, jest because he wanted to blow out his light: he wanted uncle Nate to turn it off.

"And uncle Nate jest spoke right up, smart as a whip, and said, 'Old-fashioned ways was good enough for him: blows wus made before turners, and he should blow it out.'

"And the hotel-clerk sassed him, and swore, and threatened to make him leave."

"And ruther than have a fuss, uncle Nate said he turned it out. But it rankled, uncle Nate says it did, it rankled deep. And he says he wants to vote for that special. He says he'd love to make that clerk eat humble-pie.

" Uncle Nate is a sound man: his head is level.

" And good, sound platforms, that is another reform, uncle Nate said we needed the worst kind, and he hoped I would insist on it when I got to be senator. He said there was too much talk about 'em in the papers, and too little done about 'em. Why, Elam Gowdey, uncle Nate's youngest boy, broke down the platform to his barn, and went right down through it, with a load of hay. And nothin' but that hay saved his neck from bein' broke. It spilte one of his horses.

" Uncle Nate had been urgin' him to fix the platform, or build a new one; but he was slack. But, as uncle Nate says, if such things are run by law, they will *have* to be done.

" And then, there is another thing uncle Nate and I was

talkin' about," says he, lookin' very amiable at me as I rolled out my cream biscuit — almost spooney.

UNCIVIL SERVICE.

"I shall jest run every poor Irishman and Chinaman out of the country that I can."

"What has the Irishmen done, Josiah Allen?" says I.

"Oh! they are poor. There hain't no use in our associatin' with the poor."

Says I dreamily, " Did I not read once, of One who re-nounced the throne of the universe to dwell amongst the poor? "

" Oh, wall ! most probable they wuzn't Irish."

" And what has the Chinaman done ? " says I.

" Why, they are heathens, Samantha. What does the United States want with heathens anyway? What the country *needs* is Methodists."

" Somewhere did I not once hear these words," says I musin'ly, as I set the coffee-cups on the table, — " ' You shall have the heathen for an inheritance ' — and ' preach the gospel to the heathen ' — and ' we who were sometime heathens, but have received light ' ? Did not the echo of some such words once reach my mind ? "

" Oh, wall ! if you are goin' to quote readin', why can't you quote from ' The World ' ? you can't combine Bible and politics worth a cent. And the Chinaman works too cheap — are too industrious, and reasonable in their charges, they hain't extravagant — and they are too dumb peacible, dumb 'em ! "

" Josiah Allen ! " says I firmly, " is that all the fault you find with 'em ? "

" No, it hain't. They don't want to vote ! They don't care a cent about bein' path-master or President. And I say, that after givin' a man a fair trial and a long one, if he won't try to buy or sell a vote, it is a sure sign that he can't asimulate with Americans, and be one with 'em; that he can't never be mingled in with 'em peacible. And I'll bet that I'll start the Catholics out — and the Jews. What under the sun is the use of havin' anybody here in America only jest Methodists? That is the only right

way. And if I have my way, I'll get rid of 'em, — Chinamen, Irishmen, Catholics, — the hull caboodle of 'em. I'll
jest light 'em out of the country. We can do it too.
That big statute in New-York Harbor of Liberty Enlight-
enin' the World, will jest lift her torch up high, and light
'em out of the country: — that is what we had her for."

I sithed low, and says, "I never knew that wus what
she wus there for. I s'posed it wus a gift from a land
that helped us to liberty and prosperity when we needed
'em as bad as the Irishmen and Chinamen do to-day ; and
I s'posed that torch that wus lit for us by others' help,
we should be willin' and glad to have it shine on the dark
cross-roads of others."

"Wall, it hain't meant for no such purpose: it is to
light up *our* land and *our* waters. That's what *she's* there
for."

I sithed agin, a sort of a cold sithe, and says, —

"I don't think it looks very well for us New-Englanders
a sittin' round Plymouth Rock, to be a condemnin' anybody for their religeous beliefs."

"Wall, there hain't no need of whittlin' out a stick, and
worshipin' it, as the Chinamen do."

"How are you goin' to help 'em to worship the true
God if you send 'em out of the country? Is it for the
sake of humanity you drive 'em out? or be you, like the
Isrealites of old, a worshipin' the golden calf of selfishness,
Josiah Allen?"

"I hain't never worshiped *no calf*, Samantha Allen.
That would be the last thing *I* would worship, and you
know it."

(Josiah wus very lame on his left leg where he had

been kicked by a yearlin'. The spot wus black and blue, but healin'.)

"You have blanketed that calf with thick patriotic excuses; but I fear, Josiah Allen, that the calf is there.

"Oh!" says I dreamily, "how the tread of them calves has moved down through the centuries! If every calf should amble right out, marked with its own name and the name of its owner, what a sight, what a sight it would be! On one calf, right after its owner's name, would be branded, 'Worldly Honor and Fame.'"

Josiah squirmed, for I see him, but tried to turn the squirmin' into a sickly smile; and he murmured in a meachin' voice, and with a sheepish smile, —

"'Hon. Josiah Allen. Fame.' That wouldn't look so bad on a likely yearlin' or two-year old."

But I kep' right on. "On another would be marked, 'Wealth.' Very yeller those calves would be, and a long, long drove of 'em.

"On another would be, 'Earthly Love.' Middlin' good-lookin' calves, these, and sights of 'em. But the mantillys that covered 'em would be all wet and wore with tears.

"'Culture,' 'Intellect,' 'Refinement.' These calves would march right along by the side of 'Pride,' 'Vanity,' 'Old Creeds,' 'Bigotry,' 'Selfishness.' The last-named would be too numerous to count with the naked eye, and go pushin' aginst each other, rushin' right through meetin'-housen, tearin' and actin'. Why," says I, "the ground trembles under the tread of them calves. I can hear 'em whinner," says I, fillin' up the coffee-pot.

"Calves don't whinner!" says Josiah.

Says I, "I speak parabolickly;" and says I, in a very

blind way, "Parables are used to fit the truth to weak comprehensions."

"Wall!" says he, kinder cross, "your potatoes are a burnin' down."

I turned the water off, and mashed 'em up, with plenty of cream and butter; and them, applied to his stomach internally, seemed to sooth him,—them, and the nice

THE GOLDEN CALVES OF CHRISTIANS.

tender steak, and light biscuit, and lemon puddin' and coffee, rich and yellow and fragrant.

He never said a word more about politics till after dinner. But on risin' up from the table he told me he had got to go to Jonesville to get the old mare shod. And I see sadly, as he stood to the lookin'-glass combin' out his few hairs, how every by-path his mind sot out on led up gradually to Washington, D.C. For as he stood there, and spoke of the mare's feet, he says,—

"The mare is good enough for Jonesville, Samantha. But when we get to Washington, we want sunthin' gayer, more stylish, to ride on. I calculate," says he, pullin' up his collar, and pullin' down his vest, — "I lay out to dress gay, and act gay. I calculate to make a show for once in my life, and put on style. One thing I am bound on, — I shall drive tantrum."

"How?" says I sternly.

"Why, I shall buy another mare, most probable some gay-colored one, and hitch it before the old white mare, and drive tantrum. You know, it is all the style. Mebby," says he dreamily, "I shall ride the drag. I s'pose

JOSIAH DRIVING TANTRUM.

that is fashionable. But I'll be hanged if I should think it would be easy ridin' unless you had the teeth down. Dog-carts are stylish, I hear; but our dog is so dumb lazy, you couldn't get him to go out of a walk. But tantrum I *will* drive."

I groaned, and says, "Yes, I hain't no doubt that anybody that sees you at Washington, will see tantrums, strange tantrums. But you hain't there yet."

"No, but I most probable shall be ere long."

He had actually begun to talk in high-flown, blank verse sort of a way. "Ere long!" that wus somethin' new for Josiah Allen.

Alas! every thought of his heart wus tuned to that one political key. I mentioned to him that "the bobbin to my sewin'-machine was broke, and asked him to get a new one of the agent at Jonesville."

"Yes," says he benignantly, "I will tend to your machine; and speakin' of machines, that makes me think of another thing uncle Nate and I wus talkin' about."

"Machine politics, I sha'n't favor 'em. What under the sun do they want machines to make politics with, when there is plenty of men willin', and more than willin', to make 'em? And it is as expensive agin. Machines cost so much. I tell you, they cost tarnation high."

"I can understand you without swearin', Josiah Allen."

"I hain't a swearin': 'tarnation' hain't swearin', nor never wuz. I shall use that word most likely in Washington, D.C."

"Wall," says I coldly, "there will have to be some tea and sugar got."

He did not demur. But, oh! how I see that immovible sotness of his mind!

"Yes, I will get some. But won't it be handy, Samantha, to have free trade? I shall go for that strong. Why, I can tell you, it will come handy along in the winter when the hens don't lay, and we don't make butter to turn off — it will come dretful handy to jest hitch up the mare, and go to the store, and come home with a lot of groceries of all kinds, and some fresh meat mebby. And mebby some neckties of different colors."

"Who would pay for 'em?" says I in a stern tone; for I didn't somehow like the idee.

"Why, the Government, of course."

I shook my head 2 or 3 times back and forth. I couldn't seem to get the right sense of it. "I can't understand it, Josiah. We heard a good deal about free trade, but I can't believe that is it."

"Wall, it is, jest that. Free trade is one of the prerequisits of a senator. Why, what would a man want to be a senator for, if they couldn't make by it?"

"Don't you love your country, Josiah Allen?"

"Yes, I do: but I don't love her so well as I do myself; it hain't nateral I should."

"Surely I read long ago, — was it in the English Reader?" says I dreamily, "or where was it? But surely I have heard of such things as patriotism and honor, love of country, and love of the right."

"Wall, I calculate I love my country jest as well as the next man; and," says he firmly, "I calculate I can make jest as much out of her, give me a chance. Why, I calculate to do jest as they all do. What is the use of startin' up, and bein' one by yourself?"

Says I, "That is what Pilate thought, Josiah Allen." Says I, "The majority hain't always right." Says I firmly, "They hardly ever are."

"Now, that is a regular woman's idee," says he, goin' into the bedroom for a clean shirt. And as he opened the bureau-draw, he says, —

"Another thing I shall go for, is abolishin' lots of the bureaus. Why, what is the use of any man havin' more than one bureau? It is nothin' but nonsense clutterin' up the house with so many bureaus.

"When wimmen get to votin'," says he sarcastickly, "I'll bet their first move will be to get 'em back agin. I'll

bet there hain't a women in the land, but what would love
to have 20 bureaus that they could run to."

"Then, you think wimmen *will* vote, do you, Josiah
Allen?"

"I think," says he firmly, "that it will be a wretched
day for the nation if she does. Wimmen is good in their
places," says he, as he come to me to button up his shirt-
sleeves, and tie his cravat.

"They are good in their places. But they can't have,
it hain't in 'em to have, the calm grasp of mind, the deep
outlook into the future, that men have. They can't
weigh things in the firm, careful balences of right and
wrong, and have that deep, masterly knowledge of national
affairs that we men have. They hain't got the hard horse
sense that anybody has got to have in order to make
money out of the nation. They would have some senti-
mental subjects up of right or wrong to spend their energies
and their hearts on. Look at Cicely, now. She means
well. But what would she do? What would she make
out of votin'? Not a cent. And she never would think
of passin' laws for her own personal comfort, either.
Now, there is the subsidy bill. I'll see that through if I
sweat for it.

"Why, it would be worth more than a dollar-bill to
me lots of times to make folks subside. Preachers, now,
when they get to goin' beyond the 20cthly. No preacher
has any right to go to wanderin' round up beyond them
figures in dog-days. And if they could be made to subside
when they had gone fur enough, why, it would be a perfect
boon to Jonesville and the nation.

"And sewin'-machine agents — and — and wimmen,

when they get all excited a scoldin', or talkin' about
bonnets, and things.   Why! if a man could jest lift up
his hand, and say 'Subside!' and then see 'em subside
—why, I had ruther see it than a circus any day."

A WOMAN'S PLACE.

I looked at him keenly, and says I, —
"I wish such a bill had even now passed; that is, if
wimmen could receive any benefit from it."

"Wall, you'll see it after I get to Washington, D.C., most probable. I calculate to jest straighten out things there, and get public affairs in a good runnin' order. The nation *needs* me."

"Wall," says I, wore out, "it can *have you*, as fur as I am concerned."

And I wus so completely fagged out, that I turned the subject completely round (as I s'posed) by askin' him if he laid out to sell our apples this year where he did last. The man's wife had wrote to me ahead, and wanted to know, for they had bought a new dryin'-machine, and wanted to make sure of apples ahead.

"Wall," says Josiah, drawin' on his overshoes, "I shall probable have to use the apples this fall to buy votes with."

"To buy votes?" says I, in accents of horrow.

"Yes. I wouldn't tell it out of the family. But you are all in the family, you know, and so I'll tell you. I sha'n't have to buy near so many votes on account of my plan; but I shall have to buy some, of course. You know, they all do; and I sha'n't stand no chance at all if I don't."

My groans was fearful that I groaned at this; but truly, worse was to come. He looked kinder pitiful at me (he loves me). But yet his love did not soften the firm resolve that wus spread thick over his linement as he went on, —

"I lay out to get lots of votes with my green apples," says he dreamily. "It seems as if I ought to get a vote for a bushel of apples; but there is so much iniquity and cheatin' a goin' on now in politics, that I may have to give a bushel and a half, or two bushels: and then, I shall make up a lot of the smaller ones into hard cider, and use 'em to — to advance the interests of myself and the nation in that way.

"There is hull loads of folks uncle Nate says he can bring to vote for me, by the judicious use of — wall, it hain't likely you will approve of it; but I say, stimulants

OUR LAW-MAKERS.

are necessary in medicine, and any doctor will tell you so — hard cider and beer and whiskey, and so 4th."

I riz right up, and grasped holt of his arm, and says in stern, avengin' tones, —

"Josiah Allen, will you go right against God's commands, and put the cup to your neighbor's lips, for your own gain? Do you expect, if you do, that you can escape Heaven's avengin' wrath?"

"They hain't my neighbors: I never neighbored with 'em."

Says I sternly, "If you commit this sin, you will be held accountable ; and it seems to me as if you can never be forgiven."

"Dumb it all, Samantha, if everybody else does so, where will I get my votes?"

"Go without 'em, Josiah Allen ; go down to poverty, or the tomb, but never commit this sin. 'Cursed is he that putteth the cup to his neighbor's lips.'"

"They hain't my neighbors, and it probable hain't no cup that they will drink out of: they will drink out of gobblers" (sometimes when Josiah gets excited, he calls goblets, gobblers). But I wus too wrought up and by the side of myself to notice it.

Says I, "To think a human bein', to say nothin' of a perfessor, would go to work deliberate to get a man into a state that is jest as likely as not to end in a murder, or any crime, for gain to himself." Says I, "Think of the different crimes you commit by that one act, Josiah Allen. You make a man a fool, and in that way put yourself down on a level with disease, deformity, and hereditary sin. You steal his reason away. You are a thief of the deepest dye; for you steal then, from the man you have stole from — steal the first rights of his manhood, his honor, his patriotism, his duty to God and man. You are a thief of the Government — thief of God, and right.

"Then, *you* make this man liable to commit any crime : so, if he murders, *you* are a murderer; if he commits suicide, *your* guilty soul shall cower in the presence of Him who said, 'No self-murderer shall inherit eternal life.' It is your own doom you shall read in them dreadful words."

"Good landy, Samantha! do you want to scare me to death?" and Josiah quailed and shook, and shook and quailed.

"I am only tellin' you the truth, Josiah Allen; and I should think it *would* scare anybody to death."

"If I don't do it, I shall appear like a fool: I shall be one by myself."

Oh, how Josiah duz want to be fashionable!

"No, you won't, Josiah Allen — no, you won't. If you try to do right, try to do God's will, you have His armies to surround you with a unseen wall of strength."

"Why, I hain't seen you look so sort o' skairful and riz up, for years, Samantha."

"I hain't felt so. To think of the brink you wuz a standin' on, and jest a fallin' off of."

Josiah looked quite bad. And he put his hand on his side, and says, "My heart beats as if it wuz a tryin' to get out and walk round the room. I do believe I have got population of the heart."

Says I, in a sarcasticker tone than I had used, —

"That is a disease that is very common amongst men, very common, though they hain't over and above willin' to own up to it. Too much population of the heart has ailed many a man before now, and woman too," says I in reasonable axents. "But you mean palpitation."

"Wall, I said so, didn't I? And it is jest your skairful talk that has done it."

"Wall, if I thought I could convince men as I have you, I would foller the business stiddy, of skairin' folks, and think I wuz doin' my duty." Says I, my emotions a roustin' up agin, —

" I should call it a good deal more honorable in you to get drunk yourself; and I should think more of you, if I see you a reelin' round yourself, than to see you make other folks reel. I should think it was your own reel, and you had more right to it than to anybody else's.

" Oh! to think I should have lived to see the hour, to have my companion in danger of goin' aginst the Scripter —ready to steal, or be stole, or knock down, or any thing, to buy votes, or sell 'em!"

" Wall, dumb it all, do you want me to appear as awkward as a fool? I have told you more than a dozen times I have *got* to do as the rest do, if I want to make any show at all in politics."

I said no more: but I riz right up, and walked out of the room, with my head right up in the air, and the strings of my head-dress a floatin' out behind me; and I'll bet there wus indignation in the float of them strings, and heart-ache, and agony, and — and every thing.

I thought I had convinced him, and hadn't. I felt as if I must sink. You know, that is all a woman can do — to sink. She can't do any thing else in a helpful way when her beloved companion hangs over political abysses. She can't reach out her lovin' hand, and help stiddy him : she can't do nothin' only jest sink. And what made it more curious, these despairin' thoughts come to me as I stood by the *sink*, washin' my dinner-dishes. But anon (I know it wus jest anon, for the water wus bilein' hot when I turned it out of the kettle, and it scalded my hands, onbeknown to me, as I washed out my sass-plates) this thought gripped holt of me, right in front of the sink, —

"Josiah Allen's wife, you must *not* sink. You *must* keep up. If you have no power to help your pardner to patriotism and honor, you can, if your worst fears are realized, try to keep him to home. For if his acts and words are like these in Jonesville, what will they be in Washington, D.C., if that place is all it has been depictered to you? Hold up, Samantha! Be firm, Josiah Allen's wife! John Rogers! The nine! One at the breast!"

So at last, by these almost convulsive efforts at calmness, I grew more calmer and composeder. Josiah had hitched up and gone.

And he come home clever, and all excited with a new thing.

They are buildin' a new court-house at Jonesville. It is most done, and it seemed they got into a dispute that day about the cupelow. They wanted to have the figger of Liberty sculped out on it; and they had got the man there all ready, and he had begun to sculp her as a wo-man, — the goddess of Liberty, he called her. But at the last minute a dispute had rosen: some of the leadin' minds of Jonesville, uncle Nate Gowdey amongst 'em, insisted on it that Liberty wuzn't a woman, he wuz a man. And they wanted him depictered as a man, with whiskers and pantaloons and a standin' collar, and boots and spurs — Josiah Allen wus the one that wanted the spurs.

He said the dispute waxed furious; and he says to 'em, —

"Leave it to Samantha: she'll know all about it."

And so it was agreed on that they'd leave it to me. And he drove the old mare home, almost beyond her strength, he wus so anxious to have it settled.

I wus jest makin' some cream biscuit for supper as he
come in, and asked me about it; and a minute is a minute
in makin' warm biscuit. You want to make 'em quick,
and bake 'em quick. My mind wus fairly held onto that
dough — and needed on it; but instinctively I told him
he wus in the right ont. Liberty here in the United.
States wuz a man, and, in order to be consistent, ort to
be depictered with whiskers and overcoat and a standin'
collar.

"And spurs!" says Josiah.

"Wall," I told him, "I wouldn't be particular about
the spurs." I said, "Instead of the spurs on his boots,
he might be depictered as settin' his boot-heel onto the
respectful petition of fifty thousand wimmen, who had
ventured to ask him for a little mite of what he wus
s'posed to have quantities of — Freedom.

"Or," says I, "he might be depictered as settin' on a
judgment-seat, and wavin' off into prison an intelligent
Christian woman, who had spent her whole noble, useful
life in studyin' the laws of our nation, for darin' to think
she, had as much right under our Constitution, as a low,
totally ignorant coot who would most likely think the
franchise wus some sort of a meat-stew."

Says I, "That will give Liberty jest as imperious and
showy a look as spurs would, and be fur more historick
and symbolical."

Wall, he said he would mention it to 'em; and says he,
with a contented look, —

"I told uncle Nate I knew I wus right. I knew Liberty
wus a man."

Wall, I didn't say no more: and I got him as good a

supper as the house afforded, and kep' still as death on politics; fur I could not help havin' some hopes that he might get sick of the idee of public life. And I kep' him down close all that evenin' to religion and the weather.

But, alas! my hopes wus doomed to fade away. And, as days passed by, I see the thought of bein' a senator wus ever before him. The cares and burdens of political life seemed to be a loomin' up in front of him, and in a quiet way he seemed to be fittin' himself for the duties of his position.

He come in one day with Solomon Cyphers'ses shovel, and I asked him "what it wuz?"

And he said "it wus the spoils of office."

And I says, "It is no such thing: it is Solomon Cypher'ses shovel."

"Wall," says he, "I found it out by the fence. Solomon has gone over to the other party. I am a Democrat, and this is party spoils. I am goin' to keep this as one of the spoils of office."

JONESVILLE COURT-HOUSE.

Says I firmly, "You won't keep it!"

"Why," says he, "if I am goin' to enter political life, I must begin to practise sometime. I must begin to do as

they all do. And it is a crackin' good shovel too," says
he pensively.

Says I, "You are goin' to carry that shovel right
straight home, Josiah Allen!"

And I made him.

The *idee.*

But I see in this and in many kindred things, that he
wuz a dwellin' on this thought of political life — its honors and emollients. And often, and in dark hints, he
would speak of his *Plan.* If every other means failed, if
he couldn't spare the money to buy enough votes, how his
plan wus goin' to be the makin' of him.

And I overheard him tellin' the babe once, as he wus
rockin' her to sleep in the kitchen, "how her grandpa had
got up somethin' that no other babe's grandpa had ever
thought of, and how she would probable see him in the
White House ere long."

I wus makin' nut-cakes in the buttery; and I shuddered
so at these words, that I got in most as much agin lemon
as I wanted in 'em. I wus a droppin' it into a spoon, and
it run over, I wus that shook at the thought of his plan.

I had known his plans in the past, and had hefted 'em.
And I truly felt that his plans wus liable any time to be
the death of him, and the ruination.

But he wouldn't tell!

But kep' his mind immovibly sot, as I could see. And
the very day of the shovel episode, along towards night
he rousted out of a brown study, — a sort of a dark-brown
study, — and says he, —

"Yes, I shall make out enough votes if we have a judicious committee."

"A lyin' one, do you mean?" says I coldly. But not surprized. For truly, my mind had been so strained and racked that I don't know as it would have surprized me if Josiah Allen had riz up, and knocked me down.

"Wall, in politics, you *have* to add a few orts sometimes."

I sithed, not a wonderin' sithe, but a despairin' one; and he went on, —

"I know where I shall get a hull lot of votes, anyway."

"Where?" says I.

"Why, out to that nigger settlement jest the other side of Jonesville."

"How do you know they'll vote for you?" says I.

"I'd like to see 'em vote aginst me!" says he, in a skairful way.

"Would you use intimidation, Josiah Allen?"

"Why, uncle Nate Gowdey and I, and a few others who love quiet, and love to see folks do as they ort to, lay out to take some shot-guns and *make* them niggers vote right; make 'em vote for me; shoot 'em right down if they don't. We have got the campaign all planned out."

"Josiah Allen," says I, "if you have no fear of Heaven, have you no fear of the Government? Do you want to be hung, and see your widow a breakin' her heart over your gallowses?"

"Oh! I shouldn't get hung. The Government wouldn't do nothin'. The Government feels jest as I do, — that it would be wrong to stir up old bitternesses, and race differences. The bloody shirt has been washed, and ironed out; and it wouldn't be right to dirty it up agin. The colored race is now at peace; and if they will only do right, do jest as the white men wants 'em to, Government won't never interfere with 'em."

I groaned, and couldn't help it; and he says, —

"Why, hang it all, Samantha, if I make any show at all in public life, I have got to begin to practise sometime."

"Wall," says I, "bring me in a pail of water." But as he went out after it, I murmured sternly to myself, —

"Oh! wus there ever a forerunner more needed to run?" and my soul answered, "Never! never!"

MAKING THEM DO RIGHT.

So with sithes that could hardly be sithed, so big and hefty wuz they, I commenced to make preparations for embarkin' on my tower. And no martyr that ever sot down on a hot gridiron wus animated by a more warm and martyrous feelin' of self-sacrifice. Yes, I truly felt, that if there wus dangers to be faced, and daggers run through pardners, I felt I would ruther they would pierce my own spare-ribs than Josiah's. (I say spare-ribs for oritory — my ribs are not spare, fur from it.)

I didn't really believe, if he run, he would run clear to Washington. And yet, when my mind roamed on some public men, and how fur they run, I would groan, and hurry up my preparations.

I knew my tower must be but a short one, for sugarin'-time wus approachin' with rapid strides, and Samantha must be at the hellum. But I also knew, that with a determined mind, and a willin' heart, great things could be accomplished speedily; so I commenced makin' preparations, and layin' on plans.

As become a woman of my cast-iron principles, I fixed up mostly on the inside of my head instead of the outside. I studied the map of the United States. I done several sums on the slate, to harden my mind, and help me grasp great facts, and meet difficulties bravely. I read Gass'es "Journal," — how he rode up our great rivers on a perioger, and shot bears. Expectin', as I did, to see trouble, I read over agin that book that has been my stay in so many hard-fit battle-fields of principle, — Fox'es "Book of Martyrs."

I studied G. Washington's picture on the parlor-wall, to get kinder stirred up in my mind about him, so's to realize to the full my privileges as I wept onto his tomb, and stood in the capital he had foundered.

Thomas J. come one day while I wus musin' on George; and he says, —

"What are you lookin' so close at that dear old humbug for?"

Says I firmly, and keepin' the same posture, "I am studyin' the face of the revered and noble G. Washington. I am going shortly to weep on his tomb and the capital he foundered. I am studyin' his face, and Gass'es 'Journal,' and other works," says I.

"If you are going to the capital, you had better study Dante."

Says I, "Danty who?"

And he says, "Just plain Dante." Says he, "You had better study his inscription on the door of the infern " —

Says I, "Cease instantly. You are on the very pint of swearin';" and I don't know now what he meant, and don't much care. Thomas J. is full of queer remarks, anyway. But deep. He had a sick spell a few weeks ago; and I went to see him the first thing in the mornin', after I heard of it. He had overworked, the doctor said, and his heart wuz a little weak. He looked real white; and I took holt of his hand, and says I, —

"Thomas J., I am worried about you: your pulse don't beat hardly any."

"No," says he. And he laughed with his eyes and his lips too. "I am glad I am not a newspaper this morning, mother."

And I says, "Why?"

And he says, "If I were a morning paper, mother, I shouldn't be a success, my circulation is so weak."

A jokin' right there, when he couldn't lift his head. But he got over it: he always did have them sort of sick spells, from a little child.

But a manlier, good-hearteder, level-headeder boy never lived than Thomas Jefferson Allen. He is *just right*, and always wuz. And though I wouldn't have it get out for the world, I can't help seein' it, that he goes fur ahead of Tirzah Ann in intellect, and nobleness of nater; and though I love 'em both devotedly, I *do*, and I can't help it, like him jest a little mite the best. But *this* I wouldn't have get out for a thousand dollars. I tell it in strict confidence, and s'pose it will be kep' as such. Mebby I hadn't ort to tell it at all. Mebby it hain't quite orthodox in me to feel so. But it is truthful, anyway. And sometimes I get to kinder wobblin' round inside of my mind, and a wonderin' which is the best, —to be orthodox, or truthful, —and I sort o' settle down to thinkin' I will tell the truth anyway.

Josiah, I think, likes Tirzah Ann the best.

But I studied deep, and mused. Mused on our 4 fathers, and our 4 mothers, and on Liberty, and Independence, and Truth, and the Eagle. And thinkin' I might jest as well be to work while I was a musin', I had a dress made for the occasion. It wus bran new, and the color wus Bismark Brown.

Josiah wanted me to have Ashes of Moses color.

But I said no. With my mind in the heroic state it was then, I couldn't curb it down onto Ashes of Moses, or roses, or any thing else peacible. I felt that this color, remindin' me of two grand heroes, — Bismark, John Brown, —suited me to a T.

There wus two wimmen who stood ready to make it, —Jane Bently and Martha Snyder. I chose Martha because Martha wus the name of the wife of Washington.

It wus made with a bask.

When the news got out that I wus goin' to Washington on a tower, the neighbors all wanted to send errents by me.

Betsey Bobbet wanted me to go to the Patent Office, and get her two Patent-office books, for scrap-books for poetry.

Uncle Jarvis Bently wanted me to go to the Agricultural Bureau, and get him a paper of lettis seed. And Solomon Cypher wanted me to get him a new kind of string-beans, if I could, and some cowcumber seeds.

Uncle Nate Gowdey, who talked of paintin' his house over, wanted me to ask the President what kind of paint he used on the White House, and if he put in any sperits of turpentime. And Ardelia Rumsey, who wuz goin' to be married soon, wanted me, if I see any new kinds of bed-quilt patterns to the White House, or to the senators' housen, to get the patterns for her. She said she wuz sick of sunflowers, and blazin' stars, and such. She thought mebby they'd have suthin' new, spread-eagle style, or suthin' of that kind. She said "her feller was goin' to be connected with the Government, and she thought it would be appropriate."

And I asked her "how?" And she said, "he was goin' to get a patent on a new kind of a jack-knife."

I told her "if she wanted a Government quilt, and wanted it appropriate, she ort to have it a crazy-quilt."

And she said she had jest finished a crazy-quilt, with seven thousand pieces of silk in it, and each piece trimmed with seven hundred stitches of feather stitchin': she counted 'em. And then I remembered seein' it. There wus some talk then about wimmen's rights, and a petition wus got up in Jonesville for wimmen to sign; and I remember well that Ardelia couldn't sign it for lack of time. She wanted to, but she hadn't got the quilt more'n half done then. It took the biggest heft of two years to do it. And so, of course, less important things had to be put aside till she got it finished.

· And I remember, too, that Ardelia's mother wanted to sign it; but she couldn't, owin' to a bed-spread she wus a makin'. She wuz a quiltin' in Noah's ark, and all the animals, at that time, on a Turkey-red quilt. I remember she wuz a quiltin' the camel that day, and couldn't be disturbed. So we didn't get the names. It took the old lady three years to quilt that quilt. And when it wuz done, it wuz a sight to behold. Though, as I said then, and say now, I wouldn't give much to sleep under so many animals. But folks went from fur and near to see it, and I enjoyed lookin' at it that day. And I see jest how it wuz. I see that she couldn't sign. It wuzn't to be expected that a woman could stop to tend to Justice or Freedom, or any thing else of that kind, right in the midst of a camel.

Zebulin Coon wanted me to carry a new hen-coop of hisen to get it patented. And I thought to myself, I wonder if they'll ask me to carry a cow.

And sure enough, Josiah wanted me to dicker, if I could, for a calf from Mount Vernon, — swop one of our yearlin's for it if I couldn't do no better.

But I told him right out and out, that I couldn't go into a calf-trade with my mind wrought up as I knew it would be.

Wall, it wuzn't more'n 2 or 3 days after I begun my preparations, that Dorlesky Burpy, a vegetable widow, come to see me; and the errents she sent by me wuz fur more hefty and momentous than all the rest put together, calves, hen-coop, and all.

And when she told 'em over to me, and I meditated on her reasons for sendin' 'em, and her need of havin' 'em

THE MOTHER'S BED-QUILT.

done, I felt that I would do the errents for her if a breath was left in my body. I felt that I would bear them 2 errents of hern on my tower side by side with my own private, hefty mission for Josiah.

She come for a all day's visit; and though she is a vegetable widow, and very humbly, I wuz middlin' glad to see her. But thinks'es I to myself as I carried away her things into the bedroom, "She'll want to send some errent by me;" and I wondered what it wouldn't be.

And so it didn't surprise me any when she asked me the first thing when I got back "if I would lobby a little for her in Washington."

And I looked agreeable to the idee; for I s'posed it wuz some new kind of tattin', mebby, or fancy work. And I told her "I shouldn't have much time, but I would try to buy her some if I could."

And she said "she wanted me to lobby, myself."

And then I thought mebby it wus some new kind of waltz; and I told her "I was too old to lobby, I hadn't lobbied a step since I was married."

And then she said "she wanted me to canvass some of the senators."

And I hung back, and asked her in a cautius tone "how many she wanted canvassed, and how much canvass it would take?"

I knew I had a good many things to buy for my tower; and, though I wanted to obleege Dorlesky, I didn't feel like runnin' into any great expense for canvass.

And then she broke off from that subject, and said "she wanted her rights, and wanted the Whiskey Ring broke up."

And then she says, going back to the old subject agin, "I hear that Josiah Allen has political hopes: can I canvass him?"

And I says, "Yes, you can for all me." But I mentioned cautiously, for I believe in bein' straightforward, and not holdin' out no false hopes, — I said "she must furnish her own canvass, for I hadn't a mite in the house."

But Josiah didn't get home till after her folks come after her. So he wuzn't canvassed.

But she talked a sight about her children, and how bad she felt to be parted from 'em, and how much she used to think of her husband, and how her hull life wus ruined, and how the Whiskey Ring had done it, — that, and wimmen's helpless condition under the law. And she cried, and wept, and cried about her children, and her sufferin's she had suffered; and I did. I cried onto my apron, and couldn't help it. A new apron too. And right while I wus cryin' onto that gingham apron, she made me promise to carry them two errents of hern to the President, and to get 'em done for her if I possibly could.

"She wanted the Whiskey Ring destroyed, and she wanted her rights; and she wanted 'em both in less than 2 weeks."

I wiped my eyes off, and told her I didn't believe she could get 'em done in that length of time, but I would tell the President about it, and "I thought more'n as likely as not he would want to do right by her." And says I, "If he sets out to, he can haul them babys of yourn out of that Ring pretty sudden."

And then, to kinder get her mind off of her sufferin's,

I asked her how her sister Susan wus a gettin' along. I hadn't heard from her for years — she married Philemon Clapsaddle; and Dorlesky spoke out as bitter as a bitter walnut — a green one. And says she, —

"She is in the poorhouse."

"Why, Dorlesky Burpy!" says I. "What do you mean?"

"I mean what I say. My sister, Susan Clapsaddle, is in the poorhouse."

"Why, where is their property all gone?" says I. "They was well off — Susan had five thousand dollars of her own when she married him."

"I know it," says she. "And I can tell you, Josiah Allen's wife, where their property is gone. It has gone down Philemon Clapsaddle's throat. Look down that man's throat, and you will see 150 acres of land, a good house and barns, 20 sheep, and 40 head of cattle."

"Why-ee!" says I.

"Yes, you will see 'em all down that man's throat." And says she, in still more bitter axents, "You will see four mules, and a span of horses, two buggies, a double sleigh, and three buffalo-robes. He has drinked 'em all up — and 2 horse-rakes, a cultivator, and a thrashin'- machine.

"Why! Why-ee!" says I agin. "And where are the children?"

"The boys have inherited their father's evil habits, and drink as bad as he duz; and the oldest girl has gone to the bad."

"Oh, dear! oh, dear me!" says I. And we both sot silent for a spell. And then, thinkin' I must say sunthin',

and wantin' to strike a safe subject, and a good-lookin' one,
I says, —

"Where is your aunt Eunice'es girl? that pretty girl I
see to your house once."

"That girl is in the lunatick asylum."

"Dorlesky Burpy!" says I. "Be you a tellin' the
truth?"

"Yes, I be, the livin' truth. She went to New York
to buy millinary goods for her mother's store. It wus
quite cool when she left home, and she hadn't took off
her winter clothes: and it come on brilin' hot in the city;
and in goin' about from store to store, the heat and the
hard work overcome her, and she fell down in the street
in a sort of a faintin'-fit, and was called drunk, and
dragged off to a police court by a man who wus a animal
in human shape. And he misused her in such a way, that
she never got over the horror of what befell her — when
she come to, to find herself at the mercy of a brute in a
man's shape. She went into a melancholy madness, and
wus sent to the asylum. Of course they couldn't have
wimmen in such places to take care of wimmen," says she
bitterly.

I sithed a long and mournful sithe, and sot silent agin
for quite a spell. But thinkin' I *must* be sociable, I
says, —

"Your aunt Eunice is well, I s'pose?"

"She is a moulderin' in jail," says she.

"In jail? Eunice Keeler in jail?"

"Yes, in jail." And Dorlesky's tone wus now like wormwood, wormwood and gall.

"You know, she owns a big property in tenement-houses,

and other buildings, where she lives. Of course her taxes
wus awful high; and she didn't expect to have any voice
in tellin' how that money, a part of her own property, that
she earned herself in a store, should be used.

MAN LIFTING UP EUNICE.

"But she had jest been taxed high for new sidewalks in
front of some of her buildin's.

"And then another man come into power in that ward,
and he natrully wanted to make some money out of her;
and he had a spite aginst her, too, so he ordered her to
build new sidewalks. And she wouldn't tear up a good

sidewalk to please him or anybody else, so she was put to
jail for refusin' to comply with the law."

Thinks'es I to myself, I don't believe the law would
have been so hard on her
if she hadn't been so humbly. The Burpys are a
humbly lot. But I didn't
think it out loud. And
I didn't uphold the law for
feelin' so, if it did. No:
I says in pityin' tones, —
for I wus truly sorry for
Eunice Keeler, —

"How did it end?"

"It hain't ended," says
she. "It only took place
a month ago; and she has
got her grit up, and won't
pay: and no knowin' how
it will end. She lays there
a moulderin'."

I myself don't believe
Eunice wus "mouldy;"
but that is Dorlesky's way
of talkin', — very flowery.

EUNICE IN JAIL.

"Wall," says I, "do you
think the weather is goin' to moderate?"

I truly felt that I dassent speak to her about any
human bein' under the sun, not knowin' what turn she
would give to the conversation, bein' so embittered. But
I felt the weather wus safe, and cotton stockin's, and

factory-cloth; and I kep' her down onto them subjects for more'n two hours.

But, good land! I can't blame her for bein' embittered aginst men and the laws they have made; for, if ever a woman has been tormented, she has.

It honestly seems to me as if I never see a human creeter so afflicted as Dorlesky Burpy has been, all her life.

Why, her sufferin's date back before she wus born; and that is goin' pretty fur back. You see, her father and mother had had some difficulty: and he wus took down with billious colic voyolent four weeks before Dorlesky wus born; and some think it wus the hardness between 'em, and some think it wus the gripin' of the colic at the time he made his will; anyway, he willed Dorlesky away, boy or girl, whichever it wuz, to his brother up on the Canada line.

So, when Dorlesky wus born (and born a girl, entirely onbeknown to her), she wus took right away from her mother, and gin to this brother. Her mother couldn't help herself: he had the law on his side. But it jest killed her. She drooped right away and died, before the baby wus a year old. She was a affectionate, tender-hearted woman; and her husband wus kinder overbearin', and stern always.

But it wus this last move of hisen that killed her; for I tell you, it is pretty tough on a mother to have her baby, a part of her own life, took right out of her arms, and gin to a stranger.

For this uncle of hern wus a entire stranger to Dorlesky when the will wus made. And almost like a stranger to her father, for he hadn't seen him sence he wus a boy; but he knew he hadn't any children, and s'posed he wus rich and respectable. But the truth wuz, he had been a runnin' down every way, — had lost his property and his character, wus dissipated and mean (onbeknown, it wus s'posed, to Dorlesky's father). But the will was made, and the law stood. Men are ashamed now, to think the law wus ever in voge; but it wuz, and is now in some of the States. The law wus in voge, and the poor young mother couldn't help herself. It has always been the boast of our American law, that it takes care of wimmen. It took care of her. It held her in its strong, protectin' grasp, and held her so tight, that the only way she could slip out of it wus to drop into the grave, which she did in a few months. Then it leggo.

But it kep' holt of Dorlesky: it bound her tight to her uncle, while he run through with what little property she had; while he sunk lower and lower, until at last he needed the very necessaries of life; and then he bound her out to work, to a woman who kep' a drinkin'-den, and the lowest, most degraded hant of vice.

Twice Dorlesky run away, bein' virtuous but humbly; but them strong, protectin' arms of the law that had held her mother so tight, jest reached out, and dragged her back agin. Upheld by them, her uncle could compel her to give her service wherever he wanted her to work; and he wus owin' this woman, and she wanted Dorlesky's work, so she had to submit.

But the 3d time, she made a effort so voyalent that she got away. A good woman, who, bein' nothin' but a woman, couldn't do any thing towards onclinchin' them powerful arms that wuz protectin' her, helped her to slip through 'em. And Dorlesky come to Jonesville to live with a sister of that good woman; changed her name, so's it wouldn't be so easy to find her; grew up to be a nice, industrious girl. And when the woman she was took by, died, she left Dorlesky quite a handsome property.

And finally she married Lank Rumsey, and did considerable well, it was s'posed. Her property, put with what little he had, made 'em a comfortable home; and they had two pretty little children, — a boy and a girl. But when the little girl was a baby, he took to drinkin', neglected his business, got mixed up with a whisky-ring, whipped Dorlesky — not so very hard. He went accordin' to law; and the law of the United States don't approve of a man whippin' his wife enough to endanger her life — it says it don't. He made every move of hisen lawful, and felt that Dorlesky hadn't ort to complain and feel hurt. But a good whippin' will make anybody feel hurt, law or no law. And then he parted with her, and got her property and her two little children. Why, it seemed as if every thing under the sun and moon, that *could* happen to a woman, had happened to Dorlesky, painful things, and gaulin'.

Jest before Lank parted with her, she fell on a broken sidewalk: some think he tripped her up, but it never was proved. But, anyway, Dorlesky fell, and broke her hip-bone; and her husband sued the corporation, and got ten thousand dollars for it. Of course, the law give the money to him, and she never got a cent of it. But she wouldn't never have made any fuss over that, knowin' that the law of the United States was such. But what made it gaulin' to her wuz, that, while she was layin' there achin' in splints, he took that very money and used it to court up another woman with.   Gin her presents, jewellry, bunnets, head-dresses, artificial flowers, and etcetery, out of Dorlesky's own hip-money.

And I don't know as any thing could be much more

DORLESKY'S TRIALS.

gaulin' to a woman than that wuz, — while she lay there, groanin' in splints, to have her husband take the money for her own broken bones, and dress up another woman like a doll with it.

But the law gin it to him; and he was only availin' himself of the glorious liberty of our free republic, and doin' as he was a mind to.

And it was s'posed that that very hip-money was what

made the match.   For, before she wus fairly out of splints, he got a divorce from her.   And by the help of that money, and the Whisky Ring, he got her two little children away from her.

And I wonder if there is a mother in the land, that can blame Dorlesky for gettin' mad, and wantin' her rights, and wantin' the Whisky Ring broke up, when they think it over, — how she has been fooled round with by men, willed away, and whipped and parted with and stole from. Why, they can't blame her for feelin' fairly savage about 'em — and she duz.   For as she says to me once when we wus a talkin' it over, how every thing had happened to her that could happen to a woman, and how curious it wuz, —

"Yes," says she, with a axent like boneset and vinegar, — "and what few things there are that hain't happened to me, has happened to my folks."

And, sure enough, I couldn't dispute her.   Trouble and wrongs and sufferin's seemed to be epidemic in the race of Burpy wimmen.   Why, one of her aunts on her father's side, Patty Burpy, married for her first husband Eliphalet Perkins.   He was a minister, rode on a circuit. And he took Patty on it too; and she rode round with him on it, a good deal of the time.   But she never loved to: she wus a woman who loved to be still, and be kinder settled down at home.

But she loved Eliphalet so well, she would do any thing to please him: so she rode round with him on that circuit, till she was perfectly fagged out.

He was a dretful good man to her; but he wus kinder poor, and they had hard times to get along.   But what property they had wuzn't taxed, so that helped some ; and Patty would make one doller go a good ways.

No, their property wasn't taxed till Eliphalet died. Then the supervisor taxed it the very minute the breath left his body ; run his horse, so it was said, so's to be sure to get it onto the tax-list, and comply with the law.

You see, Eliphalet's salary stopped when his breath did. And I s'pose mebby the law thought, seein' she was a havin' trouble, she might jest as well have a little more ; so it taxed all the property it never had taxed a cent for before.

But she had this to console her anyway, — that the law didn't forget her in her widowhood. No : the law is quite thoughtful of wimmen, by spells. It says, the law duz, that it protects wimmen. And I s'pose in some mysterious way, too deep for wimmen to understand, it was protectin' her now.

Wall, she suffered along, and finally married agin. I wondered why she did. But she was such a quiet, home-lovin' woman, that it was s'posed she wanted to settle down, and be kinder still and sot. But of all the bad luck she had ! She married on short acquaintance, and he proved to be a perfect wanderer. Why, he couldn't keep still. It was s'posed to be a mark.

He moved Patty thirteen times in two years; and at last he took her into a cart, — a sort of a covered wagon, — and travelled right through the Eastern States with her. He wanted to see the country, and loved to live in the wagon : it was his make. And, of course, the law give him the control of her body ; and she had to go where he moved it, or else 'part with him. And I s'pose the law thought it was guardin' and nourishin' her when it was a joltin' her over them praries and mountains and abysses. But it jest kep' her shook up the hull of the time.

It wus the regular Burpy luck.

And then, another one of her aunts, Drusilla Burpy, she married a industrius, hard-workin' man, — one that never

PATTY AND HUSBAND TRAVELLING IN THE FAR WEST.

drinked a drop, and was sound on the doctrines, and give good measure to his customers: he was a grocer-man. And a master hand for wantin' to foller the laws of his country, as tight as laws could be follered. And so, knowin' that the law approved of "moderate correction" for wimmen, and that "a man might whip his wife, but not enough to endanger her life," he bein' such a master hand for wantin' to do every thing faithful, and do his very best for his customers, it was s'posed that he wanted

to do his best for the law; and so, when he got to whippin' Drusilla, he would whip her *too* severe — he would be
too faithful to it.

You see, the way ont was, what made him whip her at
all wuz, she was cross to him. They had nine little children. She always thought that two or three children
would be about all one woman could bring up well "by
hand," when that one hand wuz so awful full of work, as
will be told more ensuin'ly. But he felt that big families
wuz a protection to the Government; and "he wanted
fourteen boys," he said, so they could all foller their
father's footsteps, and be noble, law-making, law-abiding
citizens, jest as he was.

But she had to do every mite of the housework, and
milk cows, and make butter and cheese, and cook and
wash and scour, and take all the care of the children, day
and night, in sickness and in health, and spin and weave
the cloth for their clothes (as wimmen did in them days),
and then make 'em, and keep 'em clean. And when there
wuz so many of 'em, and only about a year's difference in
their ages, some of 'em — why, I s'pose she sometimes
thought more of her own achin' back than she did of the
good of the Government; and she would get kinder discouraged sometimes, and be cross to him.

And knowin' his own motives was so high and loyal, he
felt that he ought to whip her. So he did.

And what shows that Drusilla wuzn't so bad as he
s'posed she wuz, what shows that she did have her good
streaks, and a deep reverence for the law, is, that she
stood his whippin's first-rate, and never whipped him.

Now, she wuz fur bigger than he wuz, weighed 80

pounds the most, and might have whipped him if the law had been such.

But they was both law-abidin', and wanted to keep

BEATING HIS WIFE.

every preamble; so she stood it to be whipped, and never once whipped him in all the seventeen years they lived together.

She died when her twelfth child was born : there wus
jest 13 months difference in the age of that and the one
next older.   And they said she often spoke out in her last
sickness, and said, —

"Thank fortune, I have always kept the law."

And they said the same thought wus a great comfort to
him in his last moments.

He died about a year after she did, leaving his 2nd wife
with twins and a good property.

Then, there was Abagail Burpy.   She married a sort of
a high-headed man, though one that paid, his debts, and
was truthful, and considerable good-lookin', and played
well on the fiddle.   Why, it seemed as if he had almost
every qualification for makin' a woman happy, only he
had jest this one little excentricity, — that man would lock
up Abagail Burpy's clothes every time he got mad at her.

Of course the law give her clothes to him ; and knowin'
it was one of the laws of the United States, she wouldn't
have complained only when she had company.   But it
was mortifyin', and nobody could dispute it, to have company come, and nothin' to put on.

Several times she had to withdraw into the wood-house,
and stay most of the day, shiverin', and under the cellar-
stairs, and round in clothes-presses.

But he boasted in prayer-meetin's, and on boxes before
grocery-stores, that he wus a law-abidin' citizen ; and he
wuz.   Eben Flanders wouldn't lie for anybody.

But I'll bet that Abagail Flanders beat our old Revolu-
tionary 4 mothers in thinkin' out new laws, when she
lay round under stairs, and behind barrells, in her night-
dress.

You see, when a man hides his wive's corset and petticoat, it is governin' without the "consent of the governed." And if you don't believe it, you ort to have peeked round them barrells, and seen Abagail's eyes. Why, they had hull reams of by-laws in 'em, and preambles, and "declarations of independence." So I have been told.

Why, it beat every thing I ever heard on, the lawful sufferin's of them wimmen. For there wuzn't nothin' illegal about one single trouble of theirn. They suffered accordin' to law, every one of 'em. But it wus tuff for 'em — very tuff.

And their all bein' so dretful humbly wuz and is another drawback to 'em; though that, too, is perfectly lawful, as everybody knows.

And Dorlesky looks as bad agin as she would otherways, on account of her teeth.

It wus after Lank had begun to kinder get after this other woman, and wus indifferent to his wive's looks, that Dorlesky had a new set of teeth on her upper jaw. And they sort o' sot out, and made her look so bad that it fairly made her ache to look at herself in the glass. And they hurt her gooms too. And she carried 'em back to the dentist, and wanted him to make her another set.

But the dentist acted mean, and wouldn't take 'em back, and sued Lank for the pay. And they had a lawsuit. And the law bein' such that a woman can't testify in court in any matter that is of mutual interest to husband and wife — and Lank wantin' to act mean, too, testified that " they wus good sound teeth."

And there Dorlesky sot right in front of 'em with her gooms achin', and her face all pokin' out, and lookin' like furyation, and couldn't say a word. But she had to give in to the law.

And ruther than go toothless, she wears 'em to this day. And I do believe it is the raspin' of them teeth aginst her gooms, and her discouraged and mad feelin's every time she looks in a glass, that helps to embitter her towards men, and the laws men have made, so's a woman can't have the control over her own teeth and her own bones.

Wall, Dorlesky went home about 4 P.M., I a promisin' at the last minute as sacred as I could, without usin' a book, to do her errents for her.

I urged her to stay to supper, but she couldn't; for she said the man where she worked was usin' his horses, and couldn't come after her agin. And she said that —

"Mercy on her! how could anybody eat any more supper after such a dinner as I had got?"

And it wuzn't nothin' extra, I didn't think. No better than my common run of dinners.

Wall, she hadn't been gone over an hour (she a hollerin' from the wagon, a chargin' on me solemn, about the errents, — the man she works for is deef, deef as a post, — and I a noddin' to her firm, honorable nods, that I would do 'em), and I wus a slickin' up the settin'-room, and Martha, who had jest come in, wus measurin' off my skirt-breadths, when Josiah Allen drove up, and Cicely and the boy with him.

And there I had been a layin' out to write to her that very night to tell her I wus goin' away, and to be sure and come jest as quick as I got back!

Wall, I never see the time I wuzn't glad to see Cicely,

and I felt that she could visit to Tirzah Ann's and Thomas
J.'s while I wus gone. She looked dretful pale and sad, I
thought; but she seemed glad to see me, and glad to get
back.

And the boy asked Josiah and Ury and me 47 questions
between the wagon and the front doorstep, for I counted
'em. He wus well.

I broached the subject of my tower to Cicely when
she and I wus all alone in her room. And, if you'll believe it, she all rousted up with the idee of wantin' to go
too.

She says, " You know, aunt Samantha, just how I have
prayed and labored for my boy's future ; how I have made
all the efforts that it is possible for a woman to make;
how I have thrown my heart and life into the work, —
but I have done no good. That letter," says she, takin'
one out of her pocket, and throwin' it into my lap, —
" that letter tells me just what I knew so well before, —
just how weak a woman is; that they have no power, only
the power to suffer."

It wus from that old executor, refusin' to comply with
some request she had made about her own property, — a
request of right and truth.

Oh, how glad I would have been to had him execkuted
that very minute! Why, I'd done it myself if wimmen
could execkit — but they can't.

Says she, " I'll go with you to Washington, — I and the
boy. Perhaps I can do something for him there." But
when she mentioned the boy, I demurred in my own mind,
and kep' a demurrin'. Thinks'es I, how can I stand it, as
tired as I expect to be, to have him a askin' questions all

the hull time? She see I was a demurrin'; and her pretty
face grew sadder than it had, and overcasteder.

And as I see that, I gin in at once, and says with' a
cheerful face, but a forebodin' mind, —

"Wall, Cicely, we three will embark together on our
tower."

Wall, after supper Cicely and I sot down under the
front stoop, — it was a warm evenin', — and we talked
some about other wimmen. Not runnin' talk, or gossipin'
talk, but jest plain talk, about her aunt Mary, and her
aunt Melissa, and her aunt Mary's daughter, who wus a
runnin' down, runnin' faster than ever, so I judged from
what she said. And how Susan Ann Grimshaw that was,
had a young babe. She said her aunt Mary was better
now, so she had started for the Michigan; but she had
had a dretful sick spell while she was there.

While she wuz a tellin' me this, Cicely sot on one of the
steps of the stoop: I sot up under it in my rockin'-chair.
And she looked dretful good to me. She had on a white
dress. She most always wears white in the house, when
we hain't got company; and always wears black when she
is dressed up, and when she goes out.

This dress was made of white mull. The yoke wus
made all of thin embroidery, and her white neck and
shoulders shone through it like snow. Her sleeves was
all trimmed with lace, and fell back from her pretty white
arms. Her hands wus clasped over her knees; and her
hair, which the boy had got loose a playin' with her, wus
fallin' round her face and neck. And her great, earnest
eyes wus lookin' into the West, and the light from the
sunset fallin' through the mornin'-glorys wus a fallin' over

her, till I declare, I never see any thing look so pretty in my hull life. And there was somethin' more, fur more than prettiness in her face, in her big eyes.

It wuzn't unhappiness, and it wuzn't happiness, and I don't know as I can tell what it wuz. It seemed as if she wuz a lookin' fur, fur away, further than Jonesville, further than the lake that lay beyend Jonesville, and which was pure gold now, — a sea of glass mingled with fire, — further than the cloudy masses in the western heavens, which looked like a city of shinin' mansions, fur off; but her eyes was lookin' away off, beyend them.

And I kep' still, and didn't feel like talkin' about other wimmen.

Finally she spoke out. "Aunt Samantha, what do you suppose I thought when dear aunt Mary was so ill when I was there?"

And I says, "I don't know, dear: what did you?"

"Well, I thought, that, though I loved her so dearly, I almost wished she would die while I was there."

"Why, Cicely!" says I. "Why-ee! what did you wish that for? and thinkin' so much of your aunt as you do."

"Well, you know how mother and aunt Mary loved each other, how near they were to each other. Why, mother could always tell when aunt Mary was ill or in trouble, and she was just the same in regard to mother. And I can't think that when death has freed the soul from the flesh, that they will have less spiritual knowledge of each other than when they were here; and I felt, that with such a love as theirs, death would only make their souls nearer: and you know what the Bible says, — that 'God shall make of his angels ministering spirits;' and I

LOOKING BEYEND THE SUNSET.

know He would send no other angel but my mother, to dear aunt Mary's bedside, to take her spirit home. And I thought, that, if I were there, my mother would be there right in the room with me; and I didn't know but I might *feel* her presence if I could not see her. And I *do* want my mother so sometimes, aunt Samantha," says she with the tears comin' into them soft brown eyes. "It seems as if she would tell me what to do for the boy — she always knew what was right and best to do."

Says I to myself, "For the land's sake, what won't Cicely think on next?" But I didn't say a word, mind you, not a single word would I say to hurt that child's feelin's — not for a silver dollar, I wouldn't.

I only says, in calm accents, —

"Don't for mercy's sake, child, talk of seein' your mother now."

She looked far off into the shinin' western heavens with that deep, searchin', but soft gaze, — seemin' to look clear through them cloudy mansions of rose and pearl, — and says she, —

"If I were good enough, I think I could."

And I says, "Cicely, you are goin' to take cold, with nothin' round your shoulders." Says I, "The weather is very ketchin', and it looks to me as if we wus goin' to have quite a spell of it."

And the boy overheard me, and asked me 75 questions about ketchin' the weather.

"If the weather set a trap? If it ketched with bait, or with a hook, and what it ketched? and how? and who?"

Oh my stars! what a time I did have!

The next mornin' after this Cicely wuzn't well enough

to get up. I carried up her breakfast with my own hands,
—a good one, though I am fur from bein' the one that ort
to say it.

And after breakfast, along in the forenoon, Martha, who
was makin' my dress, felt troubled in mind as to whether
she had better cut the polenay kitrin' ways of the cloth,
or not : and Miss Gowdey had jest had one made in the
height of the fashion, to Jonesville ; and so to ease Martha's
mind (she is one that gets deprested easy, when weighty
subjects are pressin' her down), I said I would run over
cross-lots, and carry home a drawin' of tea I had borrowed,
and look at the polenay, and bring back tidin's from it.
And I wus goin' there acrost the orchard, when I see the
boy a layin' on his back under a apple-tree, lookin' up into
the sky ; and says I, —

" What be you doin' here, Paul ? "

He never got up, nor moved a mite. That is one of the
peculiarities of the boy, you can't surprise him : nothin'
seems to startle him.

He lay still, and spoke out for all the world as if I had
been there with him all day.

" I am lookin' to see if I can see it. I thought I got a
glimpse of it a minute ago, but it wus only a white
cloud."

" Lookin' for what ? " says I.

" The gate of that City that comes down out of the
heavens. You know, uncle Josiah read about it this
morning, out of that big book he prays out of after breakfast. He said the gate was one pearl.

" And I asked mamma what a pearl was, and she said it
was just like that ring she wears that papa gave her. And

I asked her where the City was, and she said it was up in
the heavens.   And I asked her if I should ever see it; and
she said, if I was good, it would swing down out of the

LOOKING FOR THE CITY.

sky, sometime, and that shining gate would open, and I
should walk through it into the City.

  "And I went right to being good, that minute; and I

have been good for as many as three hours, I should think. And *say*, how long have you got to be good before you can go through? And *say*, can you see it before you go through? And SAY" —

But I had got most out of hearin' then.

" And *say* " —

I heard his last "say" just as I got out of hearin' of him.

He acted kinder disappointed at dinner-time, and said "he wus tired of watchin', and tired out of bein' good;" and he wus considerable cross all that afternoon. But he got clever agin before bedtime. And he come and leaned up aginst my lap at sundown, and asked me, I guess, about 200 questions about the City.

And his eyes looked big and dreamy and soft, and his cheeks looked rosy, and his mouth awful good and sweet. And his curls wus kinder moist, and hung down over his white forehead. I *did* love him, and couldn't help it, chin or no chin.

He had been still for quite a spell, a thinkin'; and at last he broke out, —

"Say, auntie, shall I see my father there in the City?"

And I didn't know what to tell him; for you know what it says, —

" *Without* are murderers."

But then, agin, I thought, what will become of the respectable church members who sell the fire that flames up in a man's soul, and ruins his life? What will become of them who lend their votes and their influence to make it right? They vote on Saturdays, to make the sale of this poison legal, and on Sundays go to church with their respectable families. And they expect to go right to heaven, of course; for they have improved all the means

ASKING ABOUT THE CITY.

of grace. Hired costly pews, and give big charities — in money obtained by sellin' robberies, murders, broken hearts, ruined lives.

But the boy wanted an answer; and his eyes looked questionin', but soft.

"Say, auntie, do you think we'll find him there, mamma and I? You know, that is what mamma cries so for, — she wants him so bad. And do you think he will stand just inside the gate, waiting for us? *Say!*"

But agin I thought of what it said, —

"No drunkard shall inherit eternal life."

And agin I didn't know what to say, and I hurried him off to bed.

But, after he had gone, I spoke out entirely unbeknown to myself, and says, —

"I can't see through it."

"You can't see through what?" says Josiah, who wus jest a comin' in.

"I can't see through it, why drunkards and murderers are punished, and them that make 'em drink and murder go free. I can't see through it."

"Wall, I don't see how you can see through any thing here — dark as pitch." Here he fell over a stool, which made him madder.

"Folks make fools of themselves, a follerin' up that subject." Here he stubbed his foot aginst the rockin'-chair, and most fell, and snapped out enough to take my head off, —

"The dumb fools will get so before long, that a man can't drink milk porridge without their prayin' over him."

Says I, "Be calm! stand right still in the middle of the floor, Josiah Allen, and I'll light a lamp," which I did; and he sot down cleverer, though he says, —

"You want to take away all the rights of a man.

Liquor is good for sickness, and you know it. You go onto extremes, you go too fur."

Says I calmly, "Do you s'pose, at this late hour, I am goin' to stop bein' mejum? No! mejum have I lived, and mejum will I die. I believe liquor is good for medicine: if I should say I didn't, I should be a lyin', which I am fur from wantin' to do at my age. I think it kep' mother Allen alive for years, jest as I believe arsenic broke up Bildad Smith's chills. And I s'pose folks have jest as good a right to use it for the benefit of their health, as to use any other pizen, or fire, or any thing.

"And it should be used jest like pizen and fire and etcetery. You don't want to eat pizen for a treat, or pass it round amongst your friends. You don't want to play with fire for fun, or burn yourself up with it. You don't want to use it to confligrate yourself or anybody else.

"So with liquor. You don't want to drink liquor to kill yourself with, or to kill other folks. You don't want to inebriate with it. If I had my way, Josiah Allen," says I firmly, "the hull liquor-trade should be in the hands of doctors, who wouldn't sell a drop without know-in' *positive* that it wus *needed* for sickness, or the aged and infirm. Good, honest doctors who couldn't be bought nor sold."

"Where would you find 'em?" says Josiah in a gruff tone (I mistrust his toe pained him).

Says I thoughtfully, "Surely there is one good, reliable man left in every town — that could be found."

"I don't know about it," says he, sort o' musin'ly. "I am gettin' pretty old to begin it, but I don't know but I might get to be a doctor now."

Says he, brightenin' up, "It can't take much study to deal out a dose of salts now and then, or count anybody's pult."

But says I firmly, "Give up that idee at once, Josiah Allen. I have come out alive, out of all your other plans and progects, and I hain't a goin' to be killed now at my age, by you as a doctor."

My tone wus so powerful, and even skairful, that he gin up the idee, and wound up the clock, and went to bed.

CHAPTER VI.

CICELY wus some better the next day. And two days before we sot sail for Washington, Philury Mesick, the girl Ury was payin' attention to, and who was goin' to keep my house durin' my absence on my tower, come with a small, a very small trunk, ornimented with brass nails.

Poor little thing! I wus always sorry for her, she is so little, and so freckled, and so awful willin' to do jest as anybody wants her to. She is a girl that Miss Solomon Gowdey kinder took. And I think, if there is any condition that is hard, it is to be "kinder took." Why, if I was took at all, I should want to be "*took*."

But Miss Gowdey took Philury jest enough not to pay her any regular wages, and didn't take her enough so Philury could collect any pay from her when she left. She left, because there wus a hardness between 'em, on account of a grindstun. Philury said Miss Gowdey's little boy broke the grindstun, and the boy laid it to Philury. Anyway, the grindstun wus broke, and it made a hardness. And when Philury left Miss Gowdey's, all her worldly wealth wuz held in that poor, pitiful lookin' trunk. Why, the trunk looked like Philury, and Philury looked like the trunk. It looked small, and meek, and well disposed ; and the brass nails looked some like frecks, only larger.

174

Wall, I felt sorry for her : and I s'posed, that, married or single, she would have to wear stockin's ; so I told her, that, besides her wages, she might have all the lamb's-wool yarn she wanted to spin while I was gone, after doin' the house-work.

She wus tickled enough as I told her.

"Why," says she, "I can spin enough to last me for years and years."

"Wall," says I, "so much the better. I have mistrusted," says I, "that Miss Gowdey wouldn't do much for you on account of that hardness about the grindstun ; and knowin' that you hain't got no mother, I have laid out to do middlin' well by you and Ury when you get married."

And she blushed, and said "she expected to marry Ury sometime — years and years hence."

"Wall," says I, "you can spin the yarn anyway."

Philury is a real handy little thing about the house. And so willin' and clever, that I guess, if

PHILURY.

I had asked her to jump into the oven, and bake herself, she would have done it. And so I told Josiah.

And he said "he thought a little more bakin' wouldn't hurt her." Says he, "She is pretty soft."

And says I, "Soft or not, she's good. And that is more than I can say for some folks, who *think* they know a little more."

I will stand up for my sect.

Wall, in three days' time we sot sail for Washington, D.C., I a feelin' well about Josiah. For Philury and Ury wus clever, and would do well by him. And the cubbard wus full and overflowin' with every thing good to eat. And I felt that I had indeed, in that cubbard, left him a consoler.

Josiah took us to the train about an hour and a half too early. But I wus glad we wus on time, because it would have worked Josiah up dretfully if we hadn't been. For he had spent the most of the latter part of the night in gettin' up and walkin' out to the clock to see if it wus approachin' train time: the train left at a quarter to ten.

I wus glad on his account, and also on my own; for at the last minute, as you may say, who should come a runnin' down to the depot but Sam Shelmadine, a wantin' to send a errent by me to Washington.

He kinder wunk me out to one side of the waitin'-room, and asked me "if I would try to get him a license to steal horses."

It kinder runs in the blood of the Shelmadines to love to steal, and he owned up that it did. But he wuzn't goin' into it for that, he said: he wanted the profit of it.

But I told him "I wouldn't do any such thing;" and I looked at him in such a witherin' way, that I should most probable have withered him, only he is blind with one eye, and I was on the blind side.

But he argued with me, and said it was no worse than to give licenses for other kinds of meanness.

He said they give licenses now to steal — steal folks'es senses away, and then they would steal every thing else, and murder, and tear round into every kind of wickedness. But he didn't ask that. He wanted things done fair and square: he jest wanted to steal horses. He was goin' West, and he thought he could do a good business, and lay up something. If he had a license, he shouldn't be afraid of bein' shot up, or shot.

But I refused the job with scorn; and jest as I wus refusin', the cars snorted, and I wus glad they did. They seemed to express in that wild snort something of the indignation I felt.

The *idee*.

When Cicely and the boy and I got to Washington, the shades of twilight was a shadin the earth gently; and we got a man to take us to Condelick Smith'ses.

The man was in a hack, as Cicely called it (and he had a hackin' cough, too, which made it seem more singular). We told him to take us right to Miss Condelick Smith'ses. Condelick is my own cousin on my own side, and travelin' on the road for groceries.

She keeps a nice, quiet boardin'-house. Only a few boarders, "with the comforts of a home, and congenial society," as she wrote to me when she heard I wus a comin' to Washington. She said we had *got* to go to her house; so we went, with the distinct knowledge in our minds and pocket-books, of payin' for our 3 boards.

She was very tickled to see us, and embraced us almost warmly. She had been over a hot fire a cookin'. She is humbly, but likely, I have been told and believe.

She has got a wen on her cheek, but that don't hurt her any. Wens hain't nothin' that detract from a person's moral worth.

There is only one child in the family, — Condelick, Jr., aged 13. A good, fat boy, with white hair and blue eyes, and a great capacity for blushin', but seemed to be good dispositioned.

It wus late supper time; and we had only time to go up into our rooms, and bathe our weary faces and hands, when we had to go down to supper.

Miss Condelick Smith called it dinner: she misspoke herself. Havin' so much on her hands, it is no wonder that she should make a slip once in a while. I should, myself, if my mind wuzn't like iron for strength. There wus only three or four to the table besides us: it wuz later than their· usial supper time. There wus a young couple there who had jest been married, and come there to live.

Ever sense we left home we had seen sights and sights of brides and groomses. It seemed to be a good time of year for 'em; and Cicely and I would pass the time by guessin', from their demeaners, how long they had been married. You know they act very soft the first day or two, and then harden gradually, as time passes, till sometimes they get very hard.

Wall, as I looked at this young pair, I whispered to Cicely, —

"2 days."

They acted well. Though I see with pain that the bride was tryin' to foller after the groom blindly, and I see she was a layin' up trouble for herself. Amongst other good things, they had a baked chicken for supper; and when the young husband wus asked what part of the fowl he would take, he said, —

"It was immaterial!"

And then, when they asked the bride, she blushed sweetly, and said, —

"She would take a piece of the immaterial too."

And she bein' next to me, I said to her in a low tone, but firm and motherly, —

"You are a beginner in married life; and I say to you, as one who has had stiddy practice for 20 years, begin right. Let your affections be firm as adamant, cling closely to Duty's apron-strings, but do not too blindly copy after your groom. Try to stand up on your own feet, and be a helpmate to him, not a dead weight for him to carry. Do branch right out, and tell what part of the fowl, or of life, you want, if it hain't nothin' but the gizzard or neck; and then try to get it. If you don't have any self-reliance, if you don't try to help yourself any, it is highly probable to me, that you won't get any thing more out of the fowl, or of life, than a piece of 'the immaterial.'"

She blushed, and said she would. And so Duty bein' appeased, and attended to, I calmly pursued my own meal.

The next morning Cicely was so beat out that she couldn't get up at all. She wuzn't sick, only jest tired out. And so the boy and I sot out alone.

I told Cicely I would do my errents the first thing, so as to leave my mind and my conscience clear for the rest of my stay.

And I knew there wuz a good many who would feel

SAMANTHA ADVISING THE BRIDE.

hurt, deeply hurt, if I didn't notice 'em right off the first thing. The President, and lots of 'em, I knew would take it right to heart, and feel dretfully worked up and slighted, if I didn't call on 'em.

And then, I had to carry Dorlesky's errent to the President anyway. And I thought I would tend to it right away, so I sot out in good season.

When you are a noticin' anybody, and makin' 'em perfectly happy, you feel well yourself. I was in good spirits, and quite a number of 'em. The boy wus feelin' well too. He had a little black velvet suit and a deep lace collar, and his gold curls was a hangin' down under his little black velvet cap. They made him look more babyish; but I believe Cicely kept 'em so to make him look young, she felt so dubersome about his future. But he looked sweet enough to kiss right there in the street.

I, too, looked well, very. I had on that new dress, Bismark brown, the color remindin' me of 2 noble patriots. And made by a Martha. I thought of that proudly, as I looked at George's benign face on the top of the monument, and wondered what he'd say if he see it, and hefted my emotions I had when causin' it to be made for my tower. I realized as I meandered along, that patriotism wus enwrappin' me from head to foot; for my polynay was long, and my head was completely full of Gass'es "Journal," and Starks'es "Life of Washington," and a few martyrs.

I wus carryin' Dorlesky's errents.

On the outside of my head I had a good honorable shirred silk bunnet, the color of my dress, a good solid brown (that same color, B. B.). And my usial long green veil, with a lute-string ribbon run in, hung down on one side of my bunnet in its wonted way.

It hung gracefully, and yet it seemed to me there wus both dignity and principle in its hang. It give me a sort of a dressy look, but none too dressy.

And so we wended our way down the broad, beautiful streets towards the White House.

Handsomer streets I never see. I had thought Jonesville streets wus middlin' handsome and roomy. Why, two double wagons can go by each other with perfect safety, right in front of the grocery stores, where there is lots of boxes too; and wimmen can be a walkin' there too at the same time, hefty ones.

But, good land! Loads of hay could pass each other here, and droves of dromedaries, and camels, and not touch each other, and then there would be lots of room for men and wimmen, and for

SAMANTHA AND PAUL ON THE WAY TO THE WHITE HOUSE.

wagons to rumble, and perioguers to float up and down — if perioguers could sail on dry land.

Roomier, handsomer, well shadeder streets I never want to see, nor don't expect to. Why, Jonesville streets are like tape compared with 'em; and Loontown and Toad Holler, they are like thread, No. 50 (allegory).

Bub Smith wus well acquainted with the President's hired man, so he let us in without parlay.

I don't believe in talkin big as a general thing. But thinks'es I, Here I be, a holdin' up the dignity of Jonesville: and here I be, on a deep, heart-searchin' errent to the Nation. So I said, in words and axents a good deal like them I have read of in "Children of the Abbey," and "Charlotte Temple," —

"Is the President of the United States within?"

He said he was, but said sunthin' about his not receiving calls in the mornings.

But I says in a very polite way, — for I like to put folks at their ease, presidents or peddlers or any thing, —

"It hain't no matter at all if he hain't dressed up — of course he wuzn't expectin' company. Josiah don't dress up mornin's."

And then he says something about "he didn't know but he was engaged."

Says I, "That hain't no news to me, nor the Nation. We have been a hearin' that for three years, right along. And if he is engaged, it hain't no good reason why he shouldn't speak to other wimmen, — good, honorable married ones too."

"Well," says he finally, "I will take up your card."

"No, you won't!" says I firmly. "I am a Methodist! I guess I can start off on a short tower, without takin' a pack of cards with me. And if I had 'em right here in my pocket, or a set of dominoes, I shouldn't expect to take up the time of the President of the United States a playin' games at this time of the day." Says I in deep tones, "I am a carrien' errents to the President that the world knows not of."

He blushed up red; he was ashamed; and he said " he would see if I could be admitted."

And he led the way along, and I follered, and the boy. Bub Smith had left us at the door.

The hired man seemed to think I would want to look round some; and he walked sort o' slow, out. of courtesy. But, good land! how little that hired man knew my feelin's, as he led me on, I a thinkin' to myself, —

"Here I am, a steppin' where G. Washington strode." Oh the grandeur of my feelin's! The nobility of 'em! and the quantity! Why, it was a perfect sight.

But right into these exalted sentiments the hired man intruded with his frivolous remarks, — worse than frivolous.

He says agin something about "not knowin' whether the President would be ready to receive me."

And I stepped down sudden from that lofty piller I had trod on in my mind, and says I, —

" I tell you agin, I don't care whether he is dressed up or not. I come on principle, and I shall look at him through that eye, and no other."

"Wall," says he, turnin' sort o' red agin (he was ashamed), " have you noticed the beauty of the didos?"

But I kep' my head right up in the air nobly, and never turned to the right or the left; and says I, —

" I don't see no beauty in cuttin' up didos, nor never did. I have heard that they did such things here in Washington, D.C., but I do not choose to have my attention drawed to 'em."

But I pondered a minute, and the word "meetin'-house" struck a fearful blow aginst my conscience; and I says in milder axents, —

"If I looked upon a dido at all, it would be, not with a human woman's eye, but the eye of a Methodist. My duty draws me : — point out the dido, and I will look at it through that one eye."

And he says, "I was a talkin' about the walls of this room."

And I says, "Why couldn't you say so in the first place? The idee of skairin' folks! or tryin' to," I added ; for I hain't easily skairt.

The walls wus perfectly beautiful, and so wus the ceilin' and floors. There wuzn't a house in Jonesville that could compare with it, though we had painted our meetin-house over at a cost of upwards of 28 dollars. But it didn't come up to this — not half. President Arthur has got good taste ; and I thought to myself, and I says to the hired man, as I looked round and see the soft richness and quiet beauty and grandeur of the surroundings, —

"I had just as lives have him pick me out a calico dress as to pick it out myself. And that is sayin' a great deal," says I.. "I am always very putickuler in calico : richness and beauty is what I look out for, and wear."

Jest as I wus sayin' this, the hired man opened a door into a lofty, beautiful room ; and says he, —

"Step in here, madam, into the antick room, and I'll see if the President can see you ; " and he started off sudden, bein' called. And I jest turned round and looked after him, for I wanted to enquire into it. I had heard of their cuttin' up anticks at Washington, — I had come prepared for it ; but I didn't know as they was bold enough to come right out, and have rooms devoted to that purpose. And I looked all round the room before I ventured in. But it looked neat as a pin, and not a soul in there; and thinks'es I, "It hain't probable their day for cuttin' up anticks. I guess I'll venture." So I went in.

But I sot pretty near the edge of the chair, ready to jump at the first thing I didn't like. And I kep' a close holt of the boy. I felt that I was right in the midst of dangers. I had feared and foreboded, — oh, how I had feared and foreboded about the dangers and deep perils of Washington, D.C.! And here I wuz, the very first thing, invited right in broad daylight, with no excuse or any thing, right into a antick room.

Oh, how thankful, how thankful I wuz, that Josiah Allen wuzn't there!

I knew, as he felt a good deal of the time, an antick room was what he would choose out of all others. And I felt stronger than ever the deep resolve that Josiah Allen should not run. He must not be exposed to such dangers, with his mind as it wuz, and his heft. I felt that he would suckumb.

And I wondered that President Arthur, who I had always heard was a perfect gentleman, should come to have a room called like that, but s'posed it was there when he went. I don't believe he'd countenance any thing of the kind.

I was jest a thinkin' this when the hired man come back, and said, —

"The President would receive me."

"Wall," says I calmly, "I am ready to be received."

So I follered him; and he led the way into a beautiful room, kinder round, and red colored, with lots of elegant pictures and lookin'-glasses and books.

The President sot before a table covered with books and papers: and, good land! he no need to have been afraid and hung back; he was dressed up slick — slick enough for meetin', or a parin'-bee, or any thing. He had on a sort of a gray suit, and a rose-bud in his button-hole.

He was a good-lookin' man, though he had a middlin' tired look in his kinder brown eyes as he looked up.

I had calculated to act noble on that occasion, as I appeared before him who stood in the large, lofty shoes of the revered G. W., and sot in the chair of the (nearly) angel Garfield. I had thought that likely as not, entirely unbeknown to me, I should soar right off into a eloquent oration. For I honored him as a President. I felt like neighborin' with him on account of his name —

SAMANTHA MEETING THE PRESIDENT.

Allen! (That name I took at the alter of Jonesville, and pure love.)

But how little can we calculate on future contingencies, or what we shall do when we get there! As I stood before him, I only said what I had said before on a similar occasion, these simple words, that yet mean so much, so much, —

"Allen, I have come!"

He, too, was overcome by his feelin's: I see he wuz. His face looked fairly solemn; but, as he is a perfect gentleman, he controlled himself, and said quietly these words, that, too, have a deep import,—

"I see you have."

He then shook hands with me, and I with him. I, too, am a perfect lady. And then he drawed up a chair for me with his own hands (hands that grip holt of the same hellum that G. W. had gripped holt of. O soul! be calm when I think ont), and asked me to set down; and consequently I sot.

I leaned my umberell in a easy, careless position against a adjacent chair, adjusted my green veil in long, graceful folds,—I hain't vain, but I like to look well,—and then I at once told him of my errents. I told him—

"I had brought three errents to him from Jonesville,—one for myself, and two for Dorlesky Burpy."

He bowed, but didn't say nothin': he looked tired. Josiah always looks tired in the mornin' when he has got his milkin' and barn-chores done, so it didn't surprise me. And havin' calculated to tackle him on my own errent first, consequently I tackled him.

I told him how deep my love and devotion to my pardner wuz.

And he said, "he had heard of it."

And I says, "I s'pose so. I s'pose such things will spread, bein' a sort of a rarity. I'd heard that it had got out, way beyond Loontown, and all round."

"Yes," he said, "it was spoke of a good deal."

"Wall," says I, "the cast-iron love and devotion I feel

for that man don't show off the brightest in hours of joy
and peace. It towers up strongest in dangers and trou-
bles." And then I went on to tell him how Josiah wanted
to come there as senator, and what a dangerous place I
had always heard Washington wuz, and how I had felt it
was impossible for me to lay down on my goose-feather
pillow at home, in peace and safety, while my pardner was
a grapplin' with dangers of which I did not know the
exact size and heft. And so I had made up my mind to
come ahead of him, as a forerunner on a tower, to see jest
what the dangers wuz, and see if I dast trust my companion there. "And now," says I, "I want you to tell me
candid," says I. "Your settin' in George Washington's
high chair makes me look up to you. It is a sightly place;
you can see fur: your name bein' Allen makes me feel
sort o' confidential and good towards you, and I want you
to talk real honest and candid with me." Says I solemnly,
"I ask you, Allen, not as a politician, but as a human
bein', would you dast to let Josiah come?"

Says he, "The danger to the man and the nation de-
pends a good deal on what sort of a man it is that comes."

Then was a tryin' time for me. I would not lie, neither
would I brook one word against my companion, even from
myself. So I says, —

"He is a man that has traits and qualities, and sights
of 'em."

But thinkin' that I must do so, if I got true informa-
tion of dangers, I went on, and told of Josiah's political
aims, which I considered dangerous to himself and the
nation. And I told him of The Plan, and my dark forebodin's about it.

The President didn't act surprised a mite. And finally he told me, what I had always mistrusted, but never knew, that Josiah had wrote to him all his political views and aspirations, and offered his help to the Government. And says he, "I think I know all about the man."

"Then," says I, "you see he is a good deal like other men."

And he said, sort o' dreamily, "that he was."

And then agin silence rained. He was a thinkin', I knew, on all the deep dangers that hedged in Josiah Allen and America if he come. And a musin' on all the probable dangers of the Plan. And a thinkin' it over how to do jest right in the matter, — right by Josiah, right by the nation, right by me.

Finally the suspense of the moment wore onto me too deep to bear, and I says in almost harrowin' tones of anxiety and suspense, —

"Would it be safe for my pardner to come to Washington? Would it be safe for Josiah, safe for the nation?" Says I, in deeper, mournfuler tones, —

"Would you — would you dast to let him come?"

He said, sort o' dreamily, "that those views and aspirations of Josiah's wasn't really needed at Washington, they had plenty of them there; and "—

But I says, "I *must* have a plainer answer to ease my mind and heart. Do tell me plain, — would you dast?"

He looked full at me. He has got good, honest-looking eyes, and a sensible, candid look onto him. He liked me, — I knew he did from his looks, — a calm, Methodist-Episcopal likin', — nothin' light.

And I see in them eyes that he didn't like Josiah's

political idees. I see that he was afraid, as afraid as death of that plan ; and I see that he considered Washington a dangerous, dangerous place for grangers and Josiah Allens to be a roamin' round in. I could see that he dreaded

the sufferin's for me and for the nation if the Hon. Josiah Allen was elected.

But still, he seemed to hate to speak ; and wise, cautious conservatism, and gentlemanly dignity, was wrote down on his linement. Even the red rosebud in his button-hole looked dretful good-natured, but close-mouthed.

I don't know as he would have spoke at all agin, if I hadn't uttered once more them soul-harrowin' words, " *Would you dast?* "

Pity and good feelin' then seemed to overpower for a moment the statesman and courteous diplomat.

And he said in gentle, gracious tones, "If I tell you just what I think, I would not like to say it officially, but would say it in confidence, as from an Allen to an Allen."

Says I, "It sha'n't go no further."

And so I would warn everybody that it must *not* be told.

Then says he, "I will tell you. I wouldn't dast."

Says I, "That settles it. If human efforts can avail, Josiah Allen will not be United-States senator." And says I, "You have only confirmed my fears. I knew, feelin' as he felt, that it wuzn't safe for Josiah or the nation to have him come."

Agin he reminded me that it was told to me in confidence, and agin I want to say that it *must* be kep'.

I thanked him for his kindness. He is a perfect gentleman; and he told me jest out of courtesy and politeness, and I know it. And I can be very polite too. And I am naturally one of the kindest-hearted of Jonesvillians.

So I says to him, "I won't forget your kindness to me; and I want to say right here, that Josiah and me both think well on you — first-rate."

Says he with a sort of a tired look, as if he wus a lookin' back over a hard road, "I have honestly tried to do the best I could."

Says I, "I believe it." And wantin' to encourage him still more, says I, —

"Josiah believes it, and Dorlesky Burpy, and lots of other Jonesvillians." Says I, "To set down in a chair that an angel has jest vacated, a high chair under the full glare of critical inspection, is a tegus place. I don't s'pose Garfield was really an angel, but his sufferin's and martyrdom placed him almost in that light before the world.

"And you have filled that chair, and filled it well. With dignity and courtesy and prudence. And we have been proud of you, Josiah and me both have."

He brightened up: he had been afraid, I could see, that we wuzn't suited with him. And it took a load offen him. His linement looked clearer than it had, and brighter.

"And now," says I, sithin' a little, "I have got to do Dorlesky's errents."

He, too, sithed. His linement fell. I pitied him, and would gladly have refrained from troubling him more. But duty hunched me; and when she hunches, I have to move forward.

Says I in measured tones, each tone measurin' jest about the same, — half duty, and half pity for him, —

"Dorlesky Burpy sent these errents to you. She wanted intemperance done away with — the Whiskey Ring broke right up. She wanted you to drink nothin' stronger than root-beer when you had company to dinner, she offerin' to send you a receipt for it from Jonesville; and she wanted her rights, and she wanted 'em all this week without fail."

He sithed hard. And never did I see a linement fall further than his linement fell. I pitied him. I see it wus a hard stent for him, to do it in the time she had sot.

And I says, " I think myself that Dorlesky is a little onreasonable. I myself am willin' to wait till next week. But she has suffered dretfully from intemperance, dretfully from the Rings, and dretfully from want of Rights. And her sufferin's have made her more voyalent in her demands, and impatienter."

And then I fairly groaned as I did the rest of the errent. But my promise weighed on me, and Duty poked me in the side. I wus determined to do the errent jest as I would wish a errent done for me, from borryin' a drawin' of tea to tacklin' the nation, and tryin' to get a little mess of truth and justice out of it.

" Dorlesky told me to tell you that if you didn't do these things, she would have you removed from the Presidential chair, and you should never, never, be President agin."

He trembled, he trembled like a popple-leaf. And I felt as if I should sink: it seemed to me jest as if Dorlesky wus askin' too much of him, and was threatenin' too hard.

And bein' one that loves truth, I told him that Dorlesky was middlin' disagreeable, and very humbly, but she needed her rights jest as much as if she was a dolly. And then I went on and told him all how she and her relations had suffered from want of rights, and how dretfully she had suffered from the Ring, till I declare, a talkin about them little children of hern, and her agony, I got about as fierce actin' as Dorlesky herself; and entirely unbeknown to myself, I talked powerful on intemperance and Rings — and sound.

When I got down agin onto my feet, I see he had a sort of a worried, anxious look; and he says, —

"The laws of the United States are such, that I can't interfere."

"Then," says I, "why don't you *make* the United States do right?"

And he said somethin' about the might of the majority and the powerful rings.

And that sot me off agin. And I talked very powerful, kinder allegored, about allowin' a ring to be put round the United States, and let a lot of whiskey-dealers lead her round, a pitiful sight for men and angels. Says I, "How does it look before the Nations, to see Columbia led round half tipsy by a Ring?"

He seemed to think it looked bad, I knew by his looks.

Says I, "Intemperance is bad for Dorlesky, and bad for the Nation."

He murmured somethin' about the "revenue that the liquor-trade brought to the Government."

But I says, "Every penny they give, is money right out of the people's pockets; and every dollar that the people pay into the liquor-traffic, that they may give a few cents of it into the Treasury, is costin' the people three times that dollar, in the loss that intemperance entails, — loss of labor, by the inability of drunken men to do any thing but wobble and stagger round; loss of wealth, by all the enormous losses of property and of taxation, of almshouses and madhouses, jails, police forces, paupers' coffins, and the digging of the thousands and thousands of graves that are filled yearly by them that reel into 'em." Says I, "Wouldn't it be better for the people to pay that dollar in the first place into the Treasury, than to let it filter through the dram-seller's hands, and 2 or 3 cents of it fall into the National purse at last, putrid, and heavy with all these losses and curses and crimes and shames and despairs and agonies?"

He seemed to think it would: I see by the looks of his lineament, he did. Every honorable man feels so in his heart; and yet they let the liquor ring control 'em, and lead 'em round.

Says I, "All the intellectual and moral power of the United States are jest rolled up and thrust into that Whiskey Ring, and are being drove by the whiskey-dealers jest where they want to drive 'em." Says I, "It controls New-York village, and nobody pretends to deny it; and all the piety and philanthropy and culture and philosiphy of that village has to be jest drawed along in that Ring. And," says I, in low but startlin' tones of principle, —

"Where, where, is it a drawin' 'em to? Where is it a drawin' the hull nation to? Is it a drawin' 'em down into a slavery ten times more abject and soul-destroyin' than African slavery ever was? Tell me," says I firmly, "tell me."

His mean looked impressed, but he did not try to frame a reply. I think he could not find a frame. There is no frame to that reply. It is a conundrum as boundless as truth and God's justice, and as solemnly deep in its sure consequences of evil as eternity, and as sure to come as that is.

Agin I says, "Where is that Ring a drawin' the United States? Where is it a drawin' Dorlesky?"

"Oh! Dorlesky!" says he, a comin' up out of his deep

reveryin',. but polite, — a politer demeanerd, gentlemanly appeariner man I don't want to see. "Ah, yes! I would be glad, Josiah Allen's wife, to do her errent. I think Dorlesky is justified in asking to have the Ring destroyed. But I am not the one to go to — I am not the one to do her errent."

Says I, "Who is the man, or men?"

Says he, "James G. Blaine."

Says I, "Is that so? I will go right to James G. Blaineses."

So I spoke to the boy. He had been all engaged lookin' out of the winders, but he was willin' to go.

And the President took the boy upon his knee, wantin' to do something agreeable, I s'pose, seein' he couldn't do the errent. And he says, jest to make himself pleasant to the boy, —

"Well, my little man, are you a Republican, or Democrat?"

"I am a Epispocal."

And seein' the boy seemed to be headed onto theoligy instead of politics, and wantin' to kinder show him off, I says, —

"Tell the gentleman who made you."

He spoke right up prompt, as if hurryin' to get through theoligy, so's to tackle sunthin' else. He answered as exhaustively as an exhauster could at a meetin', —

"I was made out of dust, and breathed into. I am made out of God and dirt."

Oh, how deep, how deep that child is! I never had heard him say that before. But how true it wuz! The divine and the human, linked so close together from birth

till death. No philosipher that ever philosiphized could
go deeper or higher.

I see the President looked impressed. But the boy

"I AM A EPISPOCAL."

branched off quick, for he seemed fairly burstin' with questions.

"*Say*, what is this house called the White House for?
Is it because it is to help white folks, and not help the
black ones, and Injins?"

I declare, I almost thought the boy had heard sunthin' about the elections in the South, and the Congressional vote for cuttin' down the money for the Indian schools. Legislative action to perpetuate the ignorance and brutality of a race.

The President said dreamily, " No, it wasn't for that."

" Well, is it called white like the gate of the City is? Mamma said that was white, — a pearl, you know, — because every thing was pure and white inside the City. Is it because the laws that are made here are all white and good?   And *say* " —

Here his eyes looked dark and big with excitement.

" What is George Washington up on top of that big white piller for ? "

" He was a great man."

" How much did he weigh?   How many yards did it take for his vest — forty ? "

" He did great and noble deeds — he fought and bled."

" If fighting makes folks great, why did mamma punish me when I fought with Jim Gowdey?   He stole my jackknife, and knocked me down, and set down on me, and took my chewing-gum away from me, and chewed it himself.   And I rose against him, and we fought and bled : my nose bled, and so did his.   But I got it away from him, and chewed it myself.   But mamma punished me, and said ' God wouldn't love me if I quarrelled so, and if we couldn't agree, we must get somebody to settle our trouble for us.'   Why didn't she stand me up on a big white pillow out in the door-yard, and be proud of me, and not shut me up in a dark closet ? "

" He fought for Liberty."

"Did he get it?"

"He fought that the United States might be free."

"Is it free?"

The President waved off that question, and the boy kep' on.

"Is it true what you have been talkin' about, — is there a great big ring put all round it, and is it bein' drawed along into a mean place?"

And then the boy's eyes grew black with excitement;

WAR DECLARED.

and he kep' right on without waitin' for breath, or for a answer, —

"He had heard it talked about, was it right to let anybody do wrong for money? Did the United States do it? Did it make mean things right? If it did, he wanted to get one of Tom Gowdy's white rats. He wouldn't sell it, and he wanted it. His mother wouldn't let him steal it; but if the United States could *make* it right for him to do wrong, he had got ten cents of his own, and he'd buy the right to get that white rat. And if Tom wanted to cry about it, let him.   If the United States sold him the right to do it, he guessed he could do it, no matter how much whimperin' there was, and no matter who said it was wrong.   *He wanted the rat.*"

But I see the President's eyes, which had looked kinder rested when he took him up, grew bigger and bigger with surprise and anxiety.   I guess he thought he had got his day's work in front of him.   And I told the boy we must go.   And then I says to the President, —

"That I knew he was quite a traveller, and of course he wouldn't want to die without seein' Jonesville;" and says I, "Be sure to come to our house to supper when you come."   Says I, "I can't reccomend the huntin' so much; there haint nothin' more excitin' to shoot than red squirrels and chipmunks: but there is quite good fishin' in the creek back of our house; they ketched 4 horned Asa's there last week, and lots of chubs."

He smiled real agreable, and said, "when he visited Jonesville, he wouldn't fail to take tea with me."

Says I, "So do; and, if you get lost, you jest enquire at the Corners of old Grout Nickleson, and he will set you right."

He smiled agin, and said "he wouldn't fail to enquire if he got lost."

And then I shook hands with him, thinkin' it would be expected of me (his hands are white, and not much bigger than Tirzah Ann's).   And then I removed the boy by voyalence, for he was a askin' questions agin, faster than ever; and he poured out over his shoulder a partin' dribble of questions, that lasted till we got outside.   And then he tackled me, and he asked me somewhere in the neighborhood of a 1,000 questions on the way back to Miss Smiths'es.

He begun agin on George Washington jest as quick as he ketched sight of his monument agin.

"If George Washington is up on the top of that monument for tellin' the truth, why didn't all the big men try to tell the truth so's to be stood up on pillows outdoors, and not be a layin' down in the grass? And did the little hatchet help him do right? If it did, why didn't all the big men wear them in their belts to do right with, and tell the truth with? And *say*"—

Oh, dear me suz! He asked me over 40 questions to a lamp-post, for I counted 'em; and there wuz 18 posts.

Good land! I'd ruther wash than try to answer him; but he looked so sweet and good-natured and confidin', his eyes danced so, and he was so awful pretty, that I felt in the midst of my deep fag, that I could kiss him right there in the street if it wuzn't for the looks of it: he is a beautiful child, and very deep.

CHAPTER VII.

WALL, after dinner I sot sail for James G. Blains'es, a walkin' afoot, and carryin' Dorlesky's errent. I was determined to do that errent before I slept. I am very obleegin', and am called so.

When I got to Mr. Blains'es, I was considerably tired; for though Dorlesky's errent might not be heavy as weighed by the steelyards, yet it was *very* hefty and wearin' on the moral feelin's. And my firm, unalterable determination to carry it straight, and tend to it, to the very utmost of my ability, strained on me.

I was fagged.

But I don't believe Mr. Blaine see the fag. I shook hands with him, and there was calmness in that shake. I passed the compliments of the day (how do you do, etc.), and there was peace and dignity in them compliments.

He was most probable, glad I had come. But he didn't seem quite so over-rejoiced as he probable would if he hadn't been so busy. *I* can't be so highly tickled when company comes, when I am washin' and cleanin' house.

He had piles and piles of papers on the table before him. And there was a gentleman a settin' at the end of the room a readin'.

I like James G. Blaines'es looks middlin' well. Although, like myself, he don't set up for a professional beauty. It seems as if some of the strength of the mountain pines round his old home is a holdin' up his backbone, and some of the bracin' air of the pine woods of Maine has blowed into James'es intellect, and braced it.

SAMANTHA MEETING JAMES G. BLAINE.

I think enough of James, but not too much. My likin' is jest about strong enough from a literary person to a literary person.

We are both literary, very. He is considerable taller than I am; and on that account, and a good many others, I felt like lookin' up to him.

Wall, when I have got a hard job in front of me, I don't know any better way than to tackle it to once. So consequently I tackled it.

I told James, that Dorlesky Burpy had sent two errents by me, and I had brought 'em from Jonesville on my tower.

And then I told him jest how she had suffered from the Whisky Ring, and how she had suffered from not havin' her rights; and I told him all about her relations sufferin', and that Dorlesky wanted the Ring broke, and her rights gin to her, within seven days at the longest.

He rubbed his brow thoughtfully, and says, —

"It will be difficult to accomplish so much in so short a time."

"I know it," says I. "I told Dorlesky it would. But she feels jest so, and I promised to do her errent; and I am a doin' it."

Agin he rubbed his brow in deep thought, and agin he says, —

"I don't think Dorlesky is unreasonable in her demands, only in the length of time she has set."

Says I, "That is jest what I told Dorlesky. I didn't believe you could do her errents this week. But you can see for yourself that she is right, only in the time she has sot."

"Yes," he said. "He see she wuz." And says he, "I wish the 3 could be reconciled."

"What 3?" says I.

Says he, "The liquor traffic, liberty, and Dorlesky."

And then come the very hardest part of my errent. But I had to do it. I had to.

Says I, in the deep, solemn tones befitting the threat, for I wuzn't the woman to cheat Dorlesky when she was out of sight, and use the wrong tones at the wrong times — no, I used my deepest and most skairful one — says I, "Dorlesky told me to tell you that if you didn't do her errent, you should not be the next President of the United States."

He turned pale. He looked agitated, fearful agitated.

I s'pose it was not only my words and tone that skairt him, but my mean. I put on my noblest mean; and I s'pose I have got a very noble, high-headed mean at times. I got it, I think, in the first place, by overlookin' Josiah's faults. I always said a wife ort to overlook her husband's faults; and I have to overlook so many, that it has made me about as high-headed, sometimes, as a warlike gander, but more sort o' meller-lookin', and sublime, kinder.

He stood white as a piece of a piller-case, and seemin'ly plunged down into the deepest thought. But finally he riz part way out of it, and says he, —

"I want to be on the side of Truth and Justice. I want to, awfully. And while I do not want to be President of the United States, yet at the same time I do want to be — if you'll understand that paradox," says he.

"Yes," says I sadly. "I understand that paradox. I have seen it myself, right in my own family." And I sithed. And agin silence rained; and I sot quietly in the rain, thinkin' mebby good would come of it.

Finally he riz out of his revery; and says he, with a brighter look on his linement, —

"I am not the one to go to. I am not the one to do Dorlesky's errent."

"Who is the one?" says I.

"Senator Logan," says he.

Says I, " I'll send Bub Smith to Senator Logan'ses the minute I get back; for much as I want to obleege a neighbor, I can't traipse all over Washington, walkin' afoot, and carryin' Dorlesky's errent. But Bub is trusty: I'll send him." And I riz up to go. He riz up too. He is a gentleman; and, as I said, I like his looks. He has got that grand sort of a noble look, I have seen in other literary people, or has been seen in 'em; but modesty forbids my sayin' a word further.

But jest at this minute Mr. Blaines'es hired man come in, and told him that he was wanted below; and he took up his hat and gloves.

But jest as he was startin' out, he says, turnin' to the other gentleman in the room, —

"This gentleman is a senator. Mebby he can do Dorlesky's errent for you."

" Wall," says I, " I would be glad to get it done, without goin' any further. It would tickle Dorlesky most to death, and lots and lots of other wimmen."

Mr. Blaine spoke to the gentleman; and he come forward, and Mr. Blaine introduced us. But I didn't ketch his name; because, jest as Mr. Blaine spoke it, my umberell fell, and the gentleman sprung forward to pick it up; and then he shook hands with me: and Mr. Blaine said good-bye to me, and started off.

I felt willin' and glad to have this senator do Dorlesky's errents, but I didn't like his looks from the very first minute I sot my eyes on him.

My land! talk about Dorlesky Burpy bein' disagreable

—he wus as disagreable as she is, any day. He was
kinder tall, and looked out of his eyes, and wore a vest:
I don't know as I can describe him any more close than
that. He was some bald-headed, and he kinder smiled

MR. BLAINE INTRODUCING THE SENATOR.

once in a while: I persume he will be known by this
description. It is plain, anyway, almost lucid.

But his baldness didn't look to me like Josiah Allen's
baldness; and he didn't have a mite of that smart, straight-

forward way of Blaine, or the perfect courtesy and kindness of Allen Arthur. No. I sort o' despised him from the first minute.

Wall, he was dretful polite: good land! politeness is no name for his mean. Truly, as Josiah Allen says, I don't like to see anybody too good.

He drawed a chair up, for me and for himself, and asked me, —

"If he should have the inexpressible honor and the delightful joy of aiding me in any way: if so, command him to do it," or words to that effect. I can't put down his smiles, and genteel looks, and don't want to if I could.

But tacklin' hard jobs as I always tackle 'em, I sot right down calmly in front of him, with my umberell acrost my lap, and told him over all of Dorlesky's errents. And how I had brought 'em from Jonesville on my tower. I told over all of her sufferin's, from the Ring, and from not havin' her rights; and all her sister Susan Clapsaddle's sufferin's; and all her aunt Eunice's and Patty's, and Drusilla's and Abagail's, sufferin's. I did her errent up honorable and square, as I would love to have a errent done for me. I told him all the particulers; and as I finished, I said firmly, —

"Now, can you do Dorlesky's errents? and will you?"

He leaned forward with that deceitful and sort of disagreable smile of hisen, and took up one corner of my mantilly. It wus cut tab fashion; and he took up the tab, and says he, in a low, insinuatin' voice, and lookin' close at the edge of the tab, —

"Am I mistaken, or is this pipein'? or can it be Kensington tattin'?"

I jest drawed the tab back coldly, and never dained a reply.

Again he says, in a tone of amiable anxiety, —

"Have I not heard a rumor that bangs were going out of style? I see you do not wear your lovely hair bang-like, or a pompidorus! Ah! wimmen are lovely creatures, lovely beings, every one of them." And he sithed. "*You* are very beautiful." And he sithed agin, a sort of a deceitful, love-sick sithe.

I sot demute as the Sfinx, and a chippin'-bird a tappin' his wing against her stunny breast would move it jest as much as he moved me by his talk or his sithes. But he kep' on, puttin' on a kind of a sad, injured look, as if my coldness wus ondoin' of him, —

"My dear madam, it is my misfortune that the topics I introduce, however carefully selected by me, do not seem to be congenial to you. Have you a leaning toward natural history, madam? Have you ever studied into the traits and habits of our American wad?"

"What?" says I. For truly, a woman's curiosity, however paralized by just indignation, can stand only jest so much strain. "The what?"

"The wad. The animal from which is obtained the valuable fur that tailors make so much use of."

Says I, "Do you mean waddin' 8 cents a sheet?"

"8 cents a pelt—yes, the skins are plentiful and cheap, owing to the hardy habits of the animal."

Says I, "Cease instantly. I will hear no more."

Truly, I had heard much of the flattery and the little talk that statesmen will use to wimmen, and I had heard much of their lies, etc.; but truly, I felt that the ½ had not been told. And then I thought out loud, and says, —

"I have hearn how laws of right and justice are sot one side in Washington, D.C., as bein' too triflin' to attend to, while the legislators pondered over, and passed laws regardin', hens' eggs and birds' nests. But this is goin' too fur — too fur. But," says I firmly, "I shall do Dorlesky's errents, and do 'em to the best of my ability; and you can't draw off my attention from her sufferin's and her suffragin's by talkin' about wads."

"I would love to obleege Dorlesky," says he, "because she belongs to such a lovely sex. Wimmen are the loveliest, most angelic creatures that ever walked the earth: they are perfect, flawless, like snow and roses."

Says I firmly, "That hain't no such thing. They are disagreable creeters a good deal of the time. They hain't no better than men. But they ought to have their rights all the same. Now, Dorlesky is disagreable, and kinder fierce actin', and jest as humbly as they make wimmen; but that hain't no sign she ort to be imposed upon. Josiah says, 'She hadn't ort to have a right, not a single right, because she is so humbly.' But I don't feel so."

"Who is Josiah?" says he.

Says I, "My husband."

"Ah! your husband! yes, wimmen should have husbands instead of rights. They do not need rights, they need freedom from all cares and sufferings. Sweet, lovely beings, let them have husbands to lift them above all earthly cares and trials! Oh! angels of our homes," says he, liftin' his eyes to the heavens, and kinder shettin' 'em, some as if he was goin' into a trance, "fly around, ye angels, in your native haunts! mingle not with rings, and vile laws; flee away, flee above them."

And he kinder moved his hand back and forth, in a floatin' fashion, up in the air, as if it was a woman a flyin' up there, smooth and serene. It would have impressed some folks dretful, but it didn't me. I says reasonably, —

"Dorlesky would have been glad to flew above 'em.

But the ring and the vile laws laid holt of her, unbeknown to her, and dragged her down. And there she is, all dragged and bruised and broken-hearted by it. She didn't meddle with the political ring, but the ring med-dled with her. How can she fly when the weight of this infamous traffic is a holdin' her down?"

"Ahem!" says he. "Ahem, as it were — as I was saying, my dear madam, these angelic angels of our homes are too ethereal, too dainty, to mingle with the rude crowds. We political men would fain keep them as they are now: we are willing to stand the rude buffetings of — of — voting, in order to guard these sweet, delicate creatures from any hardships. Sweet, tender beings, we would fain guard you — ah, yes! ah, yes!"

Says I, "Cease instantly, or my sickness will increase; for such talk is like thoroughwort or lobelia to my moral stomach." Says I, "You know, and I know, that these angelic, tender bein's, half clothed, fill our streets on icy midnights, huntin' up drunken husbands and fathers and sons. They are driven to death and to moral ruin by the miserable want liquor - drinkin' entails. They are starved, they are frozen, they are beaten, they are made childless and hopeless, by drunken husbands killing their own flesh and blood.

WOMAN'S RIGHTS.

SOMEBODY BLUNDERED.

They go down into the cold waves, and are drowned by drunken captains; they are cast from railways into death, by drunken engineers; they go up on the scaffold, and die of crimes committed by the direct aid of this agent of hell.

"Wimmen had ruther be a flyin' round than to do all this, but they can't. If men really believe all they say about wimmen, and I think some of 'em do, in a dreamy way — if wimmen are angels, give 'em the rights of angels. Who ever heard of a angel foldin' up her wings, and goin' to a poorhouse or jail through the fault of somebody else? Who ever heard of a angel bein' dragged off to a police court by a lot of men, for fightin' to defend her children and herself from a drunken husband that had broke her wings, and blacked her eyes, himself, got the angel into the fight, and then she got throwed into the streets and the prison by it? Who ever heard of a angel havin' to take in washin' to support a drunken son or father or husband? Who ever heard of a angel goin' out as wet nurse to get money to pay taxes on her home to a Government that in theory idolizes her, and practically despises her, and uses that same money in ways abomenable to that angel?

"If you want to be consistent — if you are bound to make angels of wimmen, you ort to furnish a free, safe place for 'em to soar in. You ort to keep the angels from bein' meddled with, and bruised, and killed, etc."

"Ahem," says he. "As it were, ahem."

But I kep' right on, for I begun to feel noble and by the side of myself.

"This talk about wimmen bein' outside and above all participation in the laws of her country, is jest as pretty as I ever heard any thing, and jest as simple. Why, you might jest as well throw a lot of snowflakes into the street, and say, ' Some of 'em are female flakes, and mustn't be trampled on.' The great march of life tramples on 'em all alike: they fall from one common sky, and are trodden down into one common ground.

" Men and wimmen are made with divine impulses and desires, and human needs and weaknesses, needin' the same heavenly light, and the same human aids and helps. The law should meet out to them the same rewards and punishments.

" Dorlesky says you call wimmens angels, and you don't give 'em the rights of the lowest beasts that crawls upon the earth. And Dorlesky told me to tell you that she didn't ask the rights of a angel: she would be perfectly contented and proud if you would give her the rights of a dog — the assured political rights of a yeller dog. She said ' yeller; ' and I am bound on doin' her errent jest as she wanted me to, word for word.

" A dog, Dorlesky says, don't have to be hung if it breaks the laws it is not allowed any hand in making. A dog don't have to pay taxes on its bone to a Government that withholds every right of citizenship from it.

" A dog hain't called undogly if it is industrious, and hunts quietly round for its bone to the best of its ability, and wants to get its share of the crumbs that fall from that table that bills are laid on.

" A dog hain't preached to about its duty to keep home sweet and sacred, and then see that home turned into a place of torment under laws that these very preachers have made legal and respectable.

"A dog don't have to see its property taxed to advance laws that it believes ruinous, and that breaks its own heart and the hearts of other dear dogs.

"A dog don't have to listen to soul-sickening speeches from them that deny it freedom and justice — about its bein' a damosk rose, and a seraphine, when it knows it hain't: it knows, if it knows any thing, that it is a dog.

"You see, Dorlesky has been kinder embittered by her trials that politics, corrupt legislation, has brought right onto her. She didn't want nothin' to do with 'em; but they come right onto her unexpected and unbeknown, and she feels jest so. She feels she must do every thing she can to alter matters. She wants to help make the laws that have such a overpowerin' influence over her, herself. She believes from her soul that they can't be much worse than they be now, and may be a little better."

"Ah! if Dorlesky wishes to influence political affairs, let her influence her children, — her boys, — and they will carry her benign and noble influence forward into the centuries."

"But the law has took her boy, her little boy and girl, away from her. Through the influence of the Whisky Ring, of which her husband was a shinin' member, he got possession of her boy. And so, the law has made it perfectly impossible for her to mould it indirectly through him. What Dorlesky does, she must do herself."

"Ah! A sad thing for Dorlesky. I trust that you have no grievance of the kind, I trust that your estimable husband is — as it were, estimable."

"Yes, Josiah Allen is a good man. As good as men

can be. You know, men or wimmen either can't be only
jest about so good anyway. But he is my choice, and he
don't drink a drop."

"Pardon me, madam; but if you are happy, as you
say, in your marriage relations, and your husband is a
temperate, good man, why do you feel so upon this subject?"

"Why, good land! if you understand the nature of a
woman, you would know that my love for him, my happiness, the content and safety I feel about him, and our boy,
makes me realize the sufferin's of Dorlesky in havin' her
husband and boy lost to her, makes me realize the depth
of a wive's, of a mother's, agony, when she sees the one
she loves goin' down, goin' down so low that she can't
reach him; makes me feel how she must yearn to help him
in some safe, sure way.

"High trees cast long shadows. The happier and more
blessed a woman's life is, the more does she feel for them
who are less blessed than she. Highest love goes lowest,
if need be. Witness the love that left Heaven, and descended onto the earth, and into it, that He might lift up
the lowly.

"The pityin' words of Him who went about pleasin'
not himself, hants me, and inspires me. I am sorry for
Dorlesky, sorry for the hull wimmen race of the nation —
and for the men too. Lots of 'em are good crecters —
better than wimmen, some on 'em. They want to do jest
about right, but don't exactly see the way to do it. In
the old slavery times, some of the masters was more to be
pitied than the slaves. They could see the injustice, feel
the wrong, they was doin'; but old chains of custom

bound 'em, social customs and idees had hardened into habits of thought.

"'They realized the size and heft of the evil, but didn't know how to grapple with it, and throw it.

"So now, many men see the great evils of this time, want to help it, but don't know the best way to lay holt of it.

"Life is a curious conundrum anyway, and hard to guess. But we can try to get the right answer to it as fur as we can. Dorlesky feels that one of the answers to the conundrum is in gettin' her rights. She feels jest so.

"I myself have got all the rights I need, or want, as fur as my own happiness is concerned. My home is my castle (a story and a half wooden one, but dear).

"My towers elevate me, the companionship of my friends give social happiness, our children are prosperous and happy. We have property enough, and more than enough, for all the comforts of life. . And, above all other things, my Josiah is my love and my theme."

"Ah! yes!" says he. "Love is a woman's empire, and in that she should find her full content — her entire happiness and thought. A womanly woman will not look outside of that lovely and safe and beautious empire."

Says I firmly, "If she hain't a idiot, she can't help it. Love is the most beautiful thing on earth, the most holy, the most satisfyin'. But which would you like best — I do not ask you as a politician, but as a human bein' — which would you like best, the love of a strong, earnest, tender nature — for in man or woman, 'the strongest are the tenderest, the loving are the daring' — which would you like best, the love and respect of such a nature, full of wit, of, tenderness, of infinite variety, or the love of a fool?

"A fool's love is wearin': it is insipid at the best, and it turns to viniger. Why! sweetened water *must* turn to viniger: it is its nater. And, if a woman is bright and true-hearted, she can't help seein' through a injustice. She may be happy in her own home. Domestic affection, social enjoyments, the delights of a cultured home and society, and the companionship of the man she loves, and who loves her, will, if she is a true woman, satisfy fully her own personal needs and desires; and she would far rather, for her own selfish happiness, rest quietly in that love — that most blessed home.

"But the bright, quick intellect that delights you, can't help seeing through an injustice, can't help seeing through shams of all kinds — sham sentiment, sham compliments, sham justice.

"The tender, lovin' nature that blesses your life, can't help feelin' pity for those less blessed than herself. She looks down through the love-guarded lattice of her home, — from which your care would fain bar out all sights of woe and squalor, — she looks down, and sees the weary toilers below, the hopeless, the wretched; she sees the steep hills they have to climb, carryin' their crosses; she sees 'em go down into the mire, dragged there by the love that should lift 'em up.

"She would not be the woman you love, if she could restrain her hand from liftin' up the fallen, wipin' tears from weepin' eyes, speakin' brave words for them who can't speak for themselves.

"The very strength of her affection that would hold you up, if you were in trouble or disgrace, yearns to help all sorrowin' hearts.

"Down in your heart, you can't help admirin' her for this: we can't help respectin' the one who advocates the right, the true, even if they are our conquerors.

"Wimmen hain't angels: now, to be candid, you know they hain't. They hain't better than men. Men are considerable likely; and it seems curious to me, that they should act so in this one thing. For men ort to be more honest and open than wimmen. They hain't had to cajole and wheedle, and spile their natures, through little trickeries and deceits, and indirect ways, that wimmen has.

"Why, cramp a tree-limb, and see if it will grow as straight and vigorous as it would in full freedom and sunshine.

"Men ort to be nobler than wimmen, sincerer, braver. And they ort to be ashamed of this one trick of theirn; for they know they hain't honest in it, they hain't generous.

"Give wimmen 2 or 3 generations of moral freedom, and see if men will laugh at 'em for their little deceits and affectations.

"No: men will be gentler, and wimmen nobler; and they will both come nearer bein' angels, though most probable they won't be angels: they won't be any too good then, I hain't a mite afraid of it."

He kinder sithed; and that sithe sort o' brought me down onto my feet agin (as it were), and a sense of my duty: and I spoke out agin,—

"Can you, and will you, do Dorlesky's errents?"

Wall, he said, "as far as giving Dorlesky her rights

THE WEARY TOILERS OF LIFE.

was concerned, he felt that natural human instinct was against the change." He said, "in savage races, who knew nothing of civilization, male force and strength always ruled."

Says I, " History can't be disputed ; and history tells of savage races where the wimmen always rule, though I don't think they ort to," says I : "ability and goodness ort to rule."

" Nature is against it," says he.

Says I firmly, "Female bees, and lots of other insects, and animals, always have a female for queen and ruler. They rule blindly and entirely, right on through the centuries. But we are more enlightened, and should *not* encourage it. In my opinion, a male bee has jest as good a right to be monarch as his female companion has. That is," says I reasonably, "if he knows as much, and is as good a calculator as she is. I love justice, I almost worship it."

Agin he sithed ; and says he, " Modern history don't seem to encourage the skeme."

But his axent was weak, weak as a cat. He knew better.

Says I, " We won't argue long on that point, for I could overwhelm you if I · approved of overwhelmin'. But I merely ask you to cast your right eye over into England, and then beyond it into France. Men have ruled exclusively in France for the last 40 or 50 years, and a woman in England : which realm has been the most peaceful and prosperous ? "

He sithed twice. And he bowed his head upon his breast, in a sad, almost meachin' way. I nearly pitied him, disagreable as he wuz. When all of a sudden he brightened up; and says he, —

"You seem to place a great deal of dependence on the Bible. The Bible is aginst the idee. The Bible teaches man's supremacy, man's absolute power and might and authority."

"Why, how you talk!" says I. "Why, in the very first chapter, the Bible tells how man was jest turned right round by a woman. It teaches how she not only turned man right round to do as she wanted him to, but turned the hull world over.

"That hain't nothin' I approve of: I don't speak of it because I like the idee. That wuzn't done in a open, honorable manner, as I believe things should be done. No: Eve ruled by indirect influence, — the 'gently influencing men' way, that politicians are so fond of. And she jest brought ruin and destruction onto· the hull world by it.

"A few years later, after men and wimmen grew wiser, when we hear of wimmen ruling Israel openly and honestly, like Miriam, Deborah, and other likely old 4 mothers, why, things went on better. They didn't act meachin', and tempt, and act indirect, I'll bet, or I wouldn't be afraid to bet, if I approved of bettin'."

He sithed powerful, and sot round oneasy in his chair. And says he, "I thought wimmen was taught by the Bible to serve, and love their homes."

"So they be. And every true woman loves to serve. Home is my supreme happiness and delight, and my best happiness is found in servin' them I love. But I must tell the truth, in the house or outdoors."

"Wall," says he faintly, "the Old Testament may teach that wimmen has some strenth and power; but in the New Testament, you will find that in every great undertakin' and plan, men have been chosen by God to carry it through."

"Why-ee!" says I. "How you talk!" says I. "Have you ever read the Bible?"

He said "He had, his grandmother owned one. And he had seen it in early youth."

And then he went on, sort o' apologizin', "He had always meant to read it through. But he had entered political life at an early age, and he believed he had never read any more of it, only portions of Gulliver's Travels. He believed," he said, "he had read as far as Lilliputions."

Says I, "That hain't in the Bible, — you mean Gallatians."

"Wall," he said, "that might be it. It was some man, he knew, and he had always heard and believed that man was the only worker God had chosen."

"Why," says I, "the one great theme of the New Testament, — the redemption of the world through the birth of the Christ, — no man had any thing to do with that whatever. Our divine Lord was born of God and woman.

"Heavenly plan of redemption for fallen humanity. God Himself called women into that work, — the divine work of helpin' a world.

"God called her. Mary had no dream of publicity, no desire for a world's work of sufferin' and renunciation. The soft airs of Gallilee wrapped her about in its sweet content, as she dreamed her quiet dreams in maiden peace, dreamed, perhaps, of domestic love and quiet and happiness.

"From that sweetest silence, the restful peace of happy, innocent girlhood, God called her to her divine work of helpin' to redeem a world from sin.

"And did not this woman's love, and willin' obedience, and sufferin', and the shame of the world, set her apart, babtize her for this work of liftin' up the fallen, helpin' the weak?

"Is it not a part of woman's life that she gave at the birth and the crucifixion? — her faith, her hope, her sufferin', her glow of divine pity and joyful martyrdom. These, mingled with the divine, the pure heavenly, have they not for 1800 years been blessin' the world? The God in Christ would awe us too much: we would shield our faces from the too blindin' glare of the pure God-like. But the tender Christ, who wept over a sinful city, and the grave of His friend, who stopped dyin' upon the cross, to comfort his mother's heart, provide for her future — it is this element in our Lord's nature that makes us dare to approach Him, dare to kneel at His feet.

"And since woman wus so blessed as to be counted worthy to be co-worker with God in the beginnin' of a world's redemption; since He called her from the quiet obscurity of womanly rest and peace, into the blessed martyrdom of renunciation and toil and sufferin', all to help a world that cared nothing for her, that cried out shame upon her, — will He not help her to carry on the work that she helped commence? Will He not approve of her continuin' in it? Will He not protect her in it?

"Yes: she cannot be harmed, since His care is over her; and the cause she loves, the cause of helpin' men and wimmen, is God's cause too, and God will take care of His own. Herods full of greed, and frightened selfishness, may try to break her heart, by efforts to kill the child she loves; but she will hold it so close to her bosom, that he can't destroy it. And the light of the divine will go before her, showin' the way she must go, over the desert, maybe; but she shall bear it into safety."

"You spoke of Herod," says he dreamily. "The name sounds familiar to me: was not Mr. Herod once in the United-States Congress?"

"No," says I. "He died some years ago. But he has relatives there now, I think, judging from recent laws. You ask who Herod was; and, as it all seems to be a new story to you, I will tell you. That when the Saviour of the world was born in Bethlehem, and a woman was tryin' to save His life, a man by the name of Herod was tryin' his best, out of selfishness, and love of gain, to murder him."

"Ah! that was not right in Herod."

"No," says I. "It hain't been called so. And what wuzn't right in him, hain't right in his relations, who are tryin' to do the same thing to-day. But," says I reasonably, "because Herod was so mean, it hain't no sign that all men was mean. Joseph, now, was likely as he could be."

"Joseph," says he pensively. "Do you allude to our senator from Connecticut, — Joseph R. Hawley?"

"No, no," says I. "He is likely, as likely can be, and is always on the right side of questions — middlin' handsome too. But I am talkin' Bible — I am talkin' about Joseph, jest plain Joseph, and nothin' else."

"Ah! I see I am not fully familiar with that work. Being so engrossed in politics, and political literature, I don't get any time to devote to less important publications."

Says I candidly, "I knew you hadn't read it, I knew it the minute you mentioned the Book of Lilliputions. But, as I was a sayin', Joseph was a likely man. He did the very best he could with what he had to do with. He had the strength to lead the way, to overcome obsticles, to keep dangers from Mary, to protect her tenderer form with the mantilly of his generous devotion.

"*But she carried the child on her bosom.*

BEARING THE BABY PEACE.

Pondering high things in her heart that Joseph had never dreamed of. That is what is wanted now, and in the future. The man and the woman walking side by side. He, a little ahead mebby, to keep off dangers by his greater strength and courage. She, a carryin' the infant

Christ of love, bearin' the baby Peace in her bosom, carrying it into safety from them that seek to murder it.

"And, as I said before, if God called woman into this work, He will enable her to carry it through. He will protect her from her own weaknesses, and from the misapprehensions and hard judgments and injustices of a gain-saying world.

"Yes, the star of hope is rising in the sky, brighter and brighter; and the wise men are even now coming from afar over the desert, seeking diligently where this ·redeemer is to be found."

He sot demute. He did not frame a reply: he had no frame, and I know it. Silence rained for some time; and finally I spoke out solemnly through the rain, —

"Will you do Dorlesky's errents? Will you give her her rights? And will you break the Whisky Ring?"

He said he would love to do Dorlesky's errents. He said I had convinced him that it would be just and right to do 'em, but the Constitution of the United States stood up firm against 'em. As the laws of the United State wuz, he could not make any move towards doin' either of the errents.

Says I, "Can't the laws be changed?"

"Be changed? Change the laws of the United States? Tamper with the glorious Constitution that our 4 fathers left us — an immortal, sacred legacy?"

He jumped right up on his feet, in his surprise, and kinder shook, as if he was skairt most to death, and tremblin' with horrow. He did it to skair me, I knew; and I wuz most skaird, I confess, he acted so horrowfied. But I knew I meant well towards the Constitution, and our old 4 fathers; and my principles stiddied me, and held me middlin' firm and serene. And when he asked me agin in tones full of awe and horrow, —

"Can it be that I heard my ear aright? or did you speak of changing the unalterable laws of the United States — tampering with the Constitution?"

Says I, "Yes, that is what I said."

Oh, how his body kinder shook, and how sort o' wild he looked out of his eyes at me!

Says I, "Hain't they never been changed?"

He dropped that skairful look in a minute, and put on a firm, judicial one. He gin up; he could not skair me to death: and says he, —

"Oh, yes! they have been changed in cases of necessity."

Says I, "For instance, durin' the late war, it was changed to make Northern men cheap blood-hounds and hunters."

"Yes," he said. "It seemed to be a case of necessity and econimy."

"I know it," says I. "Men was cheaper than any other breed of blood-hounds the planters had employed to hunt men and wimmen with, and more faithful."

"Yes," he said. "It was doubtless a case of clear econimy."

And says I, "The laws have been changed to benifit whisky-dealers."

"Wall, yes," he said. "It had been changed to enable whisky-dealers to utelize the surplufus liquor they import."

Says he, gettin' kinder animated, for he was on a congenial theme, —

"Nobody, the best calculators in drunkards, can't exactly calculate on how much whisky will be drunk in a year; and so, ruther than have the whisky-dealers suffer loss, the laws had to be changed.

"And then," says he, growin' still more candid in his

A CASE OF NECESSITY.

excitement, "we are makin' a powerful effort to change the laws now, so as to take the tax off of whisky, so it can be sold cheaper, and be obtained in greater quantities by the masses. Any such great laws for the benifit of the nation, of course, would justify a change in the Constitution and the laws; but for any frivolous cause, any trivial cause, madam, we male custodians of the sacred Constitution would stand as walls of iron before it, guarding it from any shadow of change. Faithful we will be, faithful unto death."

Says I, "As it has been changed, it can be again. And you jest said I had convinced you that Dorlesky's errents wus errents of truth and justice, and you would love to do 'em."

"Well, yes, yes — I would love to — as it were — But really, my dear madam, much as I would like to oblige you, I have not the time to devote to it. We senators and Congressmen are so driven, and hard-worked, that really we have no time to devote to the cause of Right and Justice. I don't think you realize the constant pressure of hard work, that is ageing us, and wearing us out, before our day.

"As I said, we have to watch the liquor-interest constantly, to see that the liquor-dealers suffer no loss — we *have* to do that. And then, we have to look sharp if we ·cut down the money for the Indian schools."

Says I, in a sarcastick tone, "I s'pose you worked hard for that."

"Yes," says he, in a sort of a proud tone. "We did, but we men don't· begrudge labor. if we can advance. measures of economy. You see, it was taking sights of money just to Christianize and civilize Injuns — savages. Why, the idea was worse than useless, it wus perfectly ruinous to the Indian agents. For if, through those schools, the Indians had got to be self-supporting and intelligent and Christians, why, the agents couldn't buy their wives and daughters for a yard of calico, or get them drunk, and buy a horse for a glass bead, and a farm for a pocket lookin'-glass. Well, thank fortune, we carried that important measure through; we voted strong; we cut down the money anyway. And there is one revenue that is still accruing to the Government — or, as it were, the servants of Government, the agents. You see," says he, "don't you, just how important the subjects are, that are wearing down the Congressional and senatorial mind?"

"Yes," says I sadly, "I see a good deal more than I want to."

"Yes, you see how hard-worked we are. With all the care of the North on our minds, we have to. clean out all the creeks in the South, so the planters can have smooth sailing. But we think," says he dreamily, "we think we have saved money enough out of the Indian schools, to clean out most of their creeks, and perhaps have a little left for a few New-York aldermen, to reward them for their arduous duties in drinking and voting for their constituents.

"Then, there is the Mormons: we have to make soothing laws to sooth them.

"Then, there are the Chinese. When we send them back into heathendom, we ought to send in the ship with them, some appropriate biblical texts, and some mottoes emblematical of our national eagle protecting and clawing the different nations.

"And when we send the Irish paupers back into poverty and ignorance, we ought to send in the same ship, some resolutions condemning England for her treatment of Ireland."

Says I, "Most probable the Goddess of Liberty Enlight-
enin' the World, in New-York Harbor, will hold her
torch up high, to light such ships on their way."

And he said, "Yes, he thought so." Says he, "There
is very important laws up before the House, now, about
hens' eggs — counting them." And says he, "Taking it
with all those I have spoke of and other kindred laws,
and the constant strain on our minds in trying to pass
laws to increase our own salaries, you can see just how
cramped we are for time. And though we would love to
pass some laws of Truth and Righteousness, — we fairly
ache to, — yet, not having the requisite time, we are obliged to lay 'em on the table, or under it."

"Wall," says I, "I guess I might jest a well be a goin'."

I bid him a cool good-bye, and started for the door. I
was discouraged; but he says as I went out, —

"Mebby William Wallace will do the errent for you."

Says I coldly, —

"William Wallace is dead, and you know it." And
says I with a real lot of dignity, "You needn't try to
impose on me, or Dorlesky's errent, by tryin' to send me
round amongst them old Scottish chiefs. I respect them
old chiefs, and always did; and I don't relish any light
talk about 'em."

Says he, "This is another William Wallace; and very
probable he can do the errent."

"Wall," says I, "I will send the errent to him by Bub
Smith; for I am wore out."

As I wended my way out of Mr. Blains'es, I met the
hired man, Bub Smith's friend; and he asked me, —

"If I didn't want to visit the Capitol?"

Says I, "Where the laws of the United States are made?"

"Yes," says he.

And I told him "that I was very weary, but I would fain behold it."

And he said he was going right by there on business, and he would be glad to show it to me. So we walked along in that direction.

It seems that Bub Smith saved the life of his little sister—jumped off into the water when she was most drowned, and dragged her out. And from that time the two families have thought the world of each other. That is what made him so awful good to me.

Wall, I found the Capitol was a sight to behold! Why, it beat any buildin' in Jonesville, or Loontown, or Spoon Settlement in beauty and size and grandeur. There hain't one that can come nigh it. Why, take all the meetin'-housen of these various places, and put 'em all together, and put several other meetin'-housen on top of 'em, and they wouldn't begin to show off with it.

And, oh! my land! to stand in the hall below, and look up — and up — and up — and see all the colors of the rainbow, and see what kinder curious and strange pictures there wuz way up there in the sky above me (as it were). Why, it seemed curiouser than any Northern lights I ever see in my life, and they stream up dretful curious sometimes.

And as I walked through the various lofty and magnificent halls, and realized the size and majestic proportions of the buildin', I wondered to myself that a small law, a little, unjust law, could ever be passed in such a magnificent place.

Says I to myself, "It can't be the fault of the place, anyway. They have got a chance for their souls to soar

SAMANTHA VIEWING THE CAPITOL.

if they want to." Thinks'es I, here is room and to spare, to pass by laws big as elephants and camels. And I wondered to myself that they should ever try to pass laws and resolutions as small as muskeeters and nats. Thinks'es I, I wonder them little laws don't get to strollin' round and get lost in them magnificent corriders. But I consoled myself a thinkin' that it wouldn't be no great loss if they did.

But right here, as I was a thinkin' on these deep and lofty subjects, the hired man spoke up; and says he, —

"You look fatigued, mom." (Soarin' even to yourself, is tuckerin'.) "You look very fatigued: won't you take something?"

I looked at him with a curious, silent sort of a look; for I didn't know what he meant.

Agin he looked close at me, and sort o' pityin'; and says he, "You look tired out, mom. Won't you take something?"

Says I, "What?"

Says he, "Let me treat you to something: what will you take, mom?"

Wall, I thought he was actin' dretful liberal; but I knew they had strange ways there in Washington, anyway. And I didn't know but it was their way to make some presents to every woman who come there: and I didn't want to be odd, and act awkward, and out of style; so I says, —

"I don't want to take any thing, and I don't see any reason why you should insist on it. But, if I have got to take somethin', I had jest as lives have a few yards of factory-cloth as any thing."

I thought, if he was determined to treat me, to show his good feelin's towards me, I would get somethin' useful, and that would do me some good, else what would be the use of bein' treated? And I thought, if I had *got* to take a present from a strange man, I would make a shirt for Josiah out of it: I thought that would make it all right, so fur as goodness went.

But says he, "I mean beer, or wine, or liquor of some kind."

I jest riz right up in my shoes and my dignity, and glared at him.

Says he, "There is a saloon right here handy in the buildin'."

Says I, in awful axents, "It is very appropriate to have it right here handy." Says I, "Liquor does more towards makin' the laws of the United States, from caucus to convention, than any thing else does; and it is highly proper to have some liquor here handy, so they can soak the laws in it right off, before they lay 'em onto the tables, or under 'em, or pass 'em onto the people. It is highly appropriate," says I.

"Yes," says he. "It is very handy for the senators. And let me get you a glass."

"No, you won't," says I firmly, "no, you won't. The nation suffers enough from that room now, without havin' Josiah Allen's wife let in."

Says he (his friendship for Bub Smith makin' him anxious and sot on helpin' me), "If you have any feeling of delicacy in going in there, let me make some wine here. I will get a glass of water, and make you some pure grape wine, or French brandy, or corn or rye whiskey. I have all the drugs right here." And he took out a little box out of his pocket. "My father is a importer of rare old

wines, and I know just how it is done. I have 'em all
here, — capiscum, coculus Indicus, alum, coperas, strych-
nine. I will make some of the choicest and purest im-

SAMANTHA REFUSING TO BE TREATED.

ported liquors we have in the country, in five minutes, if
you say so."

"No," says I firmly. "When I want to follow up Cleopatra's fashion, and commit suicide, I am goin' to hire a
rattlesnake, and take my poison as she did, on the outside."

"Cleopatra?" says he inquiringly. "Is she a Washington lady?"

And I says guardedly, "She has lots of relations here, I believe."

"Wall," he said, "he thought her name sounded familiar. Then, I can't do any thing for you?" he says.

"Yes," says I calmly: "you can open the front door, and let me out."

Which he did, and I was glad enough to get out into the pure air.

When I got back to the house, I found they had been to supper. Sally had had company that afternoon,—her husband's brother. He had jest left.

He lived only a few milds away, and had come in on the cars. Sally said he wanted to stay and see me the worst kind: he wanted to throw out some deep arguments aginst wimmen's suffrage. Says she, "He talks powerful about it: he would have convinced you, without a doubt."

"Wall," says I, "why didn't he stay?"

She said he had to hurry home on account of business. He had come in to the village, to get some money. There was goin' to be a lot of men, wimmen, and children sold in his neighborhood the next mornin', and he thought he should buy a girl, if he could find a likely one.

"Sold?" says I, in curious axents.

"Yes," says Sally. "They sell the inmates of the poor-house, every year, to the highest bidder,—sell their labor by the year. They have 'em get up on a auction block, and hire a auctioneer, and sell 'em at so much a head, to the crowd. Why, some of 'em bring as high as twenty dollars a year, besides board.

"Sometimes, he said, there was quite a run on old wim-

BUYING TIME.

men, and another year on young ones. He didn't know but he might buy a old woman. He said there was an old woman that he thought there was a good deal of work in, yet. She had belonged to one of the first families in the

State, and had come down to poverty late in life, through the death of some of her relations, and the villany of others. So he thought she had more strength in her than if she had always been worked. He thought, if she didn't fetch too big a price, he should buy her instead of a young one. They was so balky, he said, young ones was, and would need more to eat, bein' growin'. And she could do rough, heavy work, just as well as a younger one, and probably wouldn't complain so much; and he thought she would last a year, anyway. It was his way, he said, to put 'em right through, and, when one wore out, get another one."

I sithed; and says I, "I feel to lament that I wuzn't here so's he could have converted me." Says I, "A race of bein's, that make such laws as these, hadn't ort to be disturbed by wimmen meddlin' with 'em."

"Yes: that is what he said," says Sally, in a innocent way.

I didn't say no more. Good land! Sally hain't to blame. But with a noble scorn filling my eye, and floating out the strings of my head-dress, I moved off to bed.

Wall, the next mornin' I sent Dorlesky's errents by Bub Smith to William Wallace, for I felt a good deal fagged out. Bub did 'em well, and I know it.

But William Wallace sent him to Gen. Logan.

And Gen. Logan said Grover Cleveland was the one to go to: he wuz a sot man, and would do as he agreed. And Mr. Cleveland sent him to Mr. Edmunds.

And Mr. Edmunds told him to go to Samuel G. Tilden, or Roswell P. Flower.

And Mr. Flower sent him to William Walter Phelps.

And Mr. Phelps said that Benjamin F. Butler or Mr. Bayard was the one to do the errent.

And Mr. Bayard sent him to somebody else, and somebody else sent him to another one. And so it went on; and Bub Smith traipsed round, a carryin' them errents, from one man to another, till he was most dead.

Why, he carried them errents round all day, walkin' afoot.

Bub said most every one of 'em said the errents wuz just and right, but they couldn't do 'em, and wouldn't tell their reasons.

One or two, Bub said, opposed it, because they said right out plain, "that they wanted to drink. They wanted to drink every thing they could, and everywhere théy could, — hard cider and beer, and brandy and whisky, and every thing."

And they didn't want wimmen to vote, because they liked to have the power in their own hands: they loved to control things, and kinder boss round — loved to dearly.

These was open-hearted men who spoke as they felt. But they was exceptions. Most every one of 'em said they couldn't do it, and wouldn't tell their reasons.

Till way along towards night, a senator he had been sent to, bein' a little in liquor at the time, and bein' talkative; he owned up the reasons why the senators wouldn't do the errents.

He said they all knew in their own hearts, both of the errents was right and just, to their own souls and their own country. He said — for the liquor had made him *very* open-hearted and talkative — that they knew the course they was pursuin' in regard to intemperance was a crime against God and their own consciences. But they didn't dare to tackle unpopular subjects.

He said they knew they was elected by liquor, a good many of them, and they knew, if they voted against whisky, it would deprive 'em of thousands and thousands of voters, dillegent voters, who would vote for 'em from mornin' till night, and so they dassent tackle the ring. And if wimmen was allowed to vote, they knew it was jest the same thing as breaking the ring right in two, and destroying intemperance. So, though they knew that both the errents was jest as right as right could be, they dassent tackle 'em, for fear they wouldn't run no chance at all of bein' President of the United States.

"Good land!" says I. "What a idee! to think that doin' right would make a man unpopular. But," says I, " I am glad to know they have got a reason, if it is a poor one. I didn't know but they sent you round jest to be mean."

Wall, the next mornin' I told Bub to carry the errents right into the Senate. Says I, " You have took 'em one by one, alone, now you jest carry 'em before the hull batch on 'em together." I told him to tackle the hull crew on 'em. So he jest walked right into the Senate, a carryin' Dorlesky's errents.

And he come back skairt. He said, jest as he was a carryin' Dorlesky's errents in, a long petition come from thousands and thousands of wimmen on this very subject. A plea for justice and mercy, sent in respectful, to the law-makers of the land.

And he said the men jeered at it, and throwed it round the room, and called it all to nort, and made the meanest speeches about it you ever heard, talked nasty, and finally threw it under the table, and acted so haughty and over-bearin' towards it, that Bub said he was afraid to tackle 'em. He said "he knew they would throw Dorlesky's errents under the table, and he was afraid they would throw him under too." He was afraid — (he owned it up to me) — he was afraid they would knock him down. So he backed out with Dorlesky's errents, and never give it to 'em at all.

And I told him he did right. "For," says I, "if they wouldn't listen to the deepest, most earnest, and most prayerful words that could come from the hearts of thousands and tens of thousands of the best mothers and wives and daughters in America, the most intelligent and upright and pure-minded women in the land, loaded down with their hopes, wet with their tears — if they turned their hearts' prayers and deepest desires into ridicule, throwed 'em round under their feet, they wouldn't pay no attention to Dorlesky's errents, they wouldn't notice one little vegitable widow, humbly at that, and sort o' disagreeable." And says I, "I don't want Dorlesky's errents throwed round under foot, and she made fun of: she has went through enough trials and tribulations, besides these gentlemen — or," says I, "I beg pardon of Webster's Dictionary: I meant men."

"For," as I said to Webster's Dictionary in confidence, in a quiet thought we had about it afterwards, "they might be gentlemen in every other place on earth; but in this one move of theirn," as I observed confidentially to the Dictionary, "they was jest *men* — the male animal of the human species."

And I was ashamed enough as I looked Noah Webster's steel engraving in the face, to think I had misspoke myself, and called 'em gentlemen.

HOW WOMAN'S PRAYERS ARE ANSWERED.

Wall, from that minute I gin up doin' Dorlesky's errents. And I felt like death about it. But this thought held me up,—that I had done my best. But I didn't feel like doin' another thing all the rest of that day, only jest feel disapinted and grieved over my bad luck with the errents. I always think it is best, if you can possibly arrainge it in that way, to give up one day, or half a day, to feelin' bad over any perticuler disapintment, or to worry about any thing, and do all your worryin' up in that time, and then give it up for good, and go to feelin' happy agin. It is also best, if you have had a hull lot of things to get mad about, to set apart half a day, when you can spare the time, and do up all your resentin' in that time. It is easier, and takes less time than to keep resentin' 'em as they take place; and you can feel clever quicker than in the common way.

Wall, I felt dretful bad for Dorlesky and the hull wimmen race of the land, and for the men too. And I kep' up my bad feelin's till pretty nigh dusk. But as I see the sun go down, and the sky grow dark, I says, —

" You are goin' down now, but you are a comin' up agin. As sure as the Lord lives, the sun will shine agin; and He who holds you in His hand, holds the destinies of the nations. He will watch over you, and me and Josiah, and Dorlesky. He will help us, and take care of us."

So I begun to feel real well agin — a little after dusk.

CHAPTER VIII.

The next morning Cicely wuzn't able to leave her room, — not sick seemin'ly, but fagged out. She was a delicate little creeter always, and seemed to grow delicater every day.

So Miss Smith went with me, and she and I sallied out alone: her name bein' Sally, too, made it seem more singuler and coincidin'.

She asked me if I didn't want to go to the Patent Office.

And I told her, "Yes." And I told her of Betsy Bobbet's errent, and that Josiah had charged me expresly to go there, and get him a patent pail. He needed a new milk-pail, and thought I could get it cheaper right on the spot.

And she said that Josiah couldn't buy his pail there. But she told me what sights and sights of things there wus to be seen there; and I found out when I got there, that she hadn't told me the $\frac{1}{2}$ or the $\frac{1}{4}$ of the sights I see.

Why, I could pass a month there in perfect destraction and happiness, the sights are so numerous, and exceedingly destractin' and curious.

But I told Sally Smith plainly, that I wasn't half so much interested in apple-parers and snow-plows, and the first sewin'-machine and the last one, and steam-engines and hair-pins and pianos and thimbles, and the acres and acres of glass cases containing every thing that wus ever heard of, and every thing that never wus heard of by anybody, and etcetery, etcetery, and so 4th, and so 4th. And you might string them words out over choirs and choirs of paper, and not get half an idee of what is to be seen there.

But I told her I didn't feel half so interested in them things as I did in the copyright. I told Sally plain "that I wanted to see the place where the copyrights on books was made. And I wanted to see the man who made 'em.

And she asked me "Why? What made me so anxious?"

And I told her "the law was so curious, that I believed it would be the curiousest place, and he would be the curiousest lookin' creeter, that wuz ever seen." Says I, "I'll bet it will be better than a circus to see him."

But it wuzn't. He looked jest like any man. And he had a sort of a smart look onto him. Sally said "it was one of the clerks," but I don't believe a word of it. I believe it was the man himself, who made the law; for, as in all other emergincies of life, I follered Duty, and asked him "to change the law instantly."

And he as good as promised me he would.

I talked deep to him about it, but short. I told him Josiah had bought a mair, and he expected to own it till he or the mair died. He didn't expect to give up his right to it, and let the mair canter off free at a stated time.

SAMANTHA AND SALLY IN THE PATENT OFFICE.

And he asked me "Who Josiah was?" and I told him.

And I told him that "Josiah's farm run along one side of a pond; and if one of his sheep got over on the other side, it was sheep jest the same, and it was hisen jest the same: he didn't lose the right to it, because it happened to cross the pond."

Says he, "There would be better laws regarding copyright, if it wuzn't for selfishness on both sides of the pond."

"Wall," says I, "selfishness don't pay in the long-run." And then, thinkin' mebby if I made myself agreable and entertainin', he would change the law quicker, I made a effort, and related a little interestin' incident that I had seen take place jest before my former departure from Jonesville, on a tower.

"No, selfishness don't pay. I have seen it tried, and I know. Now, Bildad Henzy married a wife on a speculation. She was a one-legged woman. He was attached at the time to a woman with the usual number of feet; but he was so close a calculator, that he thought it would be money in his pocket to marry this one, for he wouldn't have to buy but one shoe and stockin'. But she had to jump round on that one foot, and step heavy; so she wore out more shoes than she would if she was two-footed." Says I, "Selfishness don't pay in private life or in politics."

And he said "He thought jest so," and he jest about the same as promised me he would change the law.

I hope he will. It makes me feel so strange every time I think on't, as strange as strange can be.

Why, I told Sally after we went out, and I spoke about

"the man lookin' human, and jest like anybody else;" and she said "it was a clerk;" and I said "I knew better, I knew it was the man himself."

And says I agin, "It beats all, how anybody in human shape can make such a law as that copyright law."

And she said "that was so." But I knew by her mean, that she didn't understand a thing about it; and I knew it would make me so sort o' light-headed and vacant if I went to explain it to her, that I never said a word, and fell in at once with her proposal that we should go and see the Treasury, and the Corcoran Art Gallery, and the Smithsonian Institute, one at a time.

And I found the Treasury wuz a sight to behold. Such sights and sights of money they are makin' there, and a countin'. Why, I s'pose they make more money there in a week, than Josiah and I spend in a year.

I s'pose most probable they made it a little faster, and more of it, on account of my bein' there. But they have sights and sights of it. They are dretful well off.

I asked Sally, and I spoke out kinder loud too, — I hain't one of the underhanded kind, — I asked her, "If she s'posed they'd let us take hold and make a little money for ourselves, they seemed to be so runnin' over with it. there."

And she said, "No, private citizens couldn't do that."

Says I, "Who can?"

She kinder whispered back in a skairt way, sunthin' about "speculators and legislators and rings, and etcetery."

But I answered right out loud, — I hain't one to go whisperin' round, — and says I, —

"I'll bet if Uncle Sam himself was here, and knew the

feelin's I had for him, he'd hand out a few dollars of his own accord for me to get sunthin' to remember him by. Howsumever, I don't need nor want any of his money. I hain't beholden to him nor any man. I have got over fourteen dollars by me, at this present time, egg-money."

But it was a sight to behold, to see 'em make it.

And then, as we stood out on the sidewalk agin, the Smithsonian Institute passed through my mind; and then the Corcoran Art Gallery passed through it, and several other big, noble buildin's. But I let 'em pass; and I says to Sally, —

"Let us go at once and see the man that makes the public schools." Says I, "There is a man that I honor, and almost love."

And she said she didn't know who it wuz.

But I think it was the lamb that she had in a bakin', that drew her back towards home. She owned up that her hired girl didn't baste it enough.

And she seemed oneasy.

But I stood firm, and says, "I shall see that man, lamb or no lamb."

And then Sally give in. And she found him easy enough. She knew all the time, it was the sheep that hampered her.

And, oh! I s'pose it was a sight to be remembered, to see my talk to that man. I s'pose, if it had been printed, it would have made a beautiful track — and lengthy.

Why, he looked fairly exhausted and cross before I got half through, I talked so smart (eloquence is tuckerin').

I told him how our public schools was the hope of the

nation. How they neutralized to a certain extent the other schools the nation allowed to the public, — the grog-shops, and other licensed places of ruin. I told him how pretty it looked to me to see Civilization a marchin' along from the Atlantic towards the Pacific, with a spellin'-book in one hand, and in the other the rosy, which she was a plantin' in place of the briars and brambles.

And I told him how highly I approved of compulsory education.

"Why," says I, "if anybody is a drowndin', you don't ask their consent to be drawed out of the water, you jest jump in, and yank 'em out. And when you see poor little ones, a sinkin' down in the deep waters of ignorance and brutality, why, jest let Uncle Sam reach right down, and draw 'em out." Says 1, "I'll bet that is why he is pictered as havin' such long arms for, and long legs too, — so he can wade in if the water is deep, and they are too fur from the shore for his arms to reach."

And says I, "In the case of the little Indian, and other colored children, he'll need the legs of a stork, the water is so deep round 'em. But he'll reach 'em, Uncle Sam will. He'll lift 'em right up in his long arms, and set 'em safe on the pleasant shore. You'll see that he will. Uncle Sam is a man of a thousand."

Says I, "How much it wus like him, to pass that law for children to be learnt jest what whisky is, and what it will do. Why," says I, "in that very law Christianity has took a longer stride than she could take by millions of sermons, all divided off into tenthlies and twentiethlies."

Why, I s'pose I talked perfectly beautiful to that man: I s'pose so.

And if he hadn't had a sudden engagement to go out, I should have talked longer. But I see his engagement wus a wearin' on him. His eyes looked fairly wild. I only give a bald idee of what I said. I have only give the heads of my discussion to him, jest the bald heads.

Wall, after we left there, I told Sally I felt as if I must go and see the Peace Commission. I felt as if I must make some arrangements with 'em to not have any more wars. As I told Sally, "We might jest as well call our-selves Injuns and savages at once, if we had to keep up this most savage and brutal trait of theirn." Says I firmly, "I *must*, before I go back to Jonesville, tend to it." Says I, "I didn't come here for fashion, or dry-goods; though I s'pose lots of both of 'em are to be got here." Says I, "I may tend to one or two fashionable parties, or levys as I s'pose they call 'em here. I may go to 'em ruther than hurt the feelin's of the upper 10. I want to do right: I don't want to hurt the feelin's of them 10. They have hearts, and they are sensitive. I don't think I have ever took to them 10, as much as I have to some others; but I wish 'em well.

"And I s'pose you see as grand and curious people to their parties here, as you can see together in any other place on the globe.

"I s'pose it is a sight to behold, to see 'em together. To see them, as the poet says, 'To the manner born,' and them that wasn't born in the same manor, but tryin' to act as if they was. Wealth and display, natural courtesy and refinement, walkin' side by side with pretentius vul-garity, and mebby poverty bringin' up the rear. Genius and folly, honesty and affectation, gentleness and sweet-

ness, and brazen impudence, and hatred and malice, and
envy and uncharitableness. All languages and peoples
under the sun, and differing more than stars ever did, one
from another.

"And what makes it more curious and mysterius is, the

SAMANTHA AT THE PRESIDENT'S RECEPTION.

way they dress, some on 'em. Why, they say — it has
come right straight to me by them that know — that the
ladies wear what they call full dress; and the strange and

mysterius part of it is, that the fuller the dress is, the less they have on 'em.

"This is a deep subject, and queer; and I don't s'pose you will take my word for it, and I don't want you to. But I have been *told* so.

"Why, I s'pose them upper 10 have their hands full, their 20 hands completely full. I fairly pity 'em — the hull 10 of 'em. They want me, and they need me, I s'pose, and I must tend to some of 'em.

"And then," says I, "I did calculate to pay some attention to store-clothes. I did want to get me a new calico dress, — London brown with a set flower on it. But I can do without that dress, and the upper 10 can do without me, better than the Nation can do without Peace."

I felt as if I must tend to it: I fairly hankered to do away with war, immejiately and to once. But I knew right was right, and I felt that Sally ort to be let to tend to her lamb; so Sally and I sallied homewards.

But the hired girl had tended to it well. It wus good —·very good.

CHAPTER IX.

WALL, the next mornin' Cicely wus better, and we sot sail for Mount Vernon. It was about ten o'clock A.M. when I, accompanied by Cicely and the boy, sot sail from Washington, D.C., to perform about the ostensible reason of my tower, — to weep on the tomb of the noble G. Washington.

My intentions had been and wuz, to weep for him on my tower. I had come prepared. 2 linen handkerchiefs and a large cotton one reposed in the pocket of my polenay, and I had on my new waterproof. I never do things by the ½s.

It was a beautiful seen, as we floated down the still river, to look back and see the Capitol risin' white and fair like a dream, the glitterin' snow of the monument, and the green heights, all bathed in the glory of that perfect May mornin'. It wuz a fair seen.

Happy groups of people sot on the peaceful decks, — stately gentlemen, handsome ladies, and pretty children. And in one corner, off kinder by themselves, sot that band of dusky singers, whose songs have delighted the world. Modest, good-lookin' dark girls, manly, honest-lookin' dark boys.

Only a few short years ago this black people was drove
about like dumb cattle, — bought and sold, hunted by
blood-hounds; the wimmen hunted to infamy and ruin,
the men to torture and to death. The wimmen denied
the first right of womanhood, to keep themselves pure.
The men denied the first right of manhood, to protect

GOING TO MOUNT VERNON.

the ones they loved. Deprived legally of purity and
honor, and all the rights of commonest humanity — worn
with unpaid toil, beaten, whipped, tortured, dispised and
rejected of men.

Now, a few short years have passed over this dark race,
and these children of slaves that I looked upon have been
guests of the proudest and noblest in this and in foreign
lands. Hands that hold the destinies of mighty empires
have clasped theirs in frankest friendship, and crowned
heads have bowed low before 'em to hide the tears their

sweet voices have called forth. What feelin's I felt as I looked on 'em! and my soul burned inside of me, almost to the extent of settin' my polenay on fire, a thinkin' of all this.

And pretty soon, right when I was a reveryin' — right there, when we wuz a floatin' down the still waters, their voices riz up in one of their inspired songs. They sung about their "Hard Trials," and how the "Sweet Chariot swung low," and how they had "Been Redeemed."

And I declare for't, as I listened to 'em, there wuzn't a dry eye in my head; and I wet every one of them 3 handkerchiefs that I had calculated to mourn for G. Washington on, wet as sop. But I didn't care. I knew that George had ruther not be mourned for on dry handkerchiefs, than that I should stent myself in emotions in such a time as this. He loved Liberty himself, and fit for it. And anyway, I didn't sense what I was a doin', not a mite. I took out them handkerchiefs entirely unbeknown to me, and put 'em back unbeknown.

The words of them songs hain't got hardly any sense, as we earthly bein's count sense; there are scores of great singers, whose trained voices are a hundred-fold more melodious: but these simple strains move us, thrill us; they jest get right inside of our hearts and souls, and take full possession of us.

It seems as if nothin' human of so little importance could so move us. Is it God's voice that speaks to us through them? Is it His Spirit that lifts us up, sways us to and fro, that blows upon us, as we listen to their voices? The Spirit that come down to cheer them broken hearts, lift them up in their captivity, does it now sway and melt the hearts of their captors? We read of One who watches over His sorrowing, wronged 'people, givin' them "songs in the night."

Anon, or nearly at that time, a silver bell struck out a sweet sort of a mournful note; and we jest stood right in towards the shore, and disembarked from the bark.

We clomb the long hill, and stood on top, with powerful emotions (but little or no breath); stood before the iron bars that guarded the tomb of George Washington, and Martha his wife.

I looked at the marble coffin that tried to hold George, and felt how vain it wuz to think that any tomb could hold him. That peaceful, tree-covered hill couldn't hold his tomb. Why, it wuz lifted up in every land that loved freedom. The hull liberty-lovin' earth wuz his tomb and his monument.

And that great river flowin' on and on at his feet — as long as that river rolls, George Washington shall float on it, he and his faithful Martha. It shall bear him to the sea and the ocian, and abroad to every land.

Oh! what feelin's I felt as I stood there a reveryin', my body still, but my mind proudly soarin'! To think, he wuz our Washington, and that time couldn't kill him. For he shall walk through the long centuries to come. He shall bear to the high chamber of prince and ruler, memories that shall blossom into deeds, awaken souls, rouse powers that shall never die, that shall scatter blessings over lands afar, strike the fetters from slave and serf.

The hands they folded over his peaceful breast so many years ago, are not lying there in that marble coffin: the

calm blue eyes closed so many years ago, are still lookin'
into souls. Those hands lift the low walls of the poor
boy's chamber, as he reads of victory over tyranny, of con-
querin' discouragement and defeat.

BEFORE THE TOMB OF WASHINGTON.

The low walls fade away; the dusky rafters part to
admit the infinite, infinite longin's to do and dare, infinite
resolves to emulate those deeds of valor and heroism. How
the calm blue eyes look down into the boy's impassioned
soul, how the shadowy hands beckon him upward, up the

rocky heights of noble endeavor, noble deeds! How the inspiration of this life, these deeds of might and valor, nerve the young heart for future strivings for freedom and justice and truth!

Is it not a blessed thing to thus live on forever in true, eager hearts, to nerve the hero's arm, to inspire deeds of courage and daring? The weary body may rest; but to do this, is surely not to die; no, it is to live, to be immortal, to thus become the beating heart, the living, struggling, daring soul of the future.

And right while I was thinkin' these thoughts, and lookin' off over the still landscape, the peaceful waters, this band of dark singers stood with reverent faces and uncovered heads, and begun singin' one of their sweetest melodies, —

"He rose, he rose, he rose from the dead."

Oh! as them inspired, hantin' notes rose through the soft, listenin' air, and hanted me, walked right round inside my heart and soul, and inspired me — why! how many emotions I did have, — more'n 85 a minute right along!

As I thought of how many times since the asscension of our Lord, tombs have opened, and the dead come forth alive; how Faith and Justice will triumph in the end; how you can't bury 'em deep enough, or roll a stun big enough and hard enough before the door, but what, in some calm mornin', the earliest watcher shall see a tall, fair angel standin' where the dead has lain, bearin' the message of the risen Lord, "He rose from the dead."

I thought how George W. and our other old 4 fathers

thought in the long, toilsome, weary hours before the dawnin', that fair Freedom was dead; but she rose, she rose.

I thought how the dusky race whose sweet songs was a floatin' round the grave of him who loved freedom, and gave his life for it; I thought how, durin' the dreary time when they was captives in a strange land, chained, scourged, and tortured, how they thought, through this long, long night of years, that Justice was dead, and Mercy and Pity and Righteousness.

But there come a glorious mornin' when fathers and mothers clasped their children in their arms, their own once more, in arms that was their own, to labor and protect, and they sung together of Freedom and Right, how though they wuz buried deep, and the night wuz long, and the watchers by the tomb weary, weary unto death, yet they rose, they rose from the dead.

And then I thought of the tombs that darken our land to-day, where the murdered, the legally murdered, lay buried. I thought of the graves more hopeless fur than them that entomb the dead, — the graves where lay the livin' dead. Dead souls bound to still breathin' bodies, dead hopes, ambitions, dead dreams of usefulness and respectability, happiness, dead purity, faith, honor, dead, all dead, all bound to the still breathin' body, by the festerin', putrid death-robes of helplessness and despair.

There they lie chained to their dark tombs by links slight at first, but twisted by the hard old fingers of blind habit, to chains of iron, chains linked about, and eatin' into, not only the quiverin' flesh, but the frenzied brains, the hopeless hearts, the ruined souls.

Heavy, hopeless-lookin' vaults they are indeed, whose air is putrid with the sickenin' miasma of moral loathsomness and deseese; whose walls are painted with hideous pictures of murder, rapine, lust, starvation, woe, and despair, earthly and eternal ruin. Shapes of the dreadful past, the hopeless future, that these livin' dead stare upon with broodin' frenzy by night and by day.

Oh the tombs, the countless, countless tombs, where lie these breathin' corpses! How mothers weep over them! how wives kneel, and beat their hearts out on the rocky barriers that separate them from their hearts' love, their hearts' desire! How little starvin', naked children cower in their ghostly shadows through dark midnights! how fathers weep for their children, dead to them, dead to honor, to shame, to humanity! How the cries of the mourners ascend to the sweet heavens!

And less peaceful than the graves of the departed, these tombs themselves are full of the hopeless cries of the entombed, praying for help, praying for some strong hand to reach down and lift them out of their reeking, polluted, living death.

The whole of our fair land is covered with jest such graves: its turf is tread down by the footprints of the mourners who go about the streets. They pray, they weep: the night is long, is long. But the morning will dawn at last.

And the women, — daughters, wives, mothers, — who kneel with clasped hands beside the tombs, heaviest-eyed, deepest mourners, because most helpless. Lift up your heavy eyes: the sun is even now rising, that shall gild the sky at last. The mornin' light is even now dawnin' in the east. It shall fall first upon your uplifted brows, your prayerful eyes. Most blessed of God, because you loved most, sorrowed most. To you shall it be given to behold first the tall, fair angel of Resurection and Redemption, standin' at the grave's mouth. Into your hands shall he put the key to unlock the heavy doors, where your loved has lain.

The dead shall rise. Temperance and Justice and Liberty shall rise. They shall go forth to bless our fair land. And purified and enobled, it shall be the best beloved, the fairest land of God beneath the sun. Refuge of the oppressed and tempted, inspiration of the hopeless, light of the world.

And free mothers shall clasp their free children to their hearts; and fathers and mothers and children shall join in one heavenly strain, song of freedom and of truth. And the nations shall listen to hear how "they rose, they rose, they rose from the dead."

As the tones of the sweet hymn died on the soft air, and the blessed vision passed with it; when I come down onto my feet, — for truly, I had been lifted up, and by the side of myself, — Cicely was standin' with her brown eyes lookin' over the waters, holdin' the hand of the boy; and I see every thing that the song did or could mean, in the depths of her deep, prophetic eyes. Sad eyes, too, they was, and discouraged; for the morning wus fur away — and — and the boy wus pullin' at her hand, eager to get away from where he wus.

The boy led us; and we follered him up the gradual hill to the old homestead of Washington, Mount Vernon.

Lookin' down from the broad, high porch, you can look

directly down through the trees into the river. The water calm and sort o' golden, through the green of the trees, and every thing looked peaceful and serene.

There are lots of interestin' things to be seen here,—the tombs of the rest of the Washington family; the key of the Bastile, covered with the blood and misery of a foreign land; the tree that carries us back in memory to his grave, where he rests quietly, who disturbed the sleep of empires and kingdoms; the furniture of Washington and his family,—the chairs they sot in, the tables they sot at, and the rooms' where they sot; the harpiscord, that Nelly Custis and Mrs. G. Washington harpiscorded on.

But she whose name wus once Smith longed to see somethin' else fur more.   What wus it?

It wus not the great drawin'-rooms, the guest-chambers, the halls, the grounds, the live-stock, nor the pictures, nor the flowers.

No: it wus the old garret of the mansion, the low old garret, where she sot, our Lady Washington, in her widowed dignity, with no other fire only the light of deathless love that lights palace or hovel,—sot there in the window, because she could look out from it upon the tomb of her mighty dead.

Sot lookin' out upon the river that wus sweepin' along under sun and moon, bearing on every wave and ripple the glory and beauty of his name.

Bearing it away from her mebby, she would sometimes sadly think, as she thought of happy days gone by; for though souls may soar, hearts will cling. And sometimes storms would vex the river's unquiet breast; and mebby

THE OLD HOME OF WASHINGTON.

the waves would whisper to her lovin' heart, "Never more, never more."

As she sot there looking out, waiting for that other river, whose waves crept nearer and nearer to her feet, — that other river, on which her soul should sail away to meet her glorious dead; that river which whispers "Forever, forever;" that river which is never unquiet, and whose waves are murmuring of nothing less beautiful than of meeting, of love, and of lasting repose.

CHAPTER X.

WHEN we got back from Mount Vernon, and entered our boardin'-house, Cicely went right up to her room. But I, feelin' kinder beat out (eloquent emotions are very tuckerin' on a tower), thought I would set down a few minutes in the parlor to rest, before I mounted up the stairs to my room.

But truly, as it turned out, I had better have gone right up, breath or no breath.

For, while I was a settin' there, a tall, sepulchral lookin' female, that I had noticed at the breakfast-table, come up to me; and says she, —

"I beg your pardon, mom, but I believe you are the noble and eloquent Josiah Allen's wife, and I believe you are a stoppin' here."

Says I calmly, "I hain't a stoppin'—I am stopped, as it were, for a few days."

"Wall," says she, "a friend of mine is comin' to-night, to my room, No. 17, to give a private seansy. And knowin' you are a great case to investigate into truths, I thought mebby you would love to come, and witness some of our glorious spirit manifestations."

I thanked her for her kindness, but told her "I guessed

I wouldn't go. I didn't seem to be sufferin' for a seancy."

"Oh!" says she: "it is wonderful, wonderful to see. Why, we will tie the medium up, and he will ontie himself."

"Oh!" says I. "I have seen that done, time and agin. I used to tie Thomas J. up when he was little, and naughty; and he would, in spite of me, ontie himself, and get away."

"Who is Thomas J.?" says she.

"Josiah's child by his first wife," says I.

"Wall," says she, "if we have a good circle, and the conditions are favorable, the spirits will materialize, — come before us with a body."

"Oh!" says I. "I have seen that. Thomas J. used to dress up as a ghost, and appear to us. But he didn't seem to think the conditions wus so favorable, and he didn't seem to appear so much, after his father ketched him at it, and give him a good whippin'." And says I firmly, "I guess that would be about the way with your ghosts."

And after I had said it, the idee struck me as bein' sort o' pitiful, — to go to whippin' a ghost. But she didn't seem to notice my remark, for she seemed to be a gazin' upward in a sort of a muse; and she says, —

"Oh! would you not like to talk with your departed kindred?"

"Wall, yes," says I firmly, after a minute's thought. "I would like to."

"Come to-night to our seansy, and we will call 'em, and you shall talk with 'em."

"Wall," says I candidly, "to tell the truth, bein' only

wimmen present, I'll tell you, I have got to mend my petticoat to-night. My errents have took me round to such a extent, that it has got all frayed out round the bottom, and I have got to mend the fray. But, if any of my kindred are there, you jest mention it to 'em that she that

THOMAS JEFFERSON'S GHOST.

wuz Samantha Smith is stopped at No. 16, and, if perfectly convenient, would love to see 'em. I can explain it to 'em," says I, "bein' all in the family, why I couldn't leave my room."

Says she, "You are makin' fun: you don't believe they will be there, do you?"

"Wall, to be honest with you, it looks dubersome to me. It does seem to me, that if my father or mother sot out from the other world, and come down to this boardin'-house, to No. 17, they would know, without havin' to be told, that I was in the next room to 'em; and they wouldn't want to stay with a passel of indifferent strangers, when their own child was so near."

"You don't believe in the glorious manifestations of our seansys?" says she.

"Wall, to tell you the plain truth, I don't seem to believe 'em to any great extent. I believe, if God wants to speak to a human soul below, He can, without any of your performences and foolishness; and when I say performences, and when I say foolishness, I say 'em in very polite ways: and I don't want to hurt anybody's feelin's by sayin' things hain't so, but I simply state my belief."

"Don't you believe in the communion of saints? Don't you believe God ever reveals himself to man?"

"Yes, I do! I believe that now, as in the past, the pure in heart shall see God. Why, heaven is over all, and pretty nigh to some."

And I thought of Cicely, and couldn't help it.

"I believe there are pure souls, especially when they are near to the other world, who can look in, and behold its beauty. Why, it hain't but a little ways from here, — it can't be, sense a breath of air will blow us into it. It takes sights of preparation to get ready to go, but it is only a short sail there. And you may go all over the land from house to house, and you will hear in almost every one of some dear friend who died with their faces lit up with the glow of the light shinin' from some one of the many mansions, — the dear home-light of the fatherland; died speakin' to some loved one, gone before. But I don't believe you can coax that light, and them voices, down into a cabinet, and let 'em shine and speak, at so much an evenin'."

"I thought," says she bitterly, "that you was one who never condemned any thing that you hadn't thoroughly investigated."

"I don't," says I. "I don't condemn nothin' nor nobody. I only tell my mind. I don't say there hain't no truth in it, because I don't know; and that is one of the best reasons in the world for not sayin' a thing hain't so. When you think how big a country the land of Truth is, and how many great unexplored regions lay in it, why should Josiah Allen's wife stand and lean up aginst a tree on the outmost edge of the frontier, and say what duz and what duzn't lay hid in them mysterius and beautiful regions that happier eyes than hern shall yet look into?

"No: the great future is the fulfillment of the prophecies, and blind gropin's of the present; and it is not for me, nor Josiah, nor anybody else, to talk too positive about what we hain't seen, and don't know.

"No: nor I hain't one to say it is the Devil's work, not claimin' such a close acquaintance with the gentleman named, as some do, who profess to know all his little social eccentricities. But I simply say, and say honest, that I hain't felt no drawin's towards seancys, nor felt like follerin' 'em up. But I am perfectly willin' you should have your own ideas, and foller 'em."

"Do you believe angels have appeared to men?"

"Yes, mom, I do. But I never heard of a angel bein'

stanchelled up in a box-stall, and let out of it agin at stated times, like a yearlin' colt. (Excuse my metafor, mom, I am country bred and born.) And no angel that I ever heard on, has been harnessed and tackled up with any ropes or strings whatsoever. No! whenever we hear of angels appearin' to men, they have flown down, white-winged and radiant, right out of the heavens, which is their home, and appeared to men, entirely unbeknown to them. That is the way they appeared to the shephards at Bethlahem, to the disciples on the mountain, to the women at the tomb."

"Don't you believe they could come jest as well now?"

"I don't say they couldn't. There is no place in the Bible, that I know of, where it says they shall never appear agin to man. But I s'pose, in the days I speak of, when the One Pure Heart was upon earth, Earth and Heaven drew nearer together, as it were, — the divine and the human. And if we now draw Heaven nearer to us by better, purer lives, who knows," says I dreamily (forgettin' the mejum, and other trials), "who knows but what we might, in some fair day, look up into the still heavens, and see through the clear blue, in the distance, a glimpse of the beautiful city of the redeemed?

"Who knows," says I, "if we lived for Heaven, as Jennie Dark lived for her country, in the story I have heard Thomas J. read about, but we might, like her, see visions, and hear voices, callin' us to heavenly duties? But," says I, findin' and recoverin' myself, "I don't see no use in a seansy to help us."

"Don't you admit that there is strange doin's at these seansys?"

"Yes," says I. "I never see one myself; but, from what I have heard of 'em, they are *very* strange."

"Don't you think there are things done that seem supernatural?"

"I don't know as they are any more supernatural than the telegraph and telefone and electric light, and many other seemin'ly supernatural works. And who knows but there may still be some hidden powers in nature that is the source of what you call supernatural?"

"Why not believe, with us, voices from Heaven speak through these means?"

"Because it looks dubersome to me — dretful dubersome. It don't look reasonable to me, that He, the mighty King of heaven and earth, would speak to His children through a senseless Indian jargon, or impossible and blasphemous speeches through a first sphere."

"You say you believe God has spoken to men, and why not now?"

"I tell you, I don't know but He duz. But I don't believe it is in that manner. Way back to the creation, when we read of God's speakin' to man, the voice come directly down from heaven to their souls.

"In the hush of the twilight, when every thing was still and peaceful, and Adam was alone, then he heard God's voice. He didn't have to wait for favorable conditions, or set round a table; for, what is more convincin', I don't believe he had a table to set round.

"In the dreary lonesomeness of the great desert, God spoke to the heart-broken Hagar. She didn't have to try any tests to call down the spirits. Clear and sudden out of heaven come the Lord's voice speaking to her soul in comfort and in prophecy; and her eyes was opened, and she saw waters flowin' in the midst of the desert.

"Up on the mountain top, God's voice spoke to Abraham; and Lot in the quiet of evening, at the tent's door, received the angelic visitants. Sudden, unbeknown to them, they come. They didn't have to put nobody into a trance, nor holler, so we read.

"In the hush of the temple, through the quiet of her motherly dreams, Hannah heard a voice. Hannah didn't have to say, 'If you are a spirit, rap so many times.' No: she knew the voice. God prepares the listenin' soul His own self. 'They know my voice,' so the Lord said.

"Daniel and the lions didn't have to 'form a circle' for him to see the one in shinin' raiment. No: the angel guest came down from heaven unbidden, and appeared to Daniel alone, in peril; and as he stood by the 'great river,' it said, 'Be strong, be strong!' preparin' him for conflict. And Daniel was strengthened, so the Bible says.

"God's hand is not weaker to-day, and His conflicts are bein' waged on many a battle-field. And I dare not say that He does not send His angels to comfort and sustain them who from love to Him go out into rightous warfare. But I don't believe they come through a scansy. I don't, honestly. I don't believe Daniel would have felt strengthened a mite, by seein' a materialized rag-baby hung out by a wire in front of a hemlock box, and then drawed back sudden.

"No: Adam and Enoch, and Mary and Paul and St. John, didn't have to say, before they saw the heavenly guests, 'If you are a spirit, manifest it by liftin' up some

HEAVENLY VISITORS.

table-legs.'   And they didn't have to tie a mejum into a box before they could hear God's voice.   No: we read in the Bible of eight different ones who come back from death, and appeared to their friends, besides the many who came forth from their graves at Jerusalem.   But they didn't none of 'em come in this way from round under tables, and out of little coops, and etcetery.

"And as it was in the old days, so I believe it is to-day. I believe, if God wants to speak to a human soul, livin' or dead, He don't *need* the help of ropes and boxes and things.   It don't look reasonable to think He *has* to employ such means.   And it don't look reasonable to me to think, if He wants to speak to one of His children in comfort or consolation, He will try to drive a hard bargain with 'em, and make 'em pay from fifty cents to a dollar to hear Him, children half price.   Howsomever, everybody to their own opinions."

"You are a unbeliever," says she bitterly.

"Yes, mom: I s'pose I am.   I s'pose I should be called Samantha Allen, U.S., which stands, Unbeliever in Spiritual Seansys, and also United States.   It has a noble, martyrous look to me," says I firmly.   "It makes me think of my errent."

She tosted her head in a high-headed way, which is gaulin' in the extreme to see in another female.   And she says, —

"You are not receptive to truth."

I s'pose she thought that would scare me, but it didn't. I says, —

"I believe in takin' truth direct from God's own hand and revelation.   But I don't have any faith in modern spiritual seansys. They seem to me, — and I would say it in a polite, courtous way, for I wouldn't hurt your feelin's for the world, — all mixed up with modern greed and humbug."

But, if you'll believe it, for all the pains I took to be almost over-polite to her, and not say a word to hurt her feelin's, that woman acted mad, and flounced out of the room as if she was sent.

Good land! what strange creeters there are in the world, anyway!

Wall, I had fairly forgot that the boy wus in the room. But 1,000 and 5 is a small estimate of the questions he asked me after she went out.

"What a seansy was? And did folks appear there? And would his papa appear if he should tie himself up in a box? And if I would be sorry if his papa didn't appear, if he didn't appear? And where the folks went to that I said come out of their graves? And did they die again? Or did they keep on a livin' and a livin' and a livin'? And if I wished I could keep on a livin' and a livin' and a livin'?"

Good land! it made me feel wild as a loon, and Cicely put the boy to bed.

But I happened to go into the bedroom for something; and he opened his eyes, and says he, —

"*Say!* if the dead live men's little boys that had grown up and lived and died before their pa's come out, would they come out too? and would the dead live men know that they was their little boys? and *say*" —

But I went out immegiatly, and s'pose he went to sleep.

Wall, the next mornin' I got up feelin' kinder mauger.

I felt sort o' weary in my mind as well as my body. For I had kep' up a powerful ammount of thinkin' and medetatin'. Mebby right when I would be a talkin' and a smilin' to folks about the weather or literatoor or any thing, my mind would be hard at work on problems, and I

would be a takin' silent observations, and musin' on what my eyes beheld.

And I had felt more and more satisfied of the wisdom of the conclusion I reached on my first interview with Allen Arthur, — that I dast not, I dast not let my companion go from me into Washington.

No! I felt that I dast not, as his mind was, let him go into temptation.

I felt that he wanted to make money out of the Government I loved; and after I had looked round me, and observed persons and things, I felt that he would do it.

I felt that *I* dast not let him go.

I knew that he wanted to help them that helped him, without no deep thought as to the special fitness of uncle Nate Gowdy and Ury Henzy for governmental positions. And after I had enquired round a little, and considered the heft of his mind, and the weight of example, I felt he would do it.

And I *dast* not let him go.

And, though I knew his hand was middlin' free now, still I realized that other hands just as free once had had rings slipped into 'em, and was led by 'em whithersoever the ring-makers wished to lead them.

I dast *not* let him go.

I knew that now his morals, though small (he don't weigh more'n a hundred, — bones, moral sentiments, and all), was pretty sound and firm, the most of the time. But the powerful winds that blew through them broad streets of Washington from every side, and from the outside, and from the under side, powerful breezes, some cold, and some powerful hot ones — why, I felt that them small morals, more than as likely as not, would be upsot, and blowed down, and tore all to pieces.

I dast not *let* him go.

I knew he was willin' to buy votes. If willin' to buy, — the fearful thought hanted me, — mebby he would be willin' to sell; and, the more I looked round and observed, the more I felt that he would.

I felt that I dast not let *him* go.

No, no! I dast not let him *go*.

I was a musin' on this thought at the breakfast-table where I sot with Cicely, the boy not bein' up. I was settin' to the table as calm and cool as my toast (which was *very* cool), when the hired man brought me a letter; and I opened it right there, for I see by the post-mark it was from my Josiah. And I read as follers, in dismay and anguish, for I thought he was crazy : —

Mi DEER WYF, — Kum hum, I hav got a crik in mi bak. Kum hum, mi deer Sam, kum hum, or I shal xpire. Mi gord has withurd, mi plan has faled, I am a undun Josire. Tung kant xpres mi yernin to see u. I kant tak no kumfort lookin at ure kam fisiognimy in ure fotogrof, it maks mi hart ake, u luk so swete, I fere u hav caut a bo. Kum hum, kum hum.

Ure luvin kompanien,

JOSIRE.

vers ov poetry.

Mi krik is bad, mi ink is pale:
Mi luv for u shal never fale.

I dropt my knife and fork (I had got about through eatin', anyway), and hastened to my room. Cicely follered me, anxious-eyed, for I looked bad.

I dropped into a chair; and almost buryin' my face in my white linen handkerchief, I give vent to some moans of anguish, and a large number of sithes. And Cicely says, —

"What is the matter, aunt Samantha?"

And I says, —

"Your poor uncle! your poor uncle!"

"What is the matter with him?" says she.

And I says, "He is crazy as a loon. Crazy and got a

creek, and I must start for home the first thing in the mornin.'"

SAMANTHA'S SORROW.

She says, "What do you mean?" and then I showed her the letter, and says as I did so, —

"He has had too much strain on his mind, for the size

of it. His plans have been too deep. He has grappled with too many public questions. I ortn't to have left him alone with politics. But I left him for his good. But never, never, will I leave that beloved man agin, crazy, or no crazy, creek, or no creek.

"Oh!" says I, "will he never, never more be conscious of the presence of the partner of his youth and middle age? Will he never realize the deep, constant love that has lightened up our pathway?"

I wept some. But I thought that mebby he would know my cream biscuit and other vittles, I felt that he would re*cog*nise them.

But by this time Cicely had got the letter read through; and she said "he wuzn't crazy, it was the new-fashioned way of spelling;" she said she had seen it; and so I brightened up, and felt well: though, as I told her, —

"The creek would drive me home in the mornin'." Says I, "Duty and Love draws me, a willin' captive, to the side of my sufferin' Josiah. I shall go home on that creek." Says I, "Woman's first duty is to the man she loves." Says I, "I come here on that duty, and on that duty I shall go back, and the creek."

Cicely didn't feel as if she could go the next day, for there was to be a great meetin' of the friends of temperance, in a few days, there; and she wanted to attend to it; she wanted to help all she could; and then, there wus a person high in influence that she wanted to converse with on the subject. That good little thing was willin' to do *any thing* for the sake of the boy and the Right.

But I says to her, "*I must* go, for that word 'plan' worrys me; it worrys me far more than the creek: and I see my partner is all unstrung, and I must be there to try to string him up agin."

So it wus decided, that I should start in the morning, and Cicely come on in a few days: she was all boyed up with the thought that at this meetin' she could get some help and hope for the boy.

But, after Cicely went to bed, I sot there, and got to thinkin' about the new spellin', and felt that I approved of it. My mind is such that *instantly* I can weigh and decide.

I took some of these words, photograph, philosophy, etc., in one hand, and in the other I took filosify and fotograf; and as I hefted 'em, I see the latter was easier to carry. I see they would make our language easier to learn by children and foreigners; it would lop off a lot of silent letters of no earthly use; it would make far less labor in writin', in printin', in cost of type, and would be better every way.

Cicely said a good many was opposed to it on account of bein' attached to the old way. But I don't feel so, though I love the old things with a love that makes my heart ache sometimes when changes come. But my reason tells me that it hain't best to be attached to the old way if the new is better.

Now, I s'pose our old 4 fathers was attached to the idee of hitchin' an ox onto a wagon, and ridin' after it. And our old 4 mothers liked the idee of bein' perched up on a pillion behind the old 4 fathers. I s'pose they hated the idee of gettin' off of that pillion, and onhitchin' that ox. But they had to, they had to get down, and get up into phaetons and railway cars, and steamboats.

And I s'pose them old 4 people (likely creeters they wuz too) hated the idee of usin' matches; used to love to strike fire with a flint, and trample off a mild to a neighber's on January mornin's (and their mornin's was *very* early) to borrow some coals if they had lost their flint. I s'pose they had got attached to that flint, some of 'em, and hated to give it up, thought it would be lonesome. But they had to; and the flint didn't care, it knew matches

OUR 4 PARENTS.

was better. The calm, everlasting forces of Nature don't murmur or rebel when they are changed for newer, greater helps. No: it is only human bein's who complain, and have the heartache, because they are so sot.

But whether we murmur, or whether we are calm, whether we like it, or whether we don't, we have to move our tents. We are only campin' out, here; and we have to move our tents along, and let the new things push us out of the way. The old things now, are the new ones of the past; and what seems new to us, will soon be the old.

Why, how long does it seem, only a minute, since we was a buildin' moss houses down in the woods back of the old schoolhouse? Beautiful, fresh rooms, carpeted with the green moss, with bright young faces bendin' down over 'em. Where are they now? The dust of how many years — I don't want to think how many — has sifted down over them velvet-carpeted mansions, turned them into dust.

And the same dust has sprinkled down onto the happy heads of the fresh, bright-faced little group gathered there.

Charley, and Alice! oh! the dust is very deep on her head, — the dust that shall at last lay over all our heads. And Louis! Bright blue eyes there may be

BORROWING COALS.

to-day, old Time, but none truer and tenderer than his. But long ago, oh! long ago, the dust covered you — the dust that is older than the pyramids, old, and yet new; for on some mysterious breeze it was wafted to you, it drifted down, and covered the blue eyes and the brown eyes, hid the bright faces forever.

And the years have sprinkled down into Charley's grave business head tiresome dust of dividends and railway shares. Kate and Janet, and Will and Helen and Harry — where are you all to-day, I wonder? But though I do not know that, I do know this, — that Time has not stood still with any of you. The years have moved you along, hustled you forward, as they swept by. You have had to move along, and let other bright faces stand in front of you.

You are all buildin' houses to-day that you think are more endurin'. But what you build to-day — hopes built upon worldly wealth, worldly fame, household affection, political success — ah! will they not pass away like the green moss houses down in the woods back of the old schoolhouse?

Yes, they, too, will pass away, so utterly that only their dust will remain. But God grant that we may all meet, happy children again, young with the new life of the immortals, on some happy playground of the heavenly life!

But poor little houses of moss and cedar boughs, you are broken down years and years ago, trampled down into dust, and the dust blown away by the rushin' years. Blown away, but gathered up agin by careful old Nature, nourishin' with it a newer, fresher growth.

I don't s'pose any of us really hanker after growin' old; sometimes I kinder hate to; and so I told Josiah one day.

And he says, "Why, we hain't the only ones that is growin' old. Why, everybody is as old as we be, that wuz born at the same time; and lots of folks are older.

THE OLD SCHOOLHOUSE.

Why, there is uncle Nate Gowdey, and aunt Seeny: they are as old agin, almost."

Says I, "That is a great comfort to meditate on, Josiah; but it don't take away all the sting of growin' old."

And he said "he didn't care a dumb about it, if he didn't have to work so hard." He said "he'd fairly love to grow old if he could do it easy, kinder set down to it."

(Now, that man don't work so very hard. But don't tell him I said so: he's real fractious on that subject, caused, I think, by rheumatiz, and mebby the Plan.)

I told Josiah that it wouldn't make growin' old any easier to set down, than it would to stand up.

I don't s'pose it makes much difference about our bodies, anyway; they are only wrappers for the soul: the real person is within. But then, you know, you get sort o' attached to your own body, yourself, you know, if you have lived with yourself any length of time, as we have, a good many of us.

You may not be handsome, but you sort o' like your own looks, after all. Your eyes have a sort of a good look to you. Your hands are soft and white; and they are your own too, which makes 'em nearer to you; they have done sights for you, and you can't help likin' 'em. And your mouth looks sort o' agreable and natural to you.

You don't really like to see the dimpled, soft hands change into an older person's hands; you kinder hate to change the face for an older, more care-worn face; you get sick of lookin'-glasses.

And sometimes you feel a sort of a homesick longin' for your old self — for the bright, eager face that looked back to you from the old lookin'-glass on summer mornin's,

when the winder was open out into the orchard, and the
May birds was singin' amidst the apple-blows.   The red

A MAY MORNING.

lips parted with a happy smile ; the bright, laughin' eyes,
sort o' soft too, and wistful — wishful for the good that

mebby come to you, and mebby didn't, but which the glowin' face was sure of, on that spring mornin', with the May birds singin' outside, and the May birds singin' inside.

Time may have brought you somethin' better — better than you dreamed of on that summer mornin'. But it is different, anyhow; and you can't help gettin' kinder homesick, longin', wantin' that pretty young face again, wantin' the heart back again that went with it.

Wall, I s'pose we shall have it back — sometime. I s'pose we shall get back our lost youth in the place where we first got it. And it is all right, anyway.

We must move on. You see, Time won't stop to argue with us, or dicker; and our settin' down, and coaxin' him to stop a minute, and whet his scythe, and give us a chance to get round the swath he cuts, won't ammount to nothin' only wastin' our breath. His scythe is one that don't need any grindstun, and his swath is one that must be cut.

No! Time won't lean up aginst fence corners, and wipe his brow on a bandanna, and hang round. He jest moves right on — up and down, up and down. On each side of us the ripe blades fall, and the flowers; and pretty soon the swath will come right towards us, the grass-blades will fall nearer and nearer — a turn of the gleamin' scythe, and we, too, will be gone. The sunlight will rest on the turf where our shadows were, and one blade of grass will be missed out of that broad harvest-field more than we will be, when a few short years have rolled by.

The beauty and the clamor of life will go on without us. You see, we hain't needed so much as we in our egotism think we are. The world will get along without us, while we rest in peace.

But until then we have got to move along: we can't set down anywhere, and set there. No: if we want to be fore mothers and fore fathers, we mustn't set still: we must give the babies a chance to be fore mothers and fore fathers too. It wouldn't be right to keep the babies from bein' ancestors.

We must keep a movin' on. How the summer follows the spring, and the winter follows the autumn, and the years go by! And the clouds sail on through the sky, and the shadows follow each other over the grass, and the grass fadeth.

And the sun moves down the west, and the twilight follows the sun, and at last the night comes — and then the stars shine.

Strange that all this long revery of my mind should spring from that letter of my pardner's. But so it is. Why, I sot probable 3 fourths of a hour — entirely by the side of myself. Why, I shouldn't have sensed whether I was settin' on a sofy in a Washington boarding-house (a hard one too), or a bed of flowers in Asia Minor, or in the middle of the Desert of Sarah. Why, I shouldn't have sensed Sarah or A. Minor at all, if they had stood right by me, I was so lost and unbeknown to myself.

But anon, or pretty nigh that time (for I know it was ten when I got into bed, and it probable took me ½ an hour to comb out my hair and wad it up, and ondress), I rousted up out of my revery, and realized I was Josiah Allen's wife on a tower of Principle and Discovery. I realized I was a forerunner, and on the eve of return to the bosom of my family (a linen bosom, with five pleats on a side).

Wall, I rose betimes in the mornin', or about that time, and eat a good, noble breakfast, so's to start feelin' well; embraced Cicely and the boy, who asked me 32 questions while I was embracin' him (I kissed him several times, with hugs accordin'); and then I took leave of Sally and Bub Smith. I paid for my board honorable, although Sally said she would not take any pay for so short a board. But I knew, in her condition, boards of any length should be paid for. So I insisted, and the board was paid for. I also rewarded Bub Smith for his efforts at doin' my errents, in a way that made his blushes melt into a glowin' background of joyousness.

And then, havin' asked the hired man to get a covered carriage to convey my body to the depot, and my trunk, I left Washington, D.C.

The snort of the engine as it ketched sight of me, sounded friendly to me. It seemed to say to me, —

"Forerunner, your runnin' is done, and well done! Your labors of duty and anxiety is over. Soon, soon will you be with your beloved pardner at home."

Home, the dearest word that was ever said or sung.

The passengers all looked good to me. The men's hats looked like Josiah's. They looked out of their eyes some as he did out of hisen: they looked good to me. There was one man upbraidin' his wife about some domestic matter, with crossness in his tone, but affectionate care and interest in his mean. Oh, how good, and sort o' natural, he did look to me! it almost seemed as if my Josiah was there by my side.

Never, never, does the cords of love fairly pull at your heart-strings, a drawin' you along towards your heart's home, your heart's desire, as when you have been off a movin' round on a tower. I longed for my dear home, I yearned for my Josiah.

I arrove at Jonesville as night was a lettin' down her cloudy mantilly fringed with stars (there wuzn't a star:

AT THE DEPOT.

I jest put that in for oritory, and I don't think it is wrong if I tell of it right away).

Evidently Josiah's creek wus better; for he wus at the depot with the mair, to convey my body home. He wus stirred to the very depths of his heart to see me agin; but he struggled for calmness, and told me in a voice controlled by his firm will, to "hurry and get in, for the mair wus oneasy standin' so long."

I, too, felt that I must emulate his calmness; and I says, —

"I can't get in no faster than I can. Do hold the mair still, or I can't get in at all."

"Wall, wall! hain't I a holdin' it? Jump in: there is a team behind a waitin'."

After these little interchanges of thought and affection, there was silence between us. Truly, there is happiness enough in bein' once more by the side of the one you love, whether you speak or not. And, to tell the truth, I was out of breath hurryin' so. But few words were interchanged until the peaceful haven of home was reached.

Some few words, peaceful, calm words were uttered, as to what we wus goin' to have for supper, and a desire on Josiah's part for a chicken-pie and vegitables of all kinds, and various warm cakes and pastries, compromised down to plans of tender steak, mashed potatoes, cream biscuit, lemon custard, and coffee. It wus settled in peace and calmness. He looked unstrung, very unstrung, and wan, considerable wan. But I knew that I and the supper could string him up agin; and I felt that I would not speak of the plan or the creek, or any agitatin' subject, until the supper was over, which resolve I follered. After the table was cleared, and Josiah looked like a new man, — the girl bein' out in the kitchen washin' the dishes, — I mentioned the creek; and he owned up that he didn't know as it was exactly a creek, but "it was a dumb pain, anyway, and he felt that he must see me."

It is sweet, passing sweet, to be missed, to be necessary to the happiness of one you love. But, at the same time, it is bitter to know that your pardner has prevaricated to you, and so the sweet and the bitter is mixed all through life.

I smiled and sithed simultaneous, as it were, and dropped down the creek.

Then with a calm tone, but a beatin' heart, I took up the Plan, and presented it to him. I wanted to find out the heights and depths of that *Plan* before I said a word about my own adventures at Washington, D.C. Oh, how that plan had worried me! But the minute I mentioned it, Josiah looked as if he would sink. And at first he tried to move off the subject, but I wouldn't let him. I held him up firm to that plan, and, to use a poetical image, I hitched him there.

Says I, "You know what you told me, Josiah, — you said that plan would make you beloved and revered."

He groaned.

Says I, "You know you said it would make you a lion, and me a lioness: do you remember, Josiah Allen?"

He groaned awful.

Says I firmly, "It didn't make you a lion, did it?"

He didn't speak, only sithed. But says I firmly, for I wus bound to come to the truth of it, —

"Are you a lion?"

"No," says he, "I hain't."

"Wall," says I, "then what be you?"

"I am a fool," says he bitterly, "a dumb fool."

"Wall," says I encouragingly, "you no need to have laid on plans, and I needn't have gone off on no towers of discovery, to have found that out. But now," says I in softer axents, for I see he did indeed look agitated and melancholy, —

"Tell your Samantha all about it."

Says he mournfully, "I have got to find 'The Gimlet.'"

ARE YOU A LION?

"The Gimlet!" I sithed to myself; and the wild and harrowin' thought went through me like a arrow, — that my worst apprehensions had been realized, and that man had been a writing poetry.

But then I remembered that he had promised me years ago, that he never would tackle the job agin. He begun to make a poem when we was first married; but there wuzn't no great harm done, for he had only wrote two lines when I found it out and broke it up.

Bein' jest married, I had a good deal of influence over him; and he promised me sacred, to never, *never*, as long as he lived and breathed, try to write another line of poetry agin. We was married in the spring, and these 2 lines was as follers : —

> " How happified this spring appears —
> More happier than I ever knew springs to be, *shears.*"

And I asked him what he put the "shears " in for, and he said he did it to rhyme. And then was the time, then and there, that I made him promise on the Old Testament, *never* to try to write a line of poetry agin. And I felt that he *could* not do himself and me the bitter wrong to try it agin, and still I trembled.

And right while I was tremblin', he returned, and silently laid "The Gimlet" in my lap, and sot down, and nearly buried his face in his hands. And the very first piece on which the eye of my spectacle rested, was this: " Josiah Allen on a Path-Master."

And I dropped the paper in my lap, and says I, —

" *What* have you been doing *now*, Josiah Allen? Have you been a fightin'? What path-master have you been on ?"

"I hain't been on any," says he sadly, out from under his hand. "I headed it so, to have a strong, takin' title. You know they 'pinted me path-master some time ago."

JOSIAH BEING TREATED.

I groaned and sithed to that extent that I was almost skairt at myself, not knowin' but I would have the high-stericks unbeknown to me (never havin' had 'em, I didn't

know exactly what the symptoms was), and I felt dred-
fully. But anon, or pretty nigh anon, I grew calmer, and
opened the paper, and read. It seemed to be in answer to
the men who had nominated him for path-master, and it
read as follers:—

JOSIAH ALLEN ON A PATH-MASTER.

Feller Constituents and Male Men of Jonesville and the surroundin'
and adjacent worlds!

I thank you, fellow and male citizens, I thank you heartily, and
from the depths of my bein', for the honor you have heaped onto me,
in pintin' me path-master.

But I feel it to be my duty to decline it. I feel that I must keep
entirely out of political matters, and that I cannot be induced to be
path-master, or President, or even United-States senator. I have not
got the constitution to stand it. I don't feel well a good deal of the
time. My liver is out of order, I am liable to have the ganders any
minute, I am bilious, am troubled with rheumatiz and colic, my blood
don't circulate proper, I have got a weak back, and lumbago, and
biles. And I hain't a bit well. And I dassent put too much strain on
myself, I dassent.

And then, I am a husband and a father. I have sacred duties to
perform about, nearer and more sacred duties, that I dast not put
aside for any others.

I am a husband. I took a tender and confidin' woman away from
a happy home (Mother Smith's, in the east part of Jonesville), and
transplanted her (carried her in a one-horse wagon and a mare) into
my own home. And I feel that it is my first duty to make that home
the brightest spot on earth to her. That home is my dearest and
most sacred treasure. And how can I disturb its sweet peace with
the wild turmoil of politics? I can not. I dast not.

And politics are dangerous to enter into. There is bad folks in
Jonesville 'lection day,— bad men, and bad women. And I am liable
to be led astray. I don't want to be led astray, but I feel that I am
liable to.

I have to hear swearin'. Now, I don't swear myself. (I don't call "dumb" swearin', nor never did.) I don't swear, but I think of them oaths afterwards. Twice I thought of 'em right in prayer-meetin' time, and it worrys me.

I have to see drinkin' goin' on. I don't want to drink; but they offer to treat me, old friends do, and Samantha is afraid I shall yield to the temptation; and I am most afraid of it myself.

Yes, politics is dangerous and hardenin'; and, should I enter into the wild conflict, I feel that I am in danger of losin' all them tender, winnin' qualities that first won me the love of my Samantha. I dare not imperil her peace, and mine, by the effort.

I can not, I dast not, put aside these sacred duties that Providence has laid upon me. My wive's happiness is the first thing I must consider. Can I leave her lonely and unhappy while I plunge into the wild turmoil of caurkusses and town-meetin's, and while I go to 'lection, and vote? No.

And the time I would have to spend in study in order to vote intelligent, I feel as if that time I must use in strugglin' to promote the welfare and happiness of my Samantha. No, I dassent vote, I dassent another time.

Again, another reason. I have a little grandchild growin' up around me. I owe a duty to her. I must dandle her on my knee. I must teach her the path of virtue and happiness. If I do not, who will? For though there are plenty to make laws, and to vote, little Samantha Joe has but one grandpa on her mother's side.

And then, I have sights of cares. The Methodist church is to be kep' up: I am one of the pillows of the church, and sometimes it rests heavy on me. Sometimes I have to manage every way to get the preacher's salary. I am school-trustee: I have to grapple with the deestrict every spring and fall. The teachers are high-headed; the parents always dissatisfied, and the children act like the Old Harry. I am the salesman in the cheese-factory. Anarky and quarellin' rains over me offen that cheese-factory; and its fault-findin', mistrustin' patrons, embitters my life, and rends my mind with cares.

The care of providin' for my family wears onto me; for though Samantha tends to things on the inside of the house, I have to tend to things outside, and I have to provide the food she cooks.

And then, I have a great deal of work to do. Besides my barn-chores, and all the wearin' cares I have mentioned, I have five acres of potatoes to hoe and dig, a barn to shingle, a pig-pen to new cover, a smoke-house to fix, a bed of beets and a bed of turnips to dig, — ruty bagys, — and four big beds of onions to weed — dumb 'em! and six acres of corn to husk. My barn-floor at this time is nearly covered with stooks. How dare I leave my barn in confusion, and, by my disorderly doin's, run the risk of my wive's bein' so disgusted with my want of neatness and shiftlessness, as to cause her to get dissatisfied with home and husband, and wander off into paths of dissipation and vice? Oh! I dassent, I dassent, take the resk! When I think of all the terrible evils that are liable to come onto me, I feel that I dassent vote agin, as long as I live and breathe — I dast not have any thing whatever to do with politics.

FINY. THE END.

I read it all out loud, every word of it, interrupted now and then, and sometimes oftener, by the groans of my pardner. And as I finished, I looked round at him, and I see his looks was dretful. And I says in soothin' tones — for oh! how a companion's distress calls up the tender feelin's of a lovin' female pardner!

Says I, "It hain't the worst piece in the world, Josiah Allen! It is as sensible as lots of political pieces I have read." Says I, "Chirk up!"

"It hain't the piece! It is the way it was took," says he. "Life has been a burden to me ever sense that appeared in 'The Gimlet.' Tongue can't tell the way them Jonesvillians has sneered and jeered at me, and run me down, and sot on me."

I sithed, and remained a few moments almost lost in thought; and then says I, —

"Now, if you are more composed and gathered together,

will you tell your companion how you come to write it? what you did it *for?*"

"I did it to be populer," says he, out from under his hand. "I thought I would branch off, and take a new turn, and not act so fierce and wolfish after office as most of 'em did. I thought I would get up something new and uneek."

"Wall, you have, uneeker than you probable ever will agin. But, if you wanted to be a senator, *why* did you refuse to have any thing to do with politics?"

"I did it to be *urged*," says he, in the same sad, despairin' tones. "I made the move to be loved — to be the favorite of the Nation. I thought after they read that, they would be fierce to promote me, fierce as blood-hounds. I thought it would make me the most populer man in Jonesville, and that I should be sought after, and praised up, and follered."

"What give you that idee?" says I calmly.

"Why, don't you remember Letitia Lanfear? She wrote a article sunthin' like this, only not half so smart and deep, when she was nominated for school-trustee, and it jest lifted her right up. She never had been thought any thing off in Jonesville till she wrote that, and that was the makin' of her. And she hadn't half the reason to write it that I have. She hadn't half nor a quarter the cares that I have got. She was a widder, educated high, without any children, with a comfortable income, and she lived in her brother's family, and didn't have *no* cares at all.

"And only see how that piece lifted her right up! They all said, what right feelin', what delicacy, what a noble, heart-stirrin', masterly document hern was! And I hankered, I jest hankered, after bein' praised up as she was. And I thought," says he with a deep sithe, "I

LETITIA LANFEAR.

thought I should get as much agin praise as she did. I thought I should be twice as populer, because it wus sunthin' new for a *man* to write such a article. I thought

I should be all the rage in Jonesville.   I thought I should be a lion."

"Wall, accordin' to your tell, they treat you like one, don't they?"

"Yes," says he, "speakin' in a wild animal way." Says he, growin' excited, "I wish I *wuz* a African lion right out of a jungle: I'd teach them Jonesvillians to get out of my way. I'd love, when they was snickerin', and pokin' fun at me, and actin' and jeerin' and sneerin', and callin' me all to nort, I'd love to spring onto 'em, and roar."

"Hush, Josiah," says I.   "Be calm! be calm!"

"I won't be calm! I can't see into it," he hollered. "Why, what lifted Letitia Lanfear right up, didn't lift me up. Hain't what's sass for the goose, sass for the gander?"

"No," says I sadly.   "It hain't the same sass. The geese have to get the same strength from it, — strength to swim in the same water, fly over the same fences, from the same pursuers and avengers; and they have to grow the same feathers out of it; but the sass, the sass is fur different.

"But," says I, "I don't approve of all your piece. A man, as a general thing, has as much time as a woman has. And I'd love to see the time that I couldn't do a job as short as puttin' a letter in the post-office. Why, I never see the time, even when the children was little, and in cleanin' house, or sugarin'-time, but what I could ride into Jonesville every day, to say nothin' of once a year, and lay a vote onto a pole. And you have as much time as I do, unless it is springs and falls and hayin'-time. And if *I* could do it, *you* could. I don't approve of such talk.

"And you know very well that you and I had better spend a little of our spare time a studyin' into matters, so as to vote intelligently; study into the laws that govern us both, — that hang us if we break 'em, and protect us if we obey 'em, — than to spend it a whittlin' shingles, or wonderin' whether Miss Bobbet's next baby will be a boy or a girl."

"Wall," says he, takin' his hand down, and winkin', — a sort of a shrewd, knowin' wink, but a sad and dejected one, too, as I ever see wunk, —

"I didn't have no idee of stoppin' votin'."

Says I coldly, as cold as Zero, or pretty nigh as cold-blooded as the old man, —

"Did you write that article *jest* for the speech of people? Didn't you have *no* principle to back it up?"

"Wall," says he mournfully, "I wouldn't want it to get out of the family, but I'll tell you the truth. I didn't write it on a single principle, not a darn principle. I wrote it jest for popularity, and to make 'em fierce to promote me."

I groaned aloud, and he groaned. It wus a sad and groanful time.

Says he, "I pinned my faith onto Letitia Lanfear. And I can't understand now, why a thing that made Letitia so populer, makes me a perfect outcast. Hain't we both human bein's — human Methodists and Jonesvillians?" Says he, in despairin', agonized tone, "I can't see through it."

Says I soothenly, "Don't worry about that, Josiah, for nobody can. It is too deep a conundrum to be seen through : nobody has ever seen through it."

But it seemed as if he couldn't be soothed; and agin he kinder sithed out, —

"I pinned my faith onto Letitia, and it has ondone me;" and he kinder whimpered.

But I says firmly, but gently, —

"You will hear to your companion another time, will you not? and pin your faith onto truth and justice and right?"

"No, I won't. I won't pin it onto nothin' nor nobody. I'm done with politics from this day."

And bad as we both felt, this last speech of hisen made a glimmer of light streak up, and shine into my future. Some like heat lightenin' on summer evenin's. It hain't so much enjoyment at the time, but you know it is goin' to clear the cloudy air of the to-morrow. And so its light is sweet to you, though very curious, and crinkley.

And as mournful and sort o' curious as this time seemed to me and to Josiah, yet this speech of hisen made me know that all private and public peril connected with Hon. Josiah Allen was forever past away. And that thought cast a rosy glow onto my to-morrows.

CHAPTER XI.

I found, on lookin' round the house the next mornin', that Philury had kep' things in quite good shape. Although truly the buttery looked like a lonesome desert, and the cubbards like empty tents the Arabs had left desolate.

But I knew I could soon make 'em blossom like the rosy with provisions, which I proceeded at once to do, with Philury's help.

While I wus a rollin' out the pie-crust, Philury told me "she had changed her mind about long engagements."

And while I wus a makin' the cookies, she broached it to me that "she and Ury was goin' to be married the next week."

I wus agreable to the idee, and told her so. I like 'em both. Ury is a tall, limber-jinted sort of a chap, sandy complected, and a little round shouldered, but hard-workin' and industrious, and seems to take a interest.

His habits are good: he never drinks any thing stronger than root-beer, and he never uses tobacco — never has chawed any thing to our house stronger than gum. He used that, I have thought sometimes, more than wuz for his good. And I thought it must be expensive, he con-

URY.

sumed such quantities of it. But he told me he made it himself out of beeswax and rozum.

And I told Josiah that I shouldn't say no more about it; because, although it might be a foolish habit, gum was not what you might call inebriatin'; it was not a intoxicatin' beverage, and didn't endanger the publick safety. So he kep' on a chawin' it, to home and abroad. He kep' at it all day, and at night if he felt lonesome.

I had mistrusted this, because I found a great chunk now and then on the head-board; and I tackled him about it, and he owned up.

"When he felt lonesome in the night," he said, "gum sort o' consoled him."

Well, I thought that in a great lonesome world, that needed comfort so much, if he found gum a consoler, I wouldn't break it up. So I kep' still, and would clean the head-board silently with kerosine and a woolen rag.

And Philury is a likely girl. Very freckled, but modest and unassuming. She is little, and has nice little features, and a round little face; and though she can't be said to resemble it in every particular, yet I never could think of any thing whenever I see her, but a nice little turkey-egg.

She is very obligin', and would always curchy and smile, and say "Yes'm" whenever I asked her to do any thing. She always would, and always will, I s'pose, do jest what you tell her to, — as near as she can; and she is thought a good deal of.

Wall, she has liked Ury for some time — that has been plain to see: she thought her eyes of him, and he of her. He has got eight or nine hundred dollars laid up; and I thought it was well enough for 'em to marry if they wanted to, and so I told Josiah the first time he come into the house that forenoon.

And he said "he guessed our thinkin' about it wouldn't alter it much, one way or the other."

And I said "I s'posed not." But says I, "I spoke out, because I feel quite well about it. I like 'em both, and think they'll make a happy couple: and to show my willin'ness still further, I mean to make a weddin' for her; for she hain't got no mothers, and Miss Gowdy won't have it there, for you know there has been such a hardness between 'em about that grindstun. So I'll have it here, get a good supper, and have 'em married off respectable."

He hung back a little at first, but I argued him down. Says I, —

"I have heerd you say, time and agin, that you liked 'em, and wanted 'em to do well: now, what do good wishes ammount to, unless you are willin' to back 'em up with good acts?" Says I, "I might say that I wished 'em well and happy, and that would be only a small expendature of wind, that wouldn't be no loss to me, and no petickuler help to them. But if I show my good will towards 'em by stirrin' up fruit-cakes and bride-cake, and pickin' chickens, and pressin' 'em, and makin' ice-cream and coffee and sandwitches, and workin' myself completely tired out, a wishin' 'em well, why, then they can depend on it that I am sincere in my good wishes."

"Wall," says Josiah, "if you wish me well, I wish you would get me a little sunthin' to eat before I starve: it is past eleven o'clock."

"The hand is on the pinter," says I calmly. "But start a good fire, and I will get dinner."

So he did, and I did, and he never made no further objections to my enterprise; and it was all understood that I should get their weddin' supper, and they should start from here on their tower.

And I offered, as she and Miss Gowdy didn't agree, that she might come back here, if she wanted to, and get some quiltin' done, and get ready for housekeepin'. She was tickled enough with the idee, and said she would help me enough to pay for her board. Ury's time wouldn't be out till about a month later.

I told her she needn't work any for me. But she is a dretful handy little thing about the house, or outdoors. When Josiah was sick, and when the hired man happened to be away, she would go right out to the barn, and fodder

the cattle jest as well as a man could. And Josiah said
she milked faster than he could, to save his life. Her
father had nine girls and no boys ; and he brought some
of the girls up when they was little, kinder boy-like, and
they knew all about outdoor work.

Wall, it was all decided on, that they should come right
back here jest as soon as they ended their tower. They
was a goin' to Ury's sister's, Miss Reuben Henzy's, and
laid out to be gone about four days, or from four days to
a week.

And I went to cookin' for the weddin' about a week
before it took place. I thought I would invite the minister and his wife and family, and Philury's sister-in-law's
family, — the only one of her relations who lived near us,
and she was poor ; and her classmates at Sunday school, —
there was twelve of 'em, — and our children and their
families. And I asked Miss Gowdey'ses folks, but didn't
expect they would come, owin' to that hardness about the
grindstun. But everybody else come that was invited ;
and though I am far from bein' the one that ort to say it,
the supper was successful. It was called " excellent " by
the voice, and the far deeper language of consumption.

They all seemed to enjoy it : and Ury took out his gum,
and put it under the table-leaf before he begun to eat ; and
I found it there afterwards. He was excited, I s'pose, and
forgot to take it agin when he left the table.

Philury looked pretty. She had on a travellin'-dress of
a sort of a warm brown, — a color that kinder set off her
freckles. It was woosted, and trimmed with velvet of a
darker shade ; and her hat and her gloves matched.

Her dress was picked out to suit me. Ury wanted her

to be married in a yellow tarleton, trimmed with red.
And she was jest that obleegin', clever creeter, that she
would have done it if it hadn't been for me.

I says to her and to him, —

"What use would a yeller tarleton trimmed with red
be to her after she is married, besides lookin' like fury
now?"   Says I, "Get a good, sensible dress, that will do

THE WEDDING SUPPER.

some good after marriage, besides lookin' good now."
Says I, "Marriage hain't exactly in real life like what it
is depictered in novels.   Life don't end there: folks have
to live afterwards, and dress, and ·work."   Says I, "If
marriage was really what it is painted in that literature —
if you didn't really have nothin' to do in the future, only
to set on a rainbow, and eat honey, why, then, a yaller
tarleton dress with red trimmin's would be jest the thing
to wear.   But," says I, "you will find yourself in the same

old world, with the same old dishcloths and wipin'-towels and mops a waitin' for you to grasp, with the same pair of hands. You will have to konfront brooms and wash-tubs and darnin'-needles and socks, and etcetery, etcetery. And you must prepare yourself for the enkounter."

She heerd to me; and that very day, after we had the talk, I took her to Jonesville, drivin' the old mare myself, and stood by her while she picked it out. •

And thinkin' she was young and pretty, and would want somethin' gay and bright, I bought some flannel for a mornin'-dress for her, and give it to her for a present. It was a pretty, soft gray and pink, in stripes about half a inch wide, and would be pretty for her for years, to wear in the house, and when she didn't feel well.

I knew it would wash.

She was awful tickled with it. And I bought a present for Ury on that same occasion, — two fine shirts, and two pair of socks, with gray toes and heels, to match the mornin'-dress. I do love to see things kompared, espe-cially in such a time as this.

My weddin' present for 'em was a nice cane-seat rocker, black walnut, good and stout, and very nice lookin'. And knowin' she hadn't no mother to do for her, I gave her a pair of feather pillows and a bed-quilt, — one that a aunt of mine had pieced up for me. It was a blazin' star, a bright red and yeller, and it had always sort o' dazzled me.

Ury worshiped it. I had kept it on his bed ever sense I knew what feelin's he had for it. He had said " that he didn't see how any thing so beautiful could be made out of earthly cloth." And I thought now was my time to part with it.

Wall, they had lots of good presents. I had advised the children, and the Sunday-school children, that, if they was goin' to give 'em any thing, they would give 'em somethin' that would do 'em some good.

Says I, " Perforated paper lambrequins, and feather flowers, and cotton-yarn tidies, look well; but, after all, they are not what you may call so nourishin' as some other things. And there will probable rise in their future life contingencies where a painted match-box, and a hair-pin receiver, and a card-case, will have no power to charm. Even china vases and toilet-sets, although estimable, will not bring up a large family, and educate them, especially for the ministry."

I s'pose I convinced 'em; for, as I heerd afterwards, the class had raised fifty cents apiece to get perforated paper, woosted yarn, and crystal beads. But they took it, and got her a set of solid silver teaspoons: the store-keeper threw off a dollar or two for the occasion. They was good teaspoons.

And our children got two good linen table-cloths, and a set of table-napkins; and the minister's wife brought her four towels, and the sister-in-law a patch-work bed-quilt. And Reuben Henzy's wife sent 'em the money to buy 'em a set of chairs and a extension table; and a rich uncle of hisen sent him the money for a ingrain carpet; and a rich uncle of hern in the Ohio sent her the money for a bed-room set, — thirty-two dollars, with the request that it should be light oak, with black-walnut trimmin's.

And I had all the things got, and took 'em up in one of our chambers, so folks could see 'em. And I beset Josiah Allen to give 'em for his present, a nice bedroom carpet.

But no : he had got his mind made up to give Ury a yearlin' calf, and calf it must be. But he said "he would give in to me so fur, that, seein' I wanted to make such a show, if I said so, he would take the calf up-stairs, and hitch it to the bed-post."

But I wouldn't parlay with him.

Wall, the weddin' went off first-rate : things went to suit me, all but one thing. I didn't love to see Ury chew gum all the time they was bein' married. But he took it out and held it in his hand when he said "Yes, sir," when the minister asked him, would he have this woman. And when she was asked if she would have Ury, she curchied, and said, "Yes, if you please," jest as if Ury was roast veal or mutton, and the minister was a passin' him to her. She is a good-natured little thing, and always was, and willin'.

Wall, they was married about four o'clock in the afternoon; and Josiah sot out with 'em, to take 'em to the six o'clock train, for their tower.

The company staid a half-hour or so afterwards : and the children stayed a little longer, to help me do up the work; and finally they went. And I went up into the spare chamber, and sort o' fixed Philury's things to the best advantage; for I knew the neighbors would be in to look at 'em. And I was a standin' there as calm and happy as the buro or table, — and they looked very light and cheerful, — when all of a sudden the door opened, and in walked Ury Henzy, and asked me, —

"If I knew where his overhauls was?"

You could have knocked me down with a pin-feather, as it were, I was so smut and dumb-foundered.

Says I, "Ury Henzy, is it your ghost?" says I, "or be you Ury?"

"Yes, I am Ury," says he, lookin', I thought, kinder disappointed and curious.

"Where is Philury?" says I faintly.

"YES, IF YOU PLEASE."

"She has gone on her tower," says he.

Says I, "Then, you be a ghost: you hain't Ury, and you needn't say you be."

But jest at that minute in come Josiah Allen a snickerin'; and says he, —

"I have done it now, Samantha. I have done somethin' now, that is new and uneek."

And as he see my strange and awful looks, he continued, "You know, you always say that you want a
change now and then, and somethin' new, to pass away
time."

"And I shall most probable get it," says I, groanin',
"as long as I live with you. Now tell me at once, what
you have done, Josiah Allen! I know it is your doin's."

"Yes," says he proudly, "yes, mom. Ury never would
have thought of it, or Philury. I got it up myself, out
of my own head. It is original, and I want the credit of
it all myself."

Says I faintly, "I guess you won't be troubled about
gettin' a patent for it." Says I, "What ever put it into
your head to do such a thing as this?"

"Why," says he, "I got to thinkin' of it on the way to
the cars. Philury said she would love to go and see her
sister in Buffalo; and Ury, of course, wanted to go and
see his sister in Rochester. And I proposed to 'em that
she should go first to Buffalo, and see her folks, and when
she got back, he should go to Rochester, and see his folks.
I told her that I needed Ury's help, and she could jest as
well go alone as not, after we got her ticket. And then
in a week or so, when she had got her visit made out, she
could come back, and help do the chores, and tend to
things, and Ury could go. Ury hung back at first. But
she smiled, and said she would do it."

I groaned aloud. "That clever little creeter! You
have imposed upon her, and she has stood it."

"Imposed upon her? I have made her a heroine.

Folks will make as much agin of her. I don't believe any female ever done any thing like it before, — not in any novel, or any thing."

"No," I groaned. "I don't believe they ever did."

"It will make her sought after. I told her it would. Folks will jest run after her, they will admire her so ; and so I told her."

Says I, "Josiah Allen, you did it because you didn't want to milk. Don't try to make out that you had a good motive for this awful deed. Oh, dear ! how the neighbors will talk about it ! "

"Wall, dang it all, when they are a talkin' about this, they won't be lyin' about something else."

"O Josiah Allen ! " says I. "Don't ever try to do any thing, or say any thing, or lay on any plans agin, without lettin' me know beforehand."

" I'd like to know why it hain't jest as well for 'em to go one at a time ? They are both *a goin'*. You needn't worry about *that*. I hain't a goin' to break *that* up."

I groaned awful; and he snapped out, —

"I want sunthin' to eat."

"To eat?" says I. "Can you eat with such a conscience ? Think of that poor little freckled thing way off there alone ! "

" That poor little freckled thing is with her folks by this time, as happy as a king." But though he said this sort o' defient like, he begun to feel bad about what he had done, I could see it by his looks; but he tried to keep up, and says he, " My conscience is clear, clear as a crystal goblet; and my stomack is as empty as one. I didn't eat a mouthful of supper. Cake, cake, and ice-cream, and jell! a dog couldn't eat it. I want some potatoes and meat!"

And then he started out; and I went down, and got a good supper, but I sithed and groaned powerful and frequent.

Philury got home safely from her bridal tower, lookin' clever, but considerable lonesome.

Truly, men are handy on many occasions, and in no place do they seem more useful and necessary than on a weddin' tower.

Ury seemed considerable tickled to have her back agin. And Josiah would whisper to me every chance he got, —

"That now she had got back to help him, it was Ury's turn to go, and there wuzn't nothin' fair in his not havin' a tower." Josiah always stands up for his sect.

And I would answer him every time, —

"That if I lived, Philury and Ury should go off on a tower together, like human bein's."

And Josiah would look cross and dissatisfied, and mutter somethin' about the milkin'. *There was where the shoe pinched.*

Wall, right when he was a mutterin' one day, Cicely got back from Washington. And he stopped lookin' cross, and looked placid, and sunshiny. That man thinks his eyes of Cicely, both of 'em; and so do I.

But I see that she looked fagged out.

And she told me how hard she had worked ever sence she had been gone. She had been to some of the biggest temperance meetin's, and had done every thing she could with her influence and her money. She was willin' to spend her money like rain-water, if it would help any.

But she said it seemed as if the powers against it was greater than ever, and she was heart-sick and weary.

She had had another letter from the executor, too, that worried her.

She told me that, after she went up to her room at night, and the boy was asleep.

She had took off her heavy mournin'-dress, covered with crape, and put on a pretty white loose dress; and she laid her head down in my lap, and I smoothed her shinin' hair, and says to her, —

" You are all tired out to-night, Cicely: you'll feel better in the mornin'."

But she didn't: she was sick in bed the next day, and for two or three days.

And it was arranged, that, jest as quick as she got well enough to go, I was to go with her to see the executor, to see if we couldn't make him change his mind. It was only half a day's ride on the cars, and I'd go further to please her.

But she was sick for most a week. And the boy meant to be good. He wanted to be, and I know it.

But though he was such a sweet disposition, and easy to mind, he was dretful easy led away by temptation, and other boys.

Now, Cicely had told him that he *must not* go a fishin' in the creek back of the house, there was such deep places in it; and he must not go there till he got older.

And he would *mean* to mind, I would know it by his looks. He would look good and promise. But mebby in a hour's time little Let Peedick would stroll over here, and beset the boy to go; and the next thing she'd

LED ASTRAY.

know, he would be down to the creek, fishin' with a bent pin.

And Cicely had told him he *mustn't* go in a swimmin'. But he went; and because it made his mother feel bad, he would deceive her jest as good-natured as you ever see.

Why, once he come in with his pretty brown curls all wet, and his little shirt on wrong side out.

He was kinder whistlin', and tryin' to act indifferent and innocent. And when his mother questioned him about it, he said, —

"He had drinked so much water, that it had soaked through somehow to his hair. And he turned his shirt gettin' over the fence. And we might ask Let Peedick if it wuzn't so."

We could hear Letty a whistlin' out to the barn, and we knew he stood ready to say "he see the shirt turn."

But we didn't ask.

But when the boy see that his actin' and behavin' made his mother feel real bad, he would ask her forgiveness jest as sweet; and I knew he meant to do jest right, and mebby he would for as much as an hour, or till some temptation come along — or boy.

But the good-tempered easiness to be led astray made Cicely feel like death: she had seen it in another; she see it was a inherited trait. And she could see jest how hard it was goin' to make his future: she would try her best to break him of it. But how, how was she goin' to do it, with them weak, good-natured lips, and that chin?

But she tried, and she prayed.

And, oh, how we all loved the boy! We loved him as we did the apples in our eyes.

But as I said, he was a child that had his spells. Sometimes he would be very truthful and honest, — most too
much so. That was when he had his sort o' dreamy spells.

THE BOY'S EXPLANATION.

I know one day, she that wus Kezier Lum come here a
visitin'. She is middlin' old, and dretful humbly.

Paul sot and looked at her face for a long time, with
that sort of a dreamy look of hisen; and finally he says, —

" Was you ever a young child ? "

And she says, —

" Why, law me! yes, I s'pose so."

And he says, —

" I think I would rather have died young, than to grow up, and be so homely."

SHE THAT WUS KEZIER LUM.

I riz up, and led him out of the room quick, and told him " never to talk so agin."

And he says, —

" Why, I told the truth, aunt Samantha."

" Wall, truth hain't to be spoken at all times."

" Mother punished me last night for not telling the truth, and told me to tell it always."

And then I tried to explain things to him; and he looked sweet, and said "he would try and remember not to hurt folks'es feelin's."

He never thought of doin' it in the first place, and I knew it. And I declare, I thought to myself, as I went back into the room, —

" We whip children for tellin' lies, and shake 'em for tellin' the truth. Poor little creeters! they have a hard time of it, anyway."

But when I went back into the room, I see Kezier was mad. And she said in the course of our conversation, that

" she thought Cicely was too much took up on the subject of intemperance, and some folks said she was crazy on the subject."

Kezier was always a high-headed sort of a woman, without a nerve in her body. I don't believe her teeth has got nerves; though I wouldn't want to swear to it, never havin' filled any for her.

And I says back to her, for it made me mad to see Cicely run, —

Says I, " She hain't the first one that has been called crazy, when they wus workin' for truth and right. And if the old possles stood it, to be called crazy, and drunken with new wine — why, I s'pose Cicely can."

" Wall," says she, " don't you believe she is almost crazy on that subject ? "

Says I, deep and earnest, " It is a *good* crazy, if it is. And," says I, " to s'posen the case, — s'posen the one we loved best in the world, your Ebineezer, or my Josiah, should have been ruined, and led into murder, by drinkin' milk, don't you believe we should have been sort o' crazy ever afterwards on the milk question ? "

" Why," says she, " milk won't make anybody crazy."

There it wuz — she hadn't no imagination.

Says I, " I am s'posen milk, I don't mean it." Says I, " Cicely means well."

And so she did, sweet little soul.

But day by day I could see that her eagerness to accomplish what she had sot out to, her awful anxiety about the boy's future, wus a wearin' on her: the active, keen mind, the throbbin', achin' heart, was a wearin' out the tender body.

Her eyes got bigger and bigger every day; and her face got the solemnest, curiusest look to it, that I ever see.

And her cheeks looked more and more like the pure white blow of the Sweet Cicely, only at times there would be a red upon 'em, as if a leaf out of a scarlet rose had dropped down upon their pure whiteness.

That would be in the afternoon; and there would be such a dazzlin' brightness in her eyes, that I used to wonder if it was the fire of immortality a bein' kindled there, in them big, sad eyes.

And right about this time the executor (and I wish he could have been executed with a horse-whip: he knew how she felt about it) — he wuz sot, a good man, but sot. Why, his own sir name wuz never more sot in the ground than he wuz sot on top of it. And he didn't like a woman's interference. He wrote to her that one of her stores, that he had always rented for the sale of factory-cloth and sheep's clothin', lamb's-wool blankets, and etcetery, he had had such a good offer for it, to open a new saloon and billiard-room, that he had rented it for that purpose; and he told how much more he got for it. That made 4 drinkin' saloons, that wuz in the boy's property. Every one of 'em, so Cicely felt, a drawin' some other mother's boys down to ruin.

Cicely thought of it nights a sight, so she said, — said she was afraid the curses of these mothers would fall on the boy.

And her eyes kep' a growin' bigger and solemner like, and her face grew thinner and thinner, and that red flush would burn onto her cheeks regular every afternoon, and she begun to cough bad.

But one day she felt better, and was anxious to go. So she and I went to see the executor, Condelick Post.

We left the boy with Philury. Josiah took us to the cars, and we arrove there at 1 P.M. We went to the

CONDELICK POST.

tarven, and got dinner, and then sot out for Mr. Post'ses office.

He greeted Cicely with so much politeness and courtesy, and smiled so at her, that I knew in my own mind that all she would have to do would be to tell her errent. I knew

he would do every thing jest as she wanted him to. His
smile was truly bland — I don't think I ever see a blander
one, or amiabler.

I guess she was kinder encouraged, too, for she begun
real sort o' cheerful a tellin' what she come for, — that she
wanted him to rent these buildin's for some other purpose
than drinkin' and billiard saloons.

And he went on in jest as cheerful a way, almost jokeu-
ler, to tell her " that he couldn't do any thing of the kind,
and he was doing the business to the best of his ability,
and he couldn't change it at all."

And then Cicely, in a courteus, reasonable voice, begun
to argue with him; told him jest how bad she felt about
it, and urged him to grant her request.

But no, the pyramids couldn't be no more sot than he
wuz, nor not half so polite.

And then she dropped her own sufferin's in the matter,
and argued the right of the thing.

She said when she was married, her husband took the
whole of her property, and invested it for her in these very
buildings. And in reality, it was her own property. The
most of her husband's wealth was in the mills and government bonds. But she wanted her money invested here,
because she wanted a larger interest. And she was intend-
ing to let the interest accumulate, and found a free library,
and build a chapel, for the workmen at the mills.

And says she, "Is it *right* that my own property should
be used for what I consider such wicked purposes?"

"Wicked? why, my dear madam! it brings in a larger
interest than any other investment that I have been able
to make. And you know your husband's will provides

handsomely for you — the yearly allowance is very handsome indeed."

"It is all I wish, and more than I care for. I am not speaking of that."

"Yes, it is very handsome indeed. And by the time Paul is of age, in the way I am managing the property now, he will be the richest young man in this section of the State. The revenue of which you make complaints, will be of itself a handsome property, a large patrimony."

"It will seem to be loaded with curses, weighed down with the weight of heavy hearts, broken hearts, ruined lives."

"All imagination, my dear madam! You have a vivid imagination. But there will be nothing of the kind, I assure you," says he, with a patronizing smile. "It will all be invested in government bonds, — good, honest dollars, with nothing more haunting than the American eagle on them."

"Yes, and these words, 'In God we trust.' But do you know," says she, with the red spot growin' brighter on her cheek, and her eyes brighter, — "do you know, if one did not possess great faith, they would be apt to doubt the existence of a God, who can allow such injustice?"

"What injustice, my dear madam?" says he, smilin' blandly.

"You know, Mr. Post, just how my husband died: you know he was killed by intemperance. A drinking-saloon was just as surely the cause of his death, as the sword is, that pierces through a man's heart. Intemperance was the cause of his crime. He, the one I loved better than my own self, infinitely better, was made a murderer by it. I have lost him," says she, a throwin' out her arms with a wild gesture that skairt me. "I have lost him by it."

And her eyes looked as big and wild and wretched, as if she was lookin' down the endless ages of eternity, a tryin' to find her love, and knew she couldn't. All this was in her eyes, in her voice. But she seemed to conquer her emotion by a mighty effort, tried to smother it down, and speak calmly for the sake of her boy.

"And now, after I have suffered by it as I have, is it right, is it just, that I should be compelled to allow my property to be used to make other women's hearts, other mothers' hearts, ache as mine must ache forever?"

"But, my dear madam, the law, as it is now, gives me the right to do as I am doing."

"I am pleading for justice, right: you have it in your power to grant my prayer. Women have no other weapon they can use, only just to plead, to beg for mercy."

"O my dear madam! you are quite wrong: you are entirely wrong. Women are the real rulers of the world. They, in reality, rule us men, with a rod of iron. Their dainty white hands, their rosy smiles, are the real autocrats of — of the breakfast-table, and of life."

You see, he went on, as men used to went on, to females years ago. He forgot that that Alonzo and Melissa style of talkin' to wimmen had almost entirely gone out of fashion. And it was a good deal more stylish now to talk to wimmen as if they wuz human bein's, and men wuz too.

But Cicely looked at him calm and earnest, and says, —

"Will you do as I wish you to in this matter?"

" Well, really, my dear madam, I don't quite get at your meaning."

" Will you let this store remain as it is, and rent those other saloons to honest business men for some other purpose than drinking-saloons?"

"O my dear, dear madam! What can you be thinking of? The rent that I get from those four buildings is equal in amount to any eight of the other buildings of the same size. I cannot, I cannot, consent to make any changes whatever."

" You will not, then, do as I wish?"

"I *cannot*, my dear madam: I prefer to put it in that way, — I cannot. I do not see as you do in the matter. And as the law empowers me to use my own discretion in renting the buildings, investing money, etc., I shall be obliged to do so."

Cicely got up: she was white as snow now, but as quiet as snow ever wus.

Mr. Post got up, too, about the politest actin' man I ever see, a movin' chairs out of the way, and a smilin', and a waitin' on us out. He was ready to give plenty of politeness to Cicely, but no justice.

And I guess he was kinder sorry to see how white and sad she looked, for he spoke out in a sort of a comfortin' voice, —

" You have had great sorrows, Mrs. Slide, but you have also a great deal to comfort you. Just think of how many other widows have been left in poverty, or, as you may say, penury, and you are rich."

Cicely turned then, and made the longest speech I ever heard her make.

"Yes, many a drunkard's wife is clothed in rags, and goes hungry to bed at night, with her hungry children crying for bread about her. She can lie on her cold pile of rags, with the snow sifting down on her, and think that

LICENSED WRETCHEDNESS.

her husband, a sober, honest man once, was made a low, brutal wretch by intemperance; that he drank up all his property, killed himself by strong drink, was buried in a pauper's grave, and left a starving wife and children, to live if they could. The cold of winter freezes her, the want of food makes her faint, and to see her little ones starving about her makes her heart ache, no doubt. I have plenty of money, fine clothes, dainty food, diamonds on my fingers."

Says she, stretching out her little white hands, and smilin' the bitterest smile I ever see on Cicely's face, —

"But do you not think, that, as I lie on my warm, soft couch at night, my heart is wrung by a keener pang than that drunkard's wife can ever know? I can lie and think that by my means, my wealth, I am making just such homes as that, making just such broken hearts, just such starving children, filling just such paupers' graves, — laying up a long store of curses and judgments, for my boy's inheritance. And I am powerless to do any thing but suffer."

And she opened the door, and walked right out. And Mr. Post stood and smiled till we got to the bottom of the stairs.

"Good-afternoon, *good*-afternoon, my dear madam, call again; happy to see you— *Good*-afternoon."

Wall, Cicely went right to bed the minute we got home; and she never eat a mite of supper, only drinked a cup of tea, and thanked me so pretty for bringin' it to her.

And there was such a sad and helpless, and sort of a outraged, look in her pretty brown eyes, some as a noble animal might have, who wus at bay with the cruel hunters all round it. And so I told Josiah after I went down-stairs.

And the boy overheard me, and asked me 87 questions about "a animal at bay," and what kind of a bay it was — was it the bay to a barn? or on the water? or —

Oh my land! my land! How I did suffer!

But Cicely grew worse fast, from that very day. She seemed to run right down.

CHAPTER XII.

ONE day Cicely had'been worryin' dretfully all the forenoon about the boy. And I declare, it seemed so pitiful to
hear her talk and forebode about him, with her face lookin'
so wan and white, and her big eyes so sorrowful lookin',
as if they was lookin' onto all the sadness and trouble of
the world, and couldn't help herself — such a sort of a
hopeless look, and lovin' and broken-hearted, that it was
all I could do to stand it without breakin' right down,
and cryin' with her.

But I knew her state, and held firm. And she went
over all the old grounds agin to me, that she had foreboded on; and I went over all the old grounds of soothin',
agin and agin.

Why, good land! I had had practice enough. For
every day, and every night, would she forebode and forebode, and I would soothe and soothe, till I declare for't, I
should have felt (to myself) a good deal like a bread-and-
milk poultice, or even lobelia or catnip, if my feelin's on
the subject hadn't been so dretful deep and solemn, deeper
than any poultice that was ever made — and solemner.

Why, Tirzah Ann says to me one day, — she had been
settin' with Cicely for a hour or two; and she come out a
cryin', and says she, —

"Mother, I don't see how you can stand it. It would break my heart to see Cicely's broken-hearted look, and hear her talk for half a day; and you have to hear her all the time." And she wiped her eyes.

And I says, "Tongue can't tell, Tirzah Ann, how your ma's heart does ache for her. And," says I, "if I knew myself, I had got to die and leave a boy in the world with such temptations round him, and such a chin on him, why, I don't know what I should do, and what I shouldn't do."

And says Tirzah Ann, "That is jest the way I feel, mother;" and we both of us wiped our eyes.

But I held firm before her, and reminded her every time, of what she knew already,—"that there was One who was strong, who comforted her in her hour of need, and He would watch over the boy."

And sometimes she would be soothed for a little while, and sometimes she wouldn't.

Wall, this day, as I said, she had worried and worried and worried. And at last I had soothed her down, real soothed. And she asked me before I went down-stairs, for a poem, a favorite one of hers, — "The Celestial Country." And I gin it to her. And she said I might shet the door, and she would read a spell, and she guessed she should drop to sleep.

And as I was goin' out of the room, she called me back to hear a verse or two she particularly liked, about the "endless, ageless peace of Syon:" —

> "True vision of true beauty,
> Sweet cure of all distrest."

And I stood calm, and heard her with a smooth, placid

face, though I knew my pies was a scorchin' in the oven, for I smelt 'em.   I did well by Cicely.

After she finished it, I told her it was perfectly beautiful, and I left her feelin' quite bright; and there wuzn't but

SAMANTHA LISTENING TO CICELY.

one of my pies spilte, and I didn't care if it wuz.   I wuzn't goin' to have her feelin's hurt, pies or no pies.

After I got my pies out, I went into my nearest neighbor's on a errent, tellin' Josiah to stay in Thomas Jefferson's room, just acrost from Cicely's, so's if she wanted any thing, he could get it for her.   I wuzn't gone over a hour, and, when I went back, I went up-stairs the first thing; and I found Cicely a cryin,' though there was a softer, more contented look in her eyes than I had seen there for a long time.

And I says, " What is the matter, Cicely ? "

And she says, —

" Oh ! if I had been a better woman, I could have seen my mother ! she has been here ! "

" Why, Cicely ! " says I. " Here, take some of this jell."

But she put it away, and says in a sort of a solemn, happy tone, —

"She has been here ! "

She said it jest as earnest and serene as I ever heard any thing said ; and there was a look in her eyes some as there wuz when she come home from her aunt Mary's, and told me " she almost wished her aunt had died while she was there, because she felt that her mother would be the angel sent from heaven to convey her aunt's soul home — and she could have seen her."

There was that same sort of deep, soulful, sad, and yet happy look to her eyes, as she repeated, —

" She has been here ! I was lying here, aunt Samantha, reading ' The Celestial Country,' not thinking of any thing but my book, when suddenly I felt something fanning my forehead, like a wing passing gently over my face. And then something said to me just as plain as I am speaking to you, only, instead of being spoken aloud, it was said to my soul, —

" ' You have wanted to see your mother : she is here with you.'

" And I dropped my book, and sprung up, and stood trembling, and reached out my hands, and cried, —

"'Mother! mother! where are you? Oh! how I have wanted you, mother!'

"And then that same voice said to my heart again,—

"'God will take care of the boy.'

"And as I stood there trembling, the room seemed full. You know how you would feel if your eyes were shut, and you were placed in a room full of people. You would know they were there—you would feel their presence, though you couldn't see them. You know what the Bible says,—'Seeing we are encompassed about by so great a cloud of witnesses.' That word just describes what I felt. There seemed to be all about me, a great cloud of people. And I put my arms out, and made a rush through them, as you would through a dense crowd, and said again,—

"'Mother! mother! where are you? Speak to me again.'

"And then, suddenly, there seemed to be a stir, a movement in the room, something I was conscious of with some finer, more vivid sense than hearing. It seemed to be a great crowd moving, receding. And farther off, but clear, these words came to me again, sweet and solemn,—

"'God will take care of the boy.'

"And then I seemed to be alone. And I went out into the hall; and uncle Josiah heard me, and he came out, and asked me what the matter was.

"And I told him 'I didn't know.' And my strength left me then; and he took me up in his arms, and brought me back into my room, and laid me on the lounge, and gave me some wine, and I couldn't help crying."

"What for, dear?" says I.

"Because I wasn't good enough to see my mother. If I had only been good enough, I could have seen her. For she was here, aunt Samantha, right in this room."

Her eyes wus so big and solemn and earnest, that I knew she meant what she said. But I soothed her down as well as I could, and I says, —

"Mebby you had dropped to sleep, Cicely: mebby you dremp it."

"Yes," says Josiah, who had come in, and heard my last words.

"Yes, Cicely, you dremp it."

Wall, after a while Cicely stopped cryin', and dropped to sleep.

And now what I am goin' to tell you is the *truth.* You can.believe it, or not, jest as you are a mind to; but it is the *truth.*

That night, at sundown, Thomas J. come in with a telegram for Cicely; and she says, without actin' a mite surprised, —

"Aunt Mary is dead."

And sure enough, when she opened it, it was so. She died jest before the time Cicely come out into the hall. Josiah remembered plain. The clock had jest struck two as she opened the door.

Her aunt died at two.

This is the plain truth; and I will make oath to it, and so will Josiah. And whether Cicely dremp it, or whether she didn't; whether it wus jest a coincidin' coincidence, her havin' these feelin's at exactly the time her aunt died, or not, — I don't know any more than you do. I jest put down the facts, and you can draw your own inferences

from 'em, and draw 'em jest as fur as you want to, and as
many of 'em.

But that night, way along in the night, as I lay awake
a musin' on it, and a wonderin', — for I say plain that my
specks hain't strong enough to see through the mysteries

THOMAS JEFFERSON BRINGING CICELY'S TELEGRAM.

that wrap us round on every side, — I s'posed my companion wus asleep; but he spoke out sudden like, and decided,
as if I had been a disputin' of him, —

"Yes, most probable she dremp it."

"Wall," says I, "I hain't disputed you."

"Hain't you a goin' to?" says he.

"No," says I. And that seemed to quiet him down, and he went to sleep.

And I give up, that most probable she did, or didn't, one of the two.

"MOST PROBABLE SHE DREMP IT."

But anyway, from that night, she didn't worry one bit about the boy.

She would talk to him sights about his bein' a good boy, but she would act and talk as if she was *sure* he would. She would look at him, not with the old, pitiful, agonized look, but with a sweet and happy light in her eyes.

And I guessed that she thought that the laws would be changed before the boy was of age. I thought that she felt real encouraged to think the march of civilization. was a marchin' on, pretty slow but sure, and, before the boy got old enough to go out into a world full of temptations, there would be wiser laws, purer influences, to help the boy to be a good and noble man, which is about the best thing we know of, here below.

No, she never worried one worry about him after that day, not a single worry. But she made her will, and it was fixed lawful too. She wanted Paul to stay with us till he was old enough to send off to school and college. And she wanted her property and Paul's too, if he should die before he was of age, should be used to found a school, and a home for the children of drunkards. A good school and a Christian home, to teach them and help them to be good, and good citizens.

Josiah Allen and Thomas J. and I was appinted to see to it, appinted by law. It was to be right in them buildings that wus used now for dram-shops: them very housen was to be used to send out good influences and spirits into the world instead of the vile, murderous, brutal spirits, they wus sendin' out now.

And wuzn't it sort o' pitiful to think on, that Cicely had to *die* before her property could be used as she wanted it to be, — could be used to send out blessings into the world, instead of cursings and wickedness, as it was now? It was pitiful to look on it with the eye of a woman; but

I kep' still, and tried to look on it with the eye of the United States, and **held** firm.

And we give her our solemn promises, that in case the job fell to us to do, it should be tended to, to the very best of our three abilities. Thomas J., bein' a good lawyer, could be relied on.

The executor consented to it, — I s'pose because he was so dretful polite, and he thought it would be a comfort to Cicely. He knew there wuzn't much danger of its ever takin' place, for Paul was a healthy child. And his appetite was perfectly startlin' to any one who never see a child's appetite.

I estimated, and estimated calmly, that there wuzn't a hour of the day that he couldn't eat a good, hearty meal. But truly, it needed a strong diet to keep up his strength. For oh! oh! the questions that child would ask! He would get me and Philury pantin' for breath in the house, and then go out with calmness and strength to fatigue his uncle Josiah and Ury nearly unto death.

But they loved him, and so did I, with a deep, pantin', tired-out affection. We loved him better and better as the days rolled by: the tireder we got with him seemin'ly, the more we loved him.

But one hope that had boyed me up durin' the first weeks of my intercourse with him, died out. I *did* think, that, in the course of time, he would get all asked out. There wouldn't be a thing more in heavens or on earth, or under the earth, that he hadn't enquired in perticular about.

But as days passed by, I see the fallicy of my hopes. Insperation seemed to come to him; questions would spring up spontanious in his mind; the more he asked, the more spontaniouser they seemed to spring.

Now, for instance, one evenin' he asked me about 3,000 questions about thè Atlantic Ocian, its whales and sharks and tides and steamships and islands and pirates and cable and sailors and coral and salt, and etc., etc., and

THE BOY ASKING QUESTIONS.

etcetery; and after a hour or two he couldn't think of another thing to ask, seemin'ly. And I begun to get real encouraged, though fagged to the very outmost limit of fag, when he drew a long breath, and says with a perfectly fresh, vigorous look, —

"Now less begin on the Pacific."

And I answered kindly, but with firmness, —

"I can't tackle any more ocians to-night, I am too tuckered out."

"Well," says he, glancin' out of the window at the new moon which hung like a slender golden bow in the west, "don't you think the moon to-night is shaped some like a hammock? and if I set down in it with my feet hanging out, would I be dizzy? and if I should curl my feet up, and lay back in it, and sail — and sail — and sail up into the sky, could I find out about things up in the heavens? Could I find the One up there that set me to breathing? And who made the One that made me? And where was I before I was made? — and uncle Josiah and Ury? And why wouldn't I tell him where we was before we was anywhere? and if we wasn't anywhere, did I suppose we would want to be somewhere? and *say* — SAY " —

Oh, dear me! dear me! how I did suffer!

But a better child never lived than he was, and I would have loved to seen anybody dispute it. He was a lovely child, and very deep.

And he would back up to you, and get up into your lap, with such a calm, assured air of owning you, as if you was his possession by right of discovery. And he would look up into your face with such a trustin', angelic look as he tackled you, that, no matter how tuckered out you would get, you was jest as ready for him the next time, jest as ready to be tackled and tuckered.

He was up with his mother a good deal. He would get up on the bed, and lay by her side ; and she would hold him close, and talk good to him, dretful good.

I heard her tellin' him one day, that, "if ever he had a man's influence and strength, he must use them wisely, and deal tenderly and gently by those who were weaker, and in his power. That a manly man was never ashamed of doing what was right, no matter how many opposed him; that it was manly and noble to be pure and good, and helpful to all who needed help.

"And he must remember, if he ever got tired out and discouraged trying to be good himself, and helping others to be good, that he was never alone, that his loving Father would always be with him, and *she* should. She should never be far away from her boy.

"And it would only be a little while at the longest, before she should take him in her arms again, before life here would end, and the new and glorious life begin, that he must fit himself for. That life here was so short that it wasn't worth while to spend any part of it in less worthy work than in loving and serving with all his strength God and man."

And I thought as I listened to her, that her talk had the simplicity of a child, and the wisdom of all the philosiphers.

Yes, she would talk to him dretful good, a holdin' him close in her arms, and lookin' on him with that fur-off, happy look in her eyes, that I loved and hated to see, — loved to see because it was so beautiful and sweet, hated to see because it seemed to set her so fur apart from all of us.

It seemed as though, while her body was here below, she herself was a livin' in another world than ourn: you could see its bright radience in her eyes, hear its sweet and peaceful echoes in her voice.

She was with us, and she wuzn't with us; and I'd smile and cry about it, and cry and smile, and couldn't help it, and didn't want to.

And seein' her so satisfied about the boy — why, seein' her feel so good about him, made us feel good too. And seein' her so contented and happy, made us contented and happy — some.

And so the peaceful weeks went by, Cicely growin' weaker and weaker all the time in body, but happier and happier in her mind; so sweet and serene, that we all felt, that, instead of being sad, it was somethin' beautiful to die.

And as the long, sweet days passed by, the look in her

TIRZAH ANN AND MAGGIE IN THE DEMOCRAT.

eyes grew clearer, — the look that reminded us of the summer skies in early mornin', soft and dark, with a prophecy in them of the coming brightness and glory of the full day.

The mornin' of the last day in June Cicely was not so well; and I sent for the doctor in the mornin', and told Ury to have Tirzah Ann and Maggie come home and spend the day. Which they did.

And in the afternoon she grew worse so fast, that towards night I sent for the doctor again.

He didn't give any hope, and said the end was very near.

A little before night the boys come, — Thomas Jefferson and Whitfield.

The sun went down; and it was a clear, beautiful evenin', though there was no moon. All was still in the house: the lamp was lighted, but the doors and windows was open, and the smell of the blossoms outside come in sweet; and every thing seemed so peaceful and calm, that we could not feel sorrowful, much as we loved her.

She had wanted the boy on the bed with her; and I told Josiah and the children we would go out, and leave her alone with him. Only, the doctor sot by the window, with the lamp on a little stand by the side of him, and the mornin'-glories hangin' their clusters down between him and the sweet, still night outside.

Cicely's voice was very low and faint; but we could hear her talkin' to him, good, I know, though I didn't hear her words. At last it was all still, and we heard the doctor go to the bedside; and we all went in, — Josiah and the children and me. And as we stood there, a light fell on Cicely's face, — every one in the room saw it, — a white, pure light, like no other light on earth, unless it was something like that wonderful new light — that has a soul. It was something like that clear white light, falling through a soft shade. It was jest as plainly visible to us as the lamplight at the other end of the room.

It rested there on her sweet face, on her wide-open brown eyes, on her smilin' lips. She lay there, rapt, illumined, glorified, apart from us all. For that strange, beautiful glow on her face wrapped her about, separated her from us all, who stood outside.

The boy had fallen asleep, his dimpled arms around her

neck, and his moist, rosy face against her white one. She
held him there close to her heart; but in the awe, the
wonder of what we saw, we hardly noticed the boy.

She heard voices we could not hear, for she answered
them in low tones, — contented, happy tones. She saw
faces we couldn't see, for she looked at them with won-

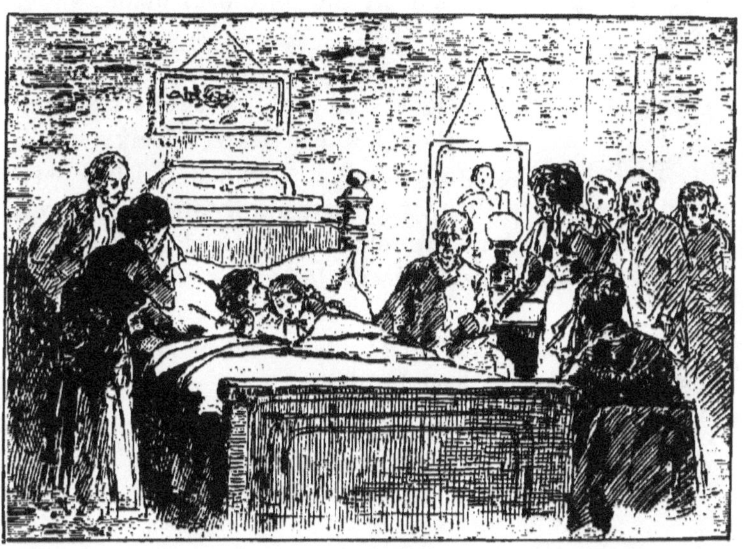

DEATH OF CICELY.

derin' rapture in her eyes. She was away from us, fur
away from us who loved her, — we who were on this earth
still. Love still held her here, human love yet held her
by a slight link to the human; but her sweet soul had got
with its true kindred, the pure in heart.

But still her arms was round the boy, — white, soft arms
of flesh, that held him close to her heart. And at the very

last, she fixed her eyes on him; and, oh! what a look that was, — a look of such full peace, and rapturous content, as if she knew all, and was satisfied with all that should happen to him. As if her care for him, her love for him, had blossomed, and bore the ripe fruit of blessedness.

At last that beautiful light grew dimmer, and more dim, till it was gone — gone with the pure soul of our sweet Cicely.

That night, way along in the night, I wuzn't sleeping, and I wuzn't crying, though I had loved Cicely so well. No: I felt lifted up in my mind, inspired, as if I had seen somethin' so beautiful that I could never forget it. I felt perhaps somethin' as our old 4 mothers did when they would see an angel standin' with furled wings outside their tents.

I thought Josiah was asleep; but it seems he wuzn't, for he spoke out sort o' decided like, —

" Most probable it was the lamp."

CHAPTER XIII.

It was a lovely mornin' about three weeks after Cicely's death. Josiah had to go to Jonesville to mill, and the boy wanted to go to ; and so I put on his little cloak and hat, and told him he might go.

We didn't act cast down and gloomy before the boy, Josiah and me didn't. He had worried for his ma dretfully, at first. But we had made every thing of him, and petted him. And I had told him that she had gone to a lovely place, and was there a waitin' for him. And I would say it to him with as cheerful a face as I could. (I knew I could do my own cryin', out to one side.)

And he believed me. He believed every word I said to him. And he would ask me sights and sights of questions about " the *place*."

And "if it was inside the gate, that uncle Josiah had read about, — that gate that was big and white, like a pearl? And if it would float down through the sky some day, and stand still in front of him? And would the gate swing open so he could see into the City? and would it be all glorious with golden streets, and shining, and full of light? And would his mamma Cicely stand just inside, and reach out her arms to him? — those pretty white arms."

And then the boy would sob and cry. And I'd soothe him, and swaller hard, and say " Yes," and didn't think it was wicked, when he would be a sobbin' so.

And then he'd ask, " Would she take him in her arms, and be glad to see her own little boy again? And would he have long to wait?"

And I'd comfort him, and tell him, " No, it wouldn't be but a little time to wait."

And didn't think it was wicked, for it wuzn't long anyway. For "our days are but shadows that flee away."

Wall, he loved us, some. .And we loved him, and did well by him; and bein' a child, we could sometimes comfort him with childish things.

And this mornin' he wus all excitement about goin' to Jonesville with his uncle Josiah. And I gin him some pennys to get some oranges for him and the babe, and they set off feelin' quite chirk.

And I sot down to mend a vest for my Josiah. And I was a settin' there a mendin' it, — one of the pockets had gin out, and it was frayed round the edges.

And I sot there a sewin' on that fray, peaceful and calm and serene as the outside of the vest, which was farmer's satin, and very smooth and shinin'. The weather also wus as mild and serene as the vest, if not serener. I had got my work all done up as slick as a pin: the floor glittered like yellow glass, the stove shone a agreable black, a good dinner was a cookin'. And I sot there, happy, as I say; for though, when I had done so much work that mornin', if that vest had belonged to anybody else, it would have looked like a stent to me, I didn't mind it, for it was for my Josiah: and love makes labor light, — light as day.

I was jest a thinkin' this, and a thinkin' that though I had jest told Josiah, from a sense of duty, that "he had broke that pocket down by luggin' round so much stuff in it, and there was no sense in actin' as if he could carry round a hull car-load of things in his vest-pocket;" though I had spoken to him thus, from a sense of duty, tryin' to keep him straight and upright in his demeaner,— still, I was a thinkin' how pleasant it wuz to work for them you loved, and that loved you : for though he had snapped me up considerable snappish, and said "he should carry round in his pockets as much as he was a minter; and if I didn't want to mend it, I could let it alone," and had throwed it down in the corner, and slammed the door considerable hard when he went out, still, I knew that this slight pettishness was only the light bubbles that rises above the sparkling wine. I knew his love for me lay pure and clear and sparklin' in the very depths of his soul.

I was a settin' there, thinkin' about it, and thinkin' how true love, such as mine and hisen, glorified a earthly existence, when all of a sudden I heard a rap come onto the kitchen door right behind me; and I says, "Come in." And a tall, slim feller entered, with light hair, and sort o' thin, and a patient, determined countenance onto him. A sort of a persistent look to him, as if he wuzn't one to be turned round by trifles. I didn't dislike his looks a mite at first, and sot him a chair.

But little did I think what was a comin'. For, if you will believe it, he hadn't much more than got sot down

when he says to me right there, in the middle of the forenoon, and right to my face, — the mean, miserable, low-
lived scamp, — says he, right there, in broad daylight, and
without blushing, or any thing, says he, —

"I called this morning, mom, to see if I couldn't sell
you a feller."

"Sell me a feller!" I jest made out to say, for I wus
fairly paralyzed by his impudence.   "Sell me a feller!"

"Yes: I have got some of the best kinds they make,
and I didn't know but I could sell you one."

Sez I, gettin' my tongue back, "Buy a feller! you ask
me, at my age, and with my respectability, and after carryin' round such principles as I have been carryin' round for
years and years, you ask me to buy a feller!"

"Yes: I didn't know but you would want one.   I have
got the best kind there is made."

"I'll let you know, young man," says I, "I'll let you
know that I have got a feller of my own, as good a one as
was ever made, one I have had for 20 years and over."

"Wall, mom," says he, with that stiddy, determined
way of hisen, "a feller that you have had for 20 years
must be out of gear by this time."

"Out of gear!" says I, speakin' up sharp.   "You will
be out of gear yourself, young man, if I hear any more
such talk out of your head."

"I hope you will excuse me, mom," says he, in that patient way of hisen.   "It hain't my way to run down anybody's else's fellers."

"Wall, I guess you hadn't better try it again in this
house," says I warmly.   "I guess it won't be very healthy
for you."

AGENT TRYING TO SELL SAMANTHA A FELLER.

"Can't I sell you some other attachment, mom? I have got 'em of all kinds."

"Sell me another attachment? No, sir. You *can't* sell me another attachment. My attachment is as firm and endurin' as the rocks, and has always been, and is one not to be bought and sold."

" I presume yours was good in the day of 'em, mom, but they must be old-fashioned. I have the very best and newest attachments of all kinds. But I make a specialty of my fellers. You'd better let me sell you a feller, mom."

I declare for't, my first thought was, to turn him right outdoors, and shet the door in his face. And then agin, I thought, I am a member of the meetin'-house. I must be patient and long sufferin', and may be here is a chance for me to do good. Thinks'es I, if I was ever eloquent in a good cause, I must be now. I must convince him of the nefariousness of his conduct. And if soarin' in eloquence can do it, why, I must soar. And so I begun.

Says I, wavin' my right hand in a broad, soarin', eloquent wave, " Young man, when you talk about buyin' and sellin' a feller, you are talkin' on a solemn subject, — buyin' and sellin' attachments! Buyin' and sellin' fellers! It hain't nothin' new to me. I've hearn tell of such things, but little did I suppose it was a subject I should ever be tackled on.

" But I have hearn of it. I have hearn of wimmen sellin' themselves to the highest bidder, with a minister for auctioneer and salesman. I have hearn of fathers and mothers sellin' beauty and innocence and youth to wicked old age for money — sellin' 'em right in the meetin'-house, under the very shadow of the steeple.

THEM THAT SELL DOVES.

" Jerusalem hain't the only village where God's holy
temple has been polluted by money-changers and them
that sell doves. Many a sweet little dove of a girl is made

by her father and mother, and other old money-changers, to walk up to God's holy altar, and swear to a lie. They think her tellin' that lie, makes the infamous bargain more sacred, makes the infamous life they have drove her into more respectable.

"There was One who cleansed from such accursed traffic the old Jewish temples, but He walks no more with humanity. If he did, would he not walk up the broad aisles of our orthodox churches in American cities, and release these doves, and overthrow the plots of these money-changers?

"But let me tell 'em, that though they can't see Him, He is there; and the lash of His righteous wrath will surely descend, not upon their bodies, but upon their guilty souls, teachin' them how much more terrible it is to sell a life, with all its rich dowery of freedom, happiness, purity, immortality."

Here my breath gin out, for I had used my very deepest principle tone; and it uses up a fearful ammount of wind, and is tuckerin' beyond what any one could imagine of tucker. You *have* to stop to collect breath.

And he looked at me with that same stiddy, patient, modest look of hisen; and says he, in that low, determined voice, —

"What you say, madam, is very true, and even beautiful and eloquent: but time is valuable to me; and as I said, I stopped here this morning to see if I could sell "—

"I know you did: I heard you with my own ears. If it had come through two or three, or even one, pair of ears besides my own, I couldn't have believed 'em — I never could have believed that any human creeter, male or female, would have dared to stand up before me, and try to sell me a feller ! *Sell* a feller to me ! Why, even in my young days, do you s'pose I would ever try to *buy* a feller?

"No, sir! fellers must come free and spontaneous, or not at all. Never was I the woman to advance one step towards **any** feller in the way of courtship — havin' no occasion for it, bein' one that had more offers than I knew what to do with, as I often tell my husband, Josiah Allen, now, in our little differences of opinion. 'Time and agin,' as I tell him, 'I might have married, but held back.' And never would I have married, never, had not love gripped holt of my very soul, and drawed me along up to the marriage alter. I loved the feller I married, and he was the only feller in the hull world for me."

Says he in that low, gentle tone, and lookin' modest and patient as a lily, but as determined and sot as ever a iron teakettle was sot over a stove, —

" You are under a mistake, mom."

Says I, " Don't you tell me that agin if you know what is good for yourself. I guess I know my own mind. I was past the age of whifflin', and foolin' round. I married that feller from pure love, and no other reason under the heavens. For there wuzn't any other reason only jest that, why I *should* marry him."

And for a moment, or two moments, my mind roamed back onto that old, mysterious question that has haunted me more or less through my natural life, for over twenty years. *Why* did I marry Josiah Allen? But I didn't revery on it long. I was too agitated, and wrought up ; and I says agin, in tones witherin' enough to wither him, —

"The idee of sellin' me a feller!"

But the chap didn't look withered a mite: he stood there firm and immovible, and says he, —

"I didn't mean no offense, mom. Sellin' attachments is what I get my living by" —

"Wall, I should ruther not get a livin'," says I, interruptin' of him. "I should ruther not live."

"As I said, mom, I get my livin' that way: and one of your neighbors told me that your feller was an old one, and sort o' givin' out; and I have got 'em with all the latest improvements, and — and she thought mebby I could sell you one."

"You miserable coot you!" says I. "Do you stop your impudent talk, or I will holler to Josiah. What do you s'pose I want with another feller? Do you s'pose I'd swap Josiah Allen for all the fellers that ever swarmed on the globe? What do you s'pose I care for the latest improvements? If a feller was made of pure gold from head to feet, with diamond eyes and a garnet nose, do you s'pose he would look so good to me as Josiah Allen duz?

"And I would thank the neighbers to mind their own business, and let my affairs alone. What if he is a gettin' old and wore out? What if he is a givin' out? He is always kinder spindlin' in the spring of the year. Some men winter harder than others: he is a little tizicky, and breathes short, and his liver may not be the liver it was once; but he will come round all right when the weather moderates. And mebby they meant to hint and insinuate sunthin' about his bein' so bald, and losin' his teeth.

"But I'll let you know, and I'll let the neighbors know, that I didn't marry that man for hair; I didn't marry that man for teeth: and a few locks more or less, or a handful of teeth, has no power over that love, — that love that makes me say from the very depths of my soul, that my feller is one of a thousand."

"I hain't disputed you, mom," says he, with his firm, patient look. "I dare presume to say that your feller was good in the day of such fellers. But every thing has its day: we make fellers far different now."

Says I sarcasticly, givin' him quite a piercin' look, "I know they do: I've seen 'em."

"Yes, they make attachments now very different: yours is old-fashioned."

"Yes, I know it is: I know that love, such love as hisen and mine, and I know that truth and fidelity and constancy, *are* old-fashioned. But I thank God that our souls are clothed with that beautiful old fashion, that seamless, flawless robe that wus cut out in Eden, and a few true souls have wore ever since."

"But your attachment will grow older and older, and give out entirely after a while. What will you do then?"

"My attachment will *never* give out."

"But mom"—

"No, you needn't argue and contend — I say it will *never* give out. It is a heavenly gift dropped down from above, entirely unbeknown. True love is not sought after, it comes; and when it comes, it stays. Talk about love gettin' old — love *never* grows old; talk about love goin' — love *never* goes: that which goes is not love, though it has been called so time and agin. Talk about love dyin' — why, it *can't* die, no more than the souls can, in which its sweet light is born. Why, it is a flame that

God Himself kindles: it is a bit of His own brightness a shinin' down through the darkness of our earthly life, and is as immortal and indestructible as His own glory.

"It is the only fountain of Eternal Youth that gushes up through this dreary earthly soil, for the refreshin' of men and wimmen, in which the weary soul can bathe itself, and find rest."

"Sometimes," says he, sort o' dreamily, "sometimes we repair old fellers."

"Wall, you won't repair my feller, I can let you know that. I won't have him repaired. The impudence of the hull idee," says I, roustin' up afresh, "goes ahead of any thing I ever dreamed of, of impudence. Repair my feller! I don't want him any different. I want him jest as he is. I would scorn to repair him. I *could* if I wanted to, — his teeth could be sharpened up, what he has got, and new ones sot in. And I could cover his head over with red curls; or I could paint it black, and paste transfer flowers onto it. I could have a sot flower sot right on the top of his bald head, and a trailin' vine runnin' round his forward. Or I could trim it round with tattin', if I wanted to, and crystal beads. I could repair him up so he would look gay. But do you

JOSIAH AFTER BEING REPAIRED.

s'pose that any artificials that was ever made, or any hair, if it was as luxuriant as Ayer'ses Vigor, could look so good to me as that old bald head that I have seen a shinin' acrost the table from me for so many years?

"I tell you, there is memories and joys and sorrows a clusterin' round that head, that I wouldn't swap for all the beauty and the treasures of the world.

"Memories of happy mornin's dewy fresh, with cool summer breezes a comin' in through the apple-blows by the open door, and the light of the happy sunrise a shinin' on that old bald head, and then gleamin' off into my happy heart.

"There is memories of pleasant evenin' hours, with the tea-table drawed up in front of the south door, and the sweet southern wind a comin' in over the roses, and the tender light of the sunset, and the waverin' shadows of the honeysuckles and mornin'-glorys, fallin' on us, wrappin' us all round, and wrappin' all of the rest of the world out."

Mebby the young chap said sunthin' here, but it was entirely unbeknown to me; though I thought I heard the murmur of his voice makin' a sort of a tinklin' accompinment to my thoughts, sunthin' like the babble of a brook a runnin' along under forest boughs, when the wind with its mighty melody is sweepin' through 'em. Great emotions was sweepin' along with power, and couldn't be stayed. And I went right on, not sensin' a thing round me, —

"There is memories of sabbath drives, in fair June mornin's, through the old lane alder and willow fringed, with the brook runnin' along on one side of it; where the speckled trout broke the Sunday quiet by dancin' up

through the brown and gold shadows of the cool water,
and the odor of the pine woods jest beyend comin' fresh
and sweet to us.

"Memories of how that road and that face looked in
the week-day dusk, as we sot out for the revival meetin',

"GOIN' TO THE REVIVAL MEETING."

when the sun had let down his long bars of gold and
crimson and yellow, and had got over 'em, and sunk down
behind 'em out of sight. And we could ketch glimpses
through the willow-sprays of them shinin' bars a layin'
down on the gray twilight field. And fur away over the
green hills and woods of the east, the moon was a risin',

big and calm and silvery. And we could hear the plaintive evenin' song of the thrush, and the crickets' happy chirp, till we got nearer the schoolhouse, when they sort o' blended in with 'There is a fountain filled with blood,' and 'Come, ye disconsolate.'

"And the moonlight, and sister Bobbet's and sister Minkly's candles, shone down and out, on that dear old bald head as his hat fell off, as he helped me out of the wagon.

"Memories of how I have seen it a bendin' over the Word, in hours of peace and happiness, and hours of anxiety and trouble, a readin' every time about the eternal hills, and the shadow of the Rock, and the Everlastin' Arms that was a holdin' us both up, me and Josiah, and the Everlastin' Love that was wrappin' us round, helpin' us onward by these very joys, these very sorrows.

"Memories of the midnight lamp lightin' it up in the chamber of the sick, in the long, lonesome hours before day-dawn.

"Memories of its bendin' over the sick ones in happier mornin's, as he carried 'em down-stairs in his arms, and sot 'em in their old places at the table.

"Memories of how it looked in the glare of the tempest, and under the rainbow when the storm had passed. It stands out from a background of winter snows and summer sunshine, and has all the shadows and brightness of them seasons a hangin' over it.

"Yes, there is memories of sorrows borne by both, and so made holier and more blessed than happiness. That head has bent with mine over a little coffin, and over open graves, when he shared my anguish. And stood by me under the silent stars, when he shared my prayers, my hopes, for the future.

"That old bald head stands up on the most sacred height of my heart, like a beacon; the glow of the soul shines on it; love gilds it. And do you s'pose any other feller's head on earth could ever look so good to me as that duz? Do you s'pose I will ever have it repaired upon? never! I *won't* repair him. I won't have him dickered and fooled with. Not at all.

"He'd look better to me than any other feller that ever walked on earth if he hadn't a tooth left in his head, or a hair on his scalp. As long as Josiah Allen has got body enough left to wrap round his soul, and keep it down here on earth, my heart is hisen, every mite of it, jest as he is too.

"And I'll thank the neighbors to mind their own business!" says I, kinder comin' to agin. For truly, I had soared up high above my kitchen, and gossipin' neighbors, and feller-agents, and all other tribulations. And as I lit down agin (as it were), I see he was a standin' on one foot, with his watch, a big silver one, in his hand, and gazin' pensively onto it; and he says, —

"Your remarks are worthy, mom — but somewhat lengthy," says he, in a voice of pain; "nearly nine moments long: but," says he, sort o' bracin' up agin on both feet, "I beg of you not to be too hasty. I did not come into this neighborhood to make dissensions or broils. I merely stated that I got the idee, from what they said, that your feller didn't work good."

"Didn't work good! You impudent creeter you! What of it? What if he don't work at all? What earthly busi-

ness is it of yourn or the neighbors? I guess he is able
to lay by for a few days if he wants to."

"You are laborin' under a mistake, mom."

"No, I hain't laborin' under no mistake! And don't you
tell me agin that I be.   We have got a good farm all paid
for, and money out on interest; and whose business is it
whether he works all day, or don't.   When I get to goin'
round to see who works, and who don't; and when I get
so low as to watch my neighbors the hull of the time, to
find out every minute they set down; when I can't find
nothin' nobler to do, — I'll spend my time talkin' about
hens' teeth, and lettis seed."

Says he, lookin' as amiable and patient as a factory-cloth
rag-babe, but as determined as a weepin' live one, with the
colic, —

"You don't seem to get my meaning.   I merely wished
to remark that I could fix over your feller if you wanted
me to " —

Oh! how burnin' indignant I wuz!   But all of a sudden,
down on this seethin' tumult of anger fell this one calmin'
word, — *Meetin'-house!*   I felt I must be calm, — calm and
impressive; so says I, —

"You need not repeat your infamous proposal.   I say to
you agin, that the form where Love has set up his temple,
is a sacred form.   Others may be more beautiful, and even
taller, but they don't have the same look to 'em.   It is one
of the strangest things," says I, fallin' agin' a little ways
down into a revery, —

"It is one of the very solemnest things I ever see,
how a emotion large and boundless enough to fill eternity
and old space itself, should all be gathered up and cen-

tered into so small a temple, and such a lookin' one, too, sometimes," says I pensively, as I thought it over, how sort o' meachin' and bashful lookin' Josiah Allen wuz, when I married to him. And how small his weight wuz by the steelyards. But it is so, curious it can be, but so it is.

" *Why* Love, like a angel, springs up in the heart unawares, as Lot entertained another, I don't know. If you should ask me why, I'd tell you plain, that I didn't know where Love come from; but if you should ask me where Love went to, I should answer agin plain, that it don't go, it stays. The only right way for pardners to come, is to come down free gifts from above, free as the sun, or the showers that fall down in a drouth — and perfectly unbeknown, like them. Such a love is oncalculatin', givin' all, unquestionin', unfearin', no dickerin', no holdin' back lookin' for better chances."

"Yes, mom," says he, a twirlin' his hat round, and standin' on one foot some like a patient old gander in the fall of the year.

"Yes, mom, what you say is very true; but your elequent remarks, your very sociable talk, has caused me to tarry a longer period than is really consistent with the claims of business. As I told you when I first come in, I merely called to see if I could sell you "—

"Yes, I know you did. And a meaner, low-liveder proposal I never heard from mortal lips, be he male, or be he female. The idee of *me*, Josiah Allen's wife, who has locked arms with principle, and has kep' stiddy company with it, for years and years — the idee of *me* buyin' a feller! I dare persume to say "—

Says I more mildly, as he took up his hat and little box he had, and started for the door, — and seein' I was goin' to get rid of him so soon, I felt softer towards him, as folks will towards burdens when they are bein' lifted from 'em, —

"I dare persume to say, you thought I was a single woman, havin' been told time and agin, that I am young-lookin' for my age, and fair complected. I won't think," says I, feelin' still softer towards him as I see him a openin' the door, —

"I won't think for a minute that you knew who it was you made your infamous proposal to. But never, never make it agin to any livin' human bein', married or single."

He looked real sort o' meachin' as I spoke; and he said in considerable of a meek voice, —

"I was talkin' to you about a new feller, jest got up by the richest firm in North America."

"What difference does it make to me who he belongs to? I don't care if he belongs to Vanderbilt, or Aster'ses family. Principle — that is what I am a workin' on ; and the same principle that would hender me from buyin' a feller that was poor as a snail, would hender me from buyin' one that had the riches of Creshus; it wouldn't make a mite of difference to me.

"As the poet Mr. Burns says, — I have heard Thomas J. repeat it time and agin, and I always liked it: I may not get the words exactly right, but the meanin' is, —

"Rank is only the E pluribus Unum stamp, on the trade dollar: a feller is a feller for all that."

But I'll be hanged if he didn't, after all my expenditure of wind and eloquence, and quotin' poetry, and every

"CAN'T I SELL YOU A FELLER?"

thing — if he didn't turn round at the foot of that door-step, and strikin' that same patient, determined attitude of hisen, say, says he, —

"You are mistaken, mom. I merely stopped this mornin' to see if I could sell you " —

But I jest shet the door in his face, and went off up-stairs into the west chamber, and went to windin' bobbin's for my carpet. And I don't know how long he stayed there, nor don't care. He had gone when I come down to get dinner, and that was all I cared for.

I told Josiah about it when he and the boy come home; and I tell you, my eyes fairly snapped, I was that mad and rousted up about it: but he said, —

" He believed it was a sewin'-machine man, and wanted to sell me a feller for my sewin'-machine. He said he had heard there was a general agent in Jonesville that was a sendin' out agents with all sorts of attachments, some with hemmers, and some with fellers."

But I didn't believe a word of it: I believe he was *mean*. A mean, low-lived, insultin' creeter.

CHAPTER XIV.

Wall, Cicely died in June; and how the days will pass by, whether we are joyful or sorrowful! And before we knew it (as it were), September had stepped down old Time's dusty track, and appeared before us, and curchied to us (allegory).

Ah, yes! time passes by swiftly. As the poet observes, In youth the days pass slowly, in middle life they trot, and in old age they canter.

But the time, though goin' fast, had passed by very quietly and peacefully to Josiah Allen and me.

Every thing on the farm wus prosperous. The children was well and happy; the babe beautiful, and growin' more lovely every day.

Ury had took his money, and bought a good little house and 4 acres of land in our neighborhood, and had took our farm for the next and ensuin' year. And they was happy and contented. And had expectations. They had (under my direction) took a tower together, and the memory of her lonely pilgrimage had seemed to pass from Philury's mind.

The boy wus a gettin' healthier all the time. And he behaved better and better, most all the time.

374

I had limited him down to not ask over 50 questions on one subject, or from 50 to 60; and so we got along first-rate.

And we loved him. Why, there hain't no tellin' how we did love him. And he would talk so pretty about his ma! I had learned him to think that he would see her bime by, and that she loved him now jest as much as ever, and that she *wanted him* to be a *good boy.*

And he wuz a beautiful boy, if his chin wuz sort o' weak. He would try to tell the truth, and do as I would tell him to — and would, a good deal of the time. And he would tell his little prayers every night, and repeat lots of Scripture passages, and would ask more'n 100 questions about 'em, if I would let him.

There was one verse I made him repeat every night after he said his prayers: "Blessed are the pure in heart, for they shall see God."

And I always would say to him, earnest and deep, that his ma was pure in heart.

And he'd say, "Does she see God now?"

And I'd say, "Yes."

And he would say, "When shall I see Him?"

And I'd say, "When you are good enough."

And he'd say, "If I was good enough, could I see Him now?"

And I would say, "Yes."

And then he would tell me that he would try to be good; and I would say, "Wall, so do."

And late one afternoon, a bright, sunny afternoon, he got tired of playin'. He had been a horse, and little Let Peedick had been a drivin' him. I had heard 'em a whinnerin' out in the yard, and a prancin', and a hitchin' each other to the post.

But he had got tired about sundown, and come in, and leaned up against my lap, and asked me about 88 questions about his ma and the City. He had never forgot what his uncle Josiah had read about it, and he couldn't seem to talk enough about it.

And says he, with a dreamy look way off into the

THE BOY AND LET PEEDICK PLAYING HORSE.

glowin' western sky, "My mamma Cicely said it would swing right down out of heaven some day, and would open, and I could walk in; and don't you believe mamma will stand just inside of the gate as she used to, and say, 'Here comes my own little boy'?"

And he wus jest a askin' me this,—and it beats all, how many times he had tackled me on this very subject,—

when Whitfield drove up in a great hurry. Little Samantha Joe had been taken sick, very sick, and extremely
sudden.

Scarlet-fever was round, and she and the boy had both
been exposed.

I was all excitement and agitation; and I hurried off
without changin' my dress, or any thing. But I told
Josiah to put the boy to bed about nine.

Wall, there was a uncommon sunset that night. The
west was all aflame with light. And as we rode on
towards Jonesville right towards it, — though very anxious about the babe, — I drawed Whitfield's attention to
it.

The hull of the west did look, for all the world, like a
great, shinin' white gate, open, and inside all full of radience, rose, and yellow, and gold light, a streamin' out, and
changin', and glowin', movin' about, as clouds will.

It seemed sometimes, as if you could almost see a
white, shadowy figure, inside the gate, a lookin' out, and
watchin' with her arms reached out; and then it would
all melt into the light again, as clouds will.

It wus the beautifulest sunset I had seen, that year, by
far. And we s'pose, from what we could learn afterwards,
that the boy, too, was attracted by that wonderful glory
in the west, and strolled out to the orchard to look at it.
It wus a favorite place with him, anyway. And there wus
a certain tree that he loved to lay under. A sick-no-further apple. It wus the very tree I found him under that
day in the spring, a lookin' up into the sky, a watchin' for
the City to come down from heaven. You could see a
good ways from there off into the west, and out over the

lake. And the sunset must have looked beautiful from there, anyway.

Wall, my poor companion Josiah wus all rousted up in his mind about the babe, and he never thought of the boy till it was half-past nine ; and then he hurried off to find

PAUL LOOKING AT THE SUNSET.

him, skairt, but s'posen he was up on his bed with his clothes on, or asleep on the lounges, or carpets, or somewhere.

But he couldn't find him : he hunted all over the house, and out in the barn, and the door-yard, and the street ; and then he rousted up Mr. Gowdey's folks, our nearest neighbors, to see if they could help find him.

Wall, Miss Gowdey, when she wus a bringin' in her clothes, — it was Monday night, — she had seen him out in the orchard under the sick-no-further tree.

And there they found him, fast asleep — where they s'pose he had fell asleep unexpected to himself.

It wus then almost eleven o'clock, and he was wet with dew: the dew was' heavy that night. And when they rousted him up, he was so hoarse he couldn't speak. And before mornin' he was in a high fever. They sent for me and the doctor at daybreak. Little Samantha Joe wus better: it only proved to be a hard cold that ailed her.

But the boy had the scarlet-fever, so the doctor said. And he grew worse fast. He didn't know me at all when I got home, but wus a talkin' fast about his mamma Cicely; and he asked me " If the gate had swung down, for him to go through into the City, and if his mamma was inside, reachin' out her arms to him ?"

And then he would get things all mixed up, and talk about things he had heard of, and things he hadn't heard of. And then he would talk about how bright it was inside the gate, and how he see it from the orchard. And so we knew he had been attracted out by the bright light in the west.

And then he would talk about the strangest things. His little tongue couldn't be still a minute; but it never could, for that matter.

Till along about the middle of the afternoon he become quiet, and grew so white and still that I knew before the doctor told me, that we couldn't keep the boy.

And I thought, and couldn't help it, of what Cicely had

worried so about; and though my heart sunk down and down, to think of givin' the boy up, — for I loved him, — yet I couldn't help thinkin' that with his temperament, and as the laws was now, the grave was about the only place of safety that the Lord Himself could find for the boy.

And it wus about sundown that he died. I had been

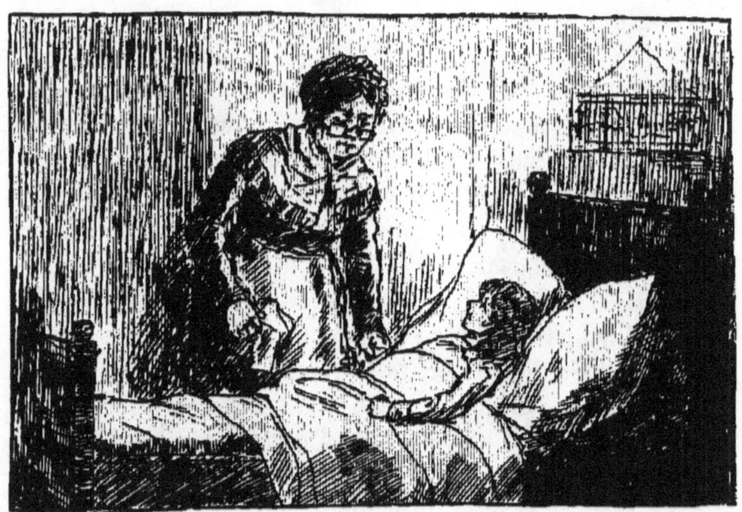

down-stairs for somethin' for him ; and as I went back into the room, I see his eyes was wide open, and looked natural.

And as I bent over him, he looked up at me, and said in a faint voice, but rational, —

"Say" —

And I couldn't help a smilin' right there, with the tears

a runnin' down my face like rain-water. He wanted to ask some question.

But he couldn't say no more. His little, eager, questionin' soul was too fur gone towards that land where the hard questions we can't answer here, will be made plain to us.

But he looked up into my face with that sort of a questionin' look, and then up over my head, and beyend it — and beyend — and I see there settled down over his face the sort of a satisfied look that he would have when I had answered his questions; and I sort o' smiled, and said to myself, I guessed the Lord had answered it.

And so he went through the gate of the City, and was safe. And that is the way God took care of the boy.